Spiked

Here's to Revenge

KL Griffiths

Cottonwood Fire LLC

This is a work of fiction. Names, characters, places, and incidents are either a product of the author's imagination or are used fictitiously. Any resemblance to actual persons, living or dead, events or locales, is entirely coincidental.

Published by Cottonwood Fire LLC

www.klgriffiths.com

FIRST EDITION

Book cover design by Creative Paramita.

Library of Congress Control Number: 2023911384

ISBN 979-8-9887038-0-8 (Paperback)

ISBN 979-8-9887038-1-5 (eBook)

For my best friend and love, Bob

Chapter 1

THE SEMI'S TAILLIGHTS BLAZED red. Twenty drum brakes groaned and coughed smoke, trying to stop 80,000 pounds on a dime. Rory jammed his brakes to avoid eating truck. The canister of fish food started to roll off the passenger seat, but he caught it in time.

Deer in the road? Dog? Rory scanned the shoulder and grassy median for a half-mangled animal. He glanced in his rearview mirror. Nothing—*hallelujah*—was splattered across the four lanes.

Whew. That was close.

Rory did not want to start the day with roadkill.

According to his GPS, he'd left home with plenty of commute time for his first day at Telluric Lake Brew Works, including a critically important detour for breakfast. The hollow in his gut bade him imagine, not eighteen white-rimmed truck wheels, but eighteen powdered sugar donuts. The adrenaline produced by the near miss, the almost accident, worked his bodily gears like an impetuous and vengeful Oz. He gunned it and passed the semi.

The trucker's hands were raised, fingers splayed in the universal what-the-hell shake at the car in front of him, a silver Lexus with a West Virginia University bumper sticker. A middle finger popped out of the Lexus' window.

Aha. The kid had brake-checked the trucker. And, by extension, Rory. Kid was lucky he wasn't a pancake. Rory, too. For the next few miles, Rory got passed by the kid and the truck. Then Rory maneuvered back into the passing lane to avoid the brake check. He counted four times the Lexus swerved in front of the truck and slammed his brakes. Kid had a death wish, maybe an exam he was trying to get out of taking. Forever.

Every time Rory tried to pass, their cat-and-mouse game made it impossible. Unless he wanted to push ninety or a hundred miles per hour—which he didn't—and leave them in the dust.

He wanted to make it alive to his first day of work. With donuts.

He planned to stop at Thigh High and pick up a dozen "Donuts-To-Thigh-For." The famous donut shop was right around the corner from Telluric, not that donuts had factored into his decision to accept the job or anything. He'd go the distance for good donuts. He had, in fact, chosen his college because of the donut-making machine in the cafeteria. He could still smell the fried dough and feel the tickle of the powdered sugar in his nose as he coated the freshly fried wonders and popped them whole into his mouth. How many t-shirts had he destroyed with grease? Too many. But that was then; his college days were history. No more donut machine. No more sleeping until noon. No more plasma donating. Rory had a bona fide job, his own (sparsely-furnished) apartment, and an opportunity to work with another of his loves: beer. Rory's life was, to anyone looking on, the American Dream.

A sharp turn in the interstate was known to slow traffic during rush hour, Rory wasn't sure how much. He'd made the trip to Telluric yesterday for orientation (and had grabbed a donut), but that was in the afternoon. Who knew what Rootsville rush hour traffic would be like?

The rumble strips caught him off guard, and he instinctively let up on the gas. To Rory's right, the lake waves crashed into a boulder wall. He engaged his wipers to take away the spritz. A barge and some motorboats dotted the horizon.

The kid in the Lexus whizzed by, deadly fast.

The semi passed, faster.

Rory's attention was fixed on the road drama, and although his pulse quickened at the dance of vengeance, he couldn't possibly predict the gruesome manifestation of Newton's first, second, and third laws about to play out. He sped up to watch the semi-driver's payback to the kid. The trucker managed to pull ahead, but only because the kid saw the ninety-degree turn in time and slammed on his brakes.

The trucker did not.

The rig fishtailed, tires smoking, trailer leaning one way then the other. A grass field would've been the semi's softish landing place as g-forces whipped his trailer out from behind him. Had the field been empty, the truck may have swung to a halt, no harm done. But parked on the grass were a flatbed of orange construction cones, an assortment of traffic construction materials, and a crane. The trailer slammed into the crane with a concussive mash of rubber and concrete and a high-pitched shred of metal. A red and white cloud erupted from the broken trailer, all flapping, flailing parts and pieces. White feathers spun and whirled in the air and a bloody hunk of flesh landed on Rory's windshield. From the sky fell twigish things that must've been bones, still flapping.

Chickens. Or parts of them. Everywhere. White and bloody feathers exploded outward as the truck jack-knifed, and the trailer was sawn in two.

From the maw of the trailer they came, flightless and dying. They scuttled into the four-lane highway to be squashed by passing cars. Or lanced by the toothy grills of those going sixty in the passing lane, commuters who were unwilling to let a few mangled chickens make them late. One chicken, caught on a Jeep's windshield wiper, flapped and twisted and flipped back into the road until another set of trying-to-swerve tires finished her off. A cloud of cartwheeling wings, beaks, and bloody chunks of meat exploded from the hole in the broken trailer, even as its two halves skidded to a stop.

Rory and other drivers slowed, drawn by the macabre. The truck driver climbed out of the cab and scrambled onto the berm. He stood in transfixed horror at the annihilation of his load.

Chickens were everywhere, blocking Rory's way. Some in the road were half dead, but others burst from the truck. Behind Rory, cars beeped.

"Places to go, people!" came a hoarse shout.

Rory put his window down and spoke, not loud enough to be heard, "Dude. Chickens are literally crossing the road. Take a breath."

The driver laid on his horn.

Rory guided his car around the one chicken strutting the highway unscathed. He winced at the crunch of bones from the still-moving leg and thigh he couldn't avoid.

"C'mon...faster, they're chickens," shouted the driver behind Rory.

Where was PETA when you needed them?

With a sigh, Rory accelerated, leaving behind mayhem and feathers and what would become the worst traffic snarl in Rootsville's history.

But the ordeal cost him extra time. No *Donuts-To-Thigh-For*. He wasn't sure he could eat after this, anyway. That was a first. And hot wings might be ruined for him forever. Rory had two incompatible philosophies dancing about in his head. One. He loved animals. All of them. They were the true innocents of the world. But two. He couldn't resist a patty melt or pulled pork or a perfectly smoked brisket. Becoming a pescatarian was too extreme a deprivation. He took care of the animals God put in his path and ate the ones God put on his plate.

Rory arrived at the intersection at Telluric with three minutes to spare. Impatiently, he smacked his steering wheel in time with the robotic pulse of the turn signal and considered the idea that his first day at Telluric, while not the best because of the no-donuts, was better than the day the chickens were having. It may have been from the crash or because it was his first day, but Rory was angsty. He'd rolled too far into the intersection trying to work up the nerve to make the left turn. Each car seemed faster than it was. When the light turned red, he got stuck there.

A left-turn arrow would be nice.

The light had gone through two iterations without a gap for him to slip through. Motorists angling around him communicated in various ways that he was a stupid asshole. They asked if he drove much or was he blind? Asked him what the hell, man? Some used sign language. Apparently, the only way to get into the brewery parking lot during rush hour was to execute a *New York*. A New York was any assertive (fine, aggressive) driving move, but especially one that involved wedging the car in between two other cars to butt into a car snake. If one didn't New York, one didn't get anywhere in that great and constipated city where Rory had learned to drive. It never left him, the New York. It hibernated. But after doing a New York, he always felt guilty. New Yorks got him middle fingers and non-verbal revilements. The chicken tragedy had stolen Rory's confidence, but now, a little New York was going to get him into Telluric's parking lot. New York. Assertive. Aggressive.

Red light. Time to go.

Out of nowhere, ear-splitting rock and roll, the sun in Rory's eyes. An obnoxious horn held, held. HELLLD until the speeding vehicle passed, dragging the tone into a lower pitch and pulling it away.

The blur of a car streaked through the intersection, made a skidding right turn into Telluric on the red light.

Another maniac driver.

Only Rory's brake-slam saved them from a collision. His seatbelt mechanism engaged, digging into his belly and the skin on his neck. The force tossed his canister of fish food into the dash and popped the lid. Neon flakes went everywhere, somehow even into Rory's mouth. His coffee sloshed in the passenger footwell and thickened into porridge as it mixed with the flakes.

Worst commute ever. And it was day one at Telluric. Bad omen.

Car horns blared.

Rory's car blocked the intersection while he watched his life pass before his eyes.

More horns. For the second time that morning, impatient drivers heckled him.

With an angry yank on the wheel, his own tires screeched as he made the turn into Telluric. A warmth in his boxers alerted Rory to the fact that he peed himself a little. Why couldn't he be more of a cool cat? Like Stonewall Jackson. A man on the wrong side, but still. Everybody had their flaws. The pain where the belt cut against his sizable belly reminded him of one of his own. How had Jackson managed to sit astride his horse (like a stone wall) while deadly bullets whizzed by? Rory was not a sit-while-the-bullets-whiz-by guy. He was not a willpower guy. He'd rather read Civil War history while popping donuts. Or while polishing off a gallon of caramel sea salt ice cream. He wanted to throttle the driver of the Trans Am for the galactically stupid and dangerous move—well beyond the mere annoyance of a New York.

His only consolation was that he was Rory Harper, beer chemist, and not a particular chicken-toting truck driver.

The Trans Am took a tire-squealing, seagull-scattering circuit of the parking lot before settling into two spaces, askew, like it was on display at the dealership. AC/DC blared from the open windows. It was forty degrees.

Peacock much?

Rory pulled into a parking space. The fish flakes that hadn't splattered in the footwell were all over the passenger seat. He tried to scrape them back into the tube. The more he swiped at them, the more of a gunky mess they made. His hands smelled gross.

Rory startled at the sudden appearance of a face in his driver's side window. A man with an oily comb-over taunted, "Me one. You zero. What's all over your windshield? Looks like blood."

Rory couldn't find his words.

The man shrugged. "Welcome to Telluric. I'm the brew master," he said, "But you can call me Master."

Rory blinked idiotically and hated himself for it.

"Aw, just kidding. My name's Arthur, but you can call me Master." And he roared as if that were even funnier.

Rory opened the door and tried to exit his car gracefully–not easy for a man of his size. Hoisting himself from the seat rendered him breathless, so he said nothing and put a hand out to shake. He hoped it had fish flakes on it.

The man—Arthur's—grip was excruciating.

"You must be the new guy. I've been here for—what in the hell is that?"

Rory followed Arthur's grimace to the grill of his Chevy Impala. It had three slits and a white, pink, and blood feather-flesh jumble that looked like a kid's finger painting with chicken legs sticking out the bottom.

"That's gross, man." Arthur set his briefcase and mug on Rory's hood. "Hang on. Got just the thing." He bounded to his car, grabbed an umbrella, and—gleefully if Rory wasn't mistaken—shoved the pointy end into the grill, dislodging chicken parts by pushing and scraping.

"You owe me an umbrella. You're welcome." Arthur didn't wait for Rory to answer. "You probably know, Dubrow just bought another packaging plant. That's why he hired you, I guess. The brewpub's got customers breaking down our doors every weekend making serious bank, and we can't keep product on the shelves. Is it enough for the great Gatsby? No, bub. Nothing will be enough for Dubrow. He hires a cellar rat and another chemist. Now I got to look after you two and do my usual duties." He dropped the umbrella.

As if Rory and "the cellar rat" were babies dropped into the fire station of his arms. And...*litter much?*

Rory picked up the umbrella and tossed it into the trash receptacle at the front entrance.

"You a tree hugger or something?" Arthur asked.

"It's an *umbrella*," Rory answered.

"We got maintenance for that."

Telluric Lake Brew Works was situated on a bluff overlooking the Black Paw River. The four-story brick warehouse had previously been the home of an ice-packing plant, its original brick smokestack outfitted with huge letters: T-L-B-W that could be seen from across the river and from the interstate. Clouds of seagulls gathered on the flat parts of the roof and the parking lot. An asphalt walking path led from the employee lot to the lakeshore where there was a public beach area. Arthur pointed.

"If you need a break, the beach bodies are just down the hill. Walking's good for the..." He pointed to his groin. "...soul."

What a guy.

To get to the elevator to the office area, employees had to pass through the brewpub where Arthur offered Rory a sample of the current test recipe, Bourbon Barrel Bite.

"It's eight-thirty in the morning," Rory protested.

"It's five o'clock somewhere." Arthur laughed uproariously and clapped Rory on the back harder than was polite. Because they'd just met, it was impossible to tell if the beer offer was a test or if Arthur was serious.

During the elevator ride from the first to the fourth floor, Rory learned Arthur drank beer like water, spent too much money on his car, could have his fill of spicy sexual escapades (partially thanks to said car), but he "preferred Hans' company to anyone else's." What did that mean? Rory searched for tells: a rainbow phone cover, an equal sign keychain, a flashy tie, colorful socks, *something*.

Nothing.

Arthur bragged that he met his conquests the old-fashioned way—at the bar, and he worked out every day. At forty-eight, he hadn't taken a single dose of Viagra.

Yes, but what type of conquests—XY or XX?

Did it matter? No, Rory decided, it didn't. The elevator doors opened. Rory hoped to leave him behind, but Arthur curled his hand around Rory's arm and led him forward.

"And here's the kitchen. Important to know, for a guy like you." His eyes rested on Rory's girth.

Like Rory hadn't parried a thousand million fat jokes. "I had the tour yesterday in orientation."

"Oh." And Arthur went on showing Rory where things were: the napkins, coffee filters, extra sugar. "We'll need more of that, now that you're here, Slim."

Arthur's gaze took in the lunch sack and fish food in Rory's hands. His brow knitted at the can of goldfish flakes. "My vote was to flush the little sucker."

As part of orientation, Rory had picked up the story of the office goldfish. He lived on the kitchen counter and was fed random pieces of crust or chips whenever the staff thought he looked hungry. "Mr. F" had come to Telluric by way of a dare, to be swallowed whole. The server who was supposed to eat him had been fired the previous evening. With no takers on swallowing the goldfish, the pub staff brought the bagged goldfish to the offices where he was transplanted into a glass vase from somebody's old flower arrangement. Gravel from the roadside was washed and spread on the bottom. By unspoken agreement, the staff would let fate decide whether Mr. F lived or died. He was a feeder fish anyway—bred to die—and scrawny and dull as "old pennies" was how the server described him.

Rory immediately liked the fish.

Arthur flicked a finger at the glass, sending Mr. F into terrified zig zags.

The vase had green fuzz growing inside it. The gravel was full of fish poo. Mr. F had defied the odds by living long enough to need a change of water and a vase scrubbing. When Rory put his face to the glass, the fish stopped his fit and looked at him.

"I think he likes me," Rory said.

"Nah. He knows you're going to feed him."

"Smart fish." Rory dropped a pinch of flakes in.

Mr. F's little "o" of a mouth opened and closed on them as his tail waggled him in place. He vacuumed along the surface, chowing the flakes and swimming in circles, making what looked like smacking motions with his mouth.

From behind, someone cleared his throat. Both men turned.

"Morning, sir." Arthur addressed Telluric's founder, Benjamin Dubrow.

Rory had learned in orientation that everyone called him "sir" to his face and "Dubrow" behind his back. Dubrow had a belly like Rory's, scored cleanly down the middle by an extra-wide tie with a Picasso vibe. He wore business slacks and converse sneakers. The dictionary definition of *incongruence* would have a picture of Benjamin Dubrow.

Dubrow grunted and pointed his mug at the fishbowl. "Thing's charmed."

"Yes," Rory said, flakes in hand.

Dubrow's gaze settled on Mr. F's vase. The flakes were settling to the bottom like neon snow. "I made a good decision, hiring you. You take care of details no one else thinks of, like purchasing honest-to-God fish food for the fish."

"Look at him," Arthur blurted. "Why is that surprising?"

Dubrow did. Look at him. "And he specializes in our product. A good choice. Yes, I made a good choice in you, Rory Harper."

After an uncomfortable three-man silence, Dubrow said, "Arthur, kindly excuse us."

Arthur opened his mouth to object but thought better of it. He left.

"What do you think of our little operation?" Dubrow asked.

Telluric wasn't exactly little. In that Dubrow was being modest. Rory accepted the job because Telluric was growing exponentially, had partnerships with the other successful local breweries, and had offered him a handsome salary package.

And the beer. Yum.

Rory's mouth worked, trying to figure out the best answer to Dubrow's question. His nervousness seemed to please Dubrow, who put a fatherly arm around him and guided him to the kitchen window that faced inland from the lake and overlooked the packaging plant. "None of this was here when I started. It was me and Arthur and a rented space, not much bigger than a garage."

Rory loved a good underdog story. Although he knew the details because he'd researched Telluric thoroughly before his interview, he listened as Dubrow reveled in history. Before starting Telluric, Dubrow had been a successful executive pulling in a six-figure salary. He had a family to support, and a mortgage to pay. He took out a second mortgage on his house (which thrilled his wife), quit his job (also thrilled), and opened a microbrewery before it became the fashionable thing to do. Starting with his grandfather's recipe for a full-bodied lager, he branched out into other brews and revolutionized the industry. He was the Columbus of IPAs, bringing to light the utility and flexibility of the all but forgotten India Pale Ale. Dubrow believed the world deserved better than the anemic bilge Americans tossed back by the gallon.

Judging by his company's success, Americans agreed with him.

"But we had our share of dark days, too," Dubrow shuddered. "Times when I questioned if I had barked up the wrong tree with my crazy ideas. My wife, may she rest in peace, she used to ride me about working too much, how Telluric was going to be the death of me. And I'd tell her not to worry. I'd sleep when I was dead."

Rory produced a small, empathetic chuckle as if he, straight out of college, could empathize with the grit it took to build an empire from the ground up. His empty stomach and a head full of chickens made it hard to concentrate.

Dubrow faced him and frowned. "Say...you look a bit off, son."

Rory never had been able to keep a poker face. "I had a rough drive in this morning. A semi overturned–"

"The chickens!" Dubrow said, "You saw it?"

"I was almost a part of it. I have chicken in my wheel wells."

Excited to have an eyewitness, Dubrow forgot about himself and insisted Rory tell him every grisly detail. His eyes gleamed when Rory told how he'd been wheel to wheel with both the trucker and the kid, both of whom wanted to have the last word.

"Revenge," Dubrow said, "is the attitude of weaklings...that's a quote from somebody smarter than me."

Arthur walked past the kitchen entry more times than seemed appropriate, lion pacing, threatening, like a guy whose girl is, for legitimate reasons, talking with someone else.

Dubrow's back was to the doorway, so only Rory could see Arthur's eavesdropping.

After more chicken talk and Dubrow's verdict that the trucker should've been more mature than the kid, Dubrow shared some recent Telluric accomplishments and finished with what felt like a threat: "...and Arthur's in charge of training and acclimating you."

Rory must have made a face because Dubrow added, "Arthur's a little rough around the edges, but he was here in the beginning when it was only me and my recipes. Arthur was my distribution arm."

"He handled distribution?"

Dubrow laughed. "He drove the beer to local bars and stores. When I met Arthur, he couldn't tell his arm from his asshole, and look at him now."

All asshole.

"Stick with Arthur, kid." Dubrow patted Rory's back in a more friendly way than Arthur had. "You two'll make the finest beer around. I won't be here forever."

Again, sounded like a threat.

Chapter 2

SUMMER WAS IN FULL swing in Rootsville. Beer sales were up. Mr. F got fatter and looked happy. Each morning Rory put several pinches of fish food in his vase. Neon flakes littered the bottom, and Rory had to clean the murky water once a week. He brought a dozen Thigh High Donuts every Friday, which made him everybody's friend.

Except, of course, Arthur's.

"You want everyone to be fat like you," he said, nodding at the donuts.

Rory wasn't sure how to respond. The statement was so outrageous. After a moment he murmured without making eye contact, "You could use a little sugar."

Arthur didn't seem to hear. "Hans is ripped," he bragged, "I need to keep up."

Hans?

"—besides, I save my calories for beer."

Telluric lab employees were given two free beers per day as a perk. The only beverage Rory ever saw in Arthur's paws was beer. Beer, beer, beer. Morning, noon, and night. But the two-beer rule didn't apply to Arthur. Just ask him; he'd tell you.

Not that Rory would ever ask him anything.

He made it his business to avoid Arthur. Although the truth was, Rory generally avoided people altogether. If a conversation was about beer or yeast counts or recipes, Rory forgot himself and could string words together, but the thought of unstructured talking time gave him the willies. By day's end, he craved a hazy, hoppy IPA but resisted the urge to take advantage of the complimentary beers. He was starving and wanted a cheesesteak or a pizza or an egg burger to complement his beer—which, while he could order food from the brewpub—the idea of the fat guy wolfing down dinner with his new colleagues...no.

Rory tried to ignore his fatness when he was around new people, to project confidence, but he often failed. Only Dubrow (because he was fat, too) and Mr. F didn't make him uncomfortable. Everyone else, he could feel their eyes on his belly. And Arthur's favorite recycled fat joke was that he feared standing too close because Rory had so much mass, he exerted a gravitational pull on bodies within arm's length.

"Dude's a black hole," Arthur would say to anyone listening. He meant Rory.

Some of the lab techs smothered their laughter, but not Carl. Carl shook his head.

"Make up your mind, Art, is he a planet or a black hole? You're screwing up your physics." Carl set his eyes back into his microscope. Under his breath, he mumbled about the yeast and scribbled notes on his electronic pad. Before Rory was hired, Carl had charge of yeast management at Telluric. He had been promoted to lab supervisor, and Rory would be taking over for him.

"Physics is for pussies," Arthur said.

Carl glanced triumphantly at Rory. Unspoken between them was: *That was the best he could do. Weak comeback, Arthur, weak.*

Rory scribbled a stick figure drawing of himself stabbing Arthur. Usually, he ripped them into tiny pieces so no one got the wrong idea. Murdering Arthur was a fantasy, but Rory had practiced so often, he had gotten good at drawing the scene. It took seconds. He held up the envelope to appreciate his art and showed it to Carl while Arthur's back was turned.

Carl clucked in admiration. "Right, you should channel some of that creativity and join us for a beer tomorrow after work."

Hearing the comment that seemed to come out of nowhere, Arthur turned.

Both Rory and Carl smiled wickedly but said nothing.

Carl continued, "Every Friday we talk...*shop*. It's highly edifying. Bring your drawings, if you want."

"Every Friday?" Rory asked.

"My wife's an EMT, so her hours are all over the place," Carl explained. "Why go home to an empty house when I can have free beer here? And you're single, right? Where else you going to go?"

"Your wife's not home because she's banging somebody else," Arthur said.

"She's banging your mother," Carl shot back. To Rory, he asked, "What do you say? Have a beer with us?"

"Tomorrow? Sure." Rory made a mental note to bring extra snacks so he wouldn't be hungry after work.

Rory brought two dozen donuts rather than the usual dozen, but he scarfed down four in his nervousness. When five o'clock rolled around, he collected the uneaten donuts and delivered them to the brewpub servers, who hugged him and attacked the box for the chocolate-dipped rainbow sprinkled.

Carl waved him over. "Finally, the new guy joins us for drinks."

"Finally? I've only been here a month." Rory poured himself a jalapeno IPA.

Silas, who was interning for the summer before going off to Cornell, nursed a club soda with a lime. Not being twenty-one, it was illegal for Silas to drink alcohol. Being an intern at a microbrewery, it was weird as shit that he didn't take advantage of the free beer and the staff's blind eyes. Everyone knew the interns drank. It was an unspoken perk of the trade.

Rory jabbed Silas in the ribs. "You work at a brewery and don't drink? What's up with that?"

Silas jabbed back, into Rory's belly. "If we put a tap in here, what kind of beer would come out?"

"Mmmmm..." Rory rubbed his chin in exaggerated thought, "Probably chocolate stout."

Rory was surprised at the ease he felt. His weight wasn't the elephant in the room, haha, because of Silas' good-natured ribbing.

"Arthur's shitting the bed," Silas said, and it was clear the idea pleased him. "The lauter tun isn't fixed yet."

Earlier that day the heating element in one of the lauter tuns went down. Arthur was beside himself trying to fix it.

"I wish it would go down every day," Silas continued.

They went around and around about what a jerk Arthur could be. Rory told the story of how Arthur scared the shit out of him at the traffic light on his first day. He didn't tell them Arthur had done the same asshole move several times in the month since Rory started. It was too embarrassing.

"On my first day," Carl said, "Arthur sent me to the store for the panel beers. I was so nervous. Sonofabitch asked me if I minded stopping at the hardware store. I wanted to make a good first impression, right? So I was eager to do whatever he asked. Arthur tells me he needs a left-handed smoke shifter and 200 feet of shoreline. I didn't think, right? Just wrote it down. I get to the hardware store, and after searching forever, I call the office and ask what aisle they're in. Arthur puts me on speaker and says, 'What's that, Carl?' So, like a dumbass, I repeat I can't find the left-handed smoke shifter or the 200 feet of shoreline. I'm not thinking, right? First-day jitters. I hear the brewpub servers laughing in the background. I wanted to go home and not come back, but..." Carl shrugged. "I like working with beer, right?" He took a pull. "And drinking it."

"I'd like to put Arthur in a choke hold while I recite poetry very slowly." Rory dreamily gulped his IPA.

"A what?" Carl asked.

"A headlock," Rory said. "I'm a red belt. Haven't cared to use it until lately. And yes, I like poetry. Don't even consider knocking it."

Carl stifled a giggle. "No shit...Poetry and Karate?"

"Taekwondo. And I haven't practiced since I was a kid. But it's like riding a bike."

"No shit..." Carl appeared to still be processing.

"Fine, it's not like a bike at all. I'm way out of practice, but I'd like to think I could pull something special out of the memory vault for Arthur." Rory curled his hands into fists. "He burns me up."

"A red belt?" asked Silas, like he hadn't even heard Rory. "That's one belt away from black."

"You know your belts. So you know I broke wood planks with this." Rory held up his meaty arm.

"Nice. I say we see how Arthur holds up against us, three on one. We've got your Taekwondo, my youth, and...and Carl," Silas said.

"My hate is stronger than your karate or your youth," Carl tipped his glass to each in turn.

"Arthur calls me the cellar rat," Silas complained.

"Oh, you found out, did you?" asked Carl.

"To my *face*," Silas said.

Rory leaned in. "We should call him 'Arthole.' Like, you're a pain in my arth-hole."

Instead of laughing, their faces went blank. Carl put his nose into his snifter. Silas gave a warning shake of his head and jutted his chin, as in *behind you*.

Rory stopped, turned.

Arthur had his fists clenched.

"Can't fix the lauter tun?" Rory asked innocently. Normally he would've been respectfully stoic, but the beer and camaraderie had given him a lovely fuzz in his head. He hiccupped.

An unreadable mixture of dark clouds passed over Arthur's face. He opened his mouth and inhaled like he was about to let fly some choice insults when Rory released an enormous belch. Arthur, apparently shocked at the disgusting (and surprising) response from the usually-shy Rory, snapped his mouth shut, narrowed his eyes, and retreated without a word.

Carl snickered. "He needs to know what an arth-hole he is. Maybe he'll turn over a new leaf if he finds out everyone hates him."

They laughed.

"I'm going to geth me another beer. Rory? Wanth another?"

When Rory screwed up his face in confusion, Carl said, "Whath? You don'th wanth another beer?" Carl went on and on using *th* instead of a *t* sound. Carl took Rory's name, Arthole, and created a sort of dialect with the *th* sound, the inside joke on Arthur, or Arthole, as he would be known forevermore, behind his back.

Because of Rory.

This would get back to Arthur.

Rory downed his second beer and shared Taekwondo stories. Like the time he couldn't break his board for his belt test, how his hand hurt so bad he thought it must be broken. The idea of slamming his throbbing, swelling hand down a second time was almost unthinkable. But he did. And he did it without hesitating or holding back. Rory had swung his hand into the board under the full conviction that bone and board would break. And he was correct. They did. A fifth metacarpal fracture. Or, as the orthopedic surgeon said, "The disintegration of your pinky finger." The hand would be stronger when it healed, the surgeon promised. The next time Rory would need to break a board, it would be a piece of cake.

But there was no next time.

"Why'd you stop practicing?" Silas asked.

Rory shrugged. "I don't know. It stopped being fun, I guess."

But that was only part of the truth. Rory's next belt test was for black, and he would have to break not two, but three boards. He remembered how it loomed in his horizon like a coming storm. The idea of the test grew bigger and bigger until it blotted out the joy of sparring. Rory didn't care what the surgeon said. Every time he thought about breaking boards, it got worse. Not the pain. The fear. What if, this time, he didn't break it on the first try? What if he had to go a second time against three boards, and with a re-broken hand? Because no way could he walk away from unbroken boards. No way.

Rory dropped out of Taekwondo.

He'd convinced his teenage self that he knew enough martial arts to kick any kid's ass. The black belt was only for bragging rights.

But as he pulled on his beer, Rory knew the black belt was a mountain he should have climbed. He had the regret of a man standing at base camp who wondered what the view was like from the peak. Never mind he had put on a hundred pounds in the wake of his Taekwondo days. Some students gained the freshman fifteen; Rory gained the freshman fifty. And he hadn't stopped there.

That wasn't beer talk. That was deep, philosophical shit that should remain buried. Rory turned the conversation to Silas and Cornell and how exciting it was to be all potential, everything still spread out before you.

"You're in the Friday five o'clock of life," Rory told him. "Enjoy it."

Carl harrumphed. "That puts me in the Saturday afternoon of life, am I right? Plenty of weekend left, and I intend to enjoy every minute."

Technically, Rory was in the Saturday morning of life, having recently graduated college. He had a car and his own place, a Spartan, unfurnished apartment with a mattress on the floor and his dog-eared poetry anthology, a thick tome he used to help him sleep. His one decoration was framed parking tickets from his early college days. His refrigerator was stocked with microwavable meals, deli meats, cheeses, olive salads, and whole cheesecakes in plastic containers. He had no girlfriend, no roommate, no television. He wasn't into TV. Rory didn't even have a cat. His parents lived hundreds of miles away, didn't know one microbrewery from another and were not pleased their overweight son had a degree in fermentation science. His father could hardly keep a straight face when he said the words *fermentation science*, like it was casserole science or ironing science.

"You're going to college for beer-drinking? Look at you—you'll be dead from a heart attack before you're thirty," his dad had said.

His parents couldn't understand because they drank shitty beer.

There were days even in his first month—Rory admitted to Carl and Silas—that he considered looking for another job. Telluric wasn't the only brewery around, Rory said, "Maybe another company would be populated with one hundred percent human beings...not with assholes like Arthur."

"Assholes everywhere," Carl agreed. "But none as big as our Arthole."

They laughed and Rory rose to leave, "See you artholes tomorrow." As he approached the hallway, he heard steps rushing away, as if someone had been eavesdropping the whole time.

Chapter 3

RORY DID NOT PULL into the intersection to execute a New York. He waited dutifully behind the white line for the light and kept his eyes peeled for Trans Ams. In the two months since he started at Telluric, he'd learned a few things, like how to pull into work without getting killed.

The Trans Am was already parked askew in its usual two spaces. Great way to start the day: alive. And thanks to the dozen donuts beside him—French crullers—he skipped across the parking lot. Fridays were the best because he felt like Santa carrying in sweet, deep-fried happiness to share with his co-workers.

The glass doors parted, and the smell of fermenting yeast greeted him. The TV monitor mounted overhead announced today was sensory panel day. Oh, now things were looking up. Telluric's staff would gather in the taproom after lunch. *After lunch* was key, especially if they were testing double IPAs or stouts. Beer with the alcohol content of wine could quickly turn a person loopy, especially on an empty stomach (never a problem for Rory). But maybe as an extra precaution, he'd order a pizza to make sure he had enough carbs. Pizza Palace had excellent Friday specials.

Sensory panels served different functions. Today was a true-to-style test. The job of the tasters was to determine if the beer, as made, fit within the guidelines for the given style. A Flanders Red couldn't taste like a strong Scotch Ale, and if it did...*Houston, we have a problem.* The next step would be to figure out why the Flanders tasted like an ale. What had happened to cause the change? If there were problems, the beer would be pulled at every stage of the production line to find out what had gone wrong. Infections, they were called. Or sometimes an intern mixed up the recipe.

So far, the only infection Rory encountered at Telluric was Arthur. Rory daydreamed of punching him in the face, of riposting Arthur's mockery with a witty, humiliating comeback in front of the line cooks or the chemists or the servers. Rory daydreamed because he knew he'd never do anything to Arthur. Oh, he'd call him names behind his back. He, Carl, and Silas muttered their secret *th* dialect, and it was a salve, an *us vs. him* mentality. But it wasn't satisfying, the name-calling. Rory and Carl and Silas—they were a clutch of chickens preening their feathers while Arthur, the wolf, paced outside their coop.

Rory held a pinch of fish flakes over Mr. F's water.

"BOO!" came a booming voice.

He fumbled the canister and some flakes went flying.

"Gotcha, Slim." Arthur's voice trailed away down the hall.

Rory wiped up the flakes with a damp paper towel. Arthole thought he was sooo funny.

But once immersed in his work, the morning flew by. Carl leaned into Rory's office, scanned the hall conspiratorially, and whispered, "Wanth anything for lunch? I'm getting the panel beerths for today."

Only Carl and Arthur–those running the panel–would know which beers were bought and which were chosen from Telluric. Running the panel with Arthur was a job no one wanted.

Rory made a mock sad face. "Sucks to be you, man. Thanks, but I got a pizza coming. IPAs today, am I right?"

"You know that's clathified informathon." Carl winked and smiled, which meant it was IPA day.

Arthur was insanely private about the panels. Knowing they were IPAs didn't give anyone an edge because the purpose was to determine if the beers tasted like the style they supposedly were. Competitors' beers were thrown in as a control. The moment the glasses were poured, the deep orange or hazy yellow colors gave away India Pale Ales. Deep, chocolatey browns meant porters. Lagers were pale and clear and tasted like mass-produced piss brine, if you asked Rory. It was fun to see the high alcohol content affect the staff, to watch them stumble to the john halfway through the panel. How fast a wee bit of double-imperial IPA could send you to the moon. Mercifully, the beer dulled their egos and gave interns or servers the confidence to weigh in on new recipes or admit the beer tasted oddly like popcorn. This was actually a common infection, but it was fun to watch someone taste it for the first time. Besides the surprising taste, diacetyl could be confirmed by the—ew—palate slickness it produced.

True-to-styles winnowed the wheat from the chaff. You knew your beer. Or you didn't.

Rory may not have been much to look at. Or more precisely, too much to look at, but he was the Jedi master of beer tastings. He could predict Telluric Love Child (TLC) the company's most well-known product, with a hundred percent accuracy. He'd only been there for two months, but once his reputation got out, chemists, salespeople, even the barrel rep tried to stump Rory in spontaneous after-hours tastings. Most of Rory's complimentary beers were spent proving he could pick out TLC no matter what beer it was up against. This enraged Arthur, who often failed to correctly guess TLC. Arthur mistook it for Sunnylicious. What a scandal, a chief science officer failing to recognize his own beer.

On one of the many occasions where Rory guessed correctly and Arthur had not, Arthur grumbled to the interns that Sunnylicious was a suss move.

"Suss? You were beat, fair and square."

"I have a head cold."

"Sure you do." Dubrow overheard, and that was the worst strike of all. Arthur couldn't stand to look bad in Dubrow's eyes.

Rory never brought it up, but others did. Arthur needed to be brought down a peg or ten thousand, and the brewers, lab workers, and even brewpub staff didn't miss a chance to rip on Arthur every time there was a sensory panel.

The servers gathered by the oak barrels. The lab techs hadn't arrived and could always be counted on to be late. From behind the bar, Carl prepped flights and set out the tasting sheets, pencils, pretzels, and waters.

"Where's the cellar rat?" Arthur called out, as he swaggered into the pub.

"I don't know where our *intern, Silas* is." Rory didn't look up. Telluric didn't even have a cellar. The cylinders were right next door, in a glass-plated room. They could be seen from the brewpub.

Arthur cleared his throat and directed his speech to the servers. "Okay, noobs, here's how it goes. The beers are numbered so you won't know which is which. See these papers here? You're going to receive one for each beer. We've got seven beers today. Not going to tell you what they are. That's for y–"

"IPA!" Someone yell-coughed.

Arthur narrowed his eyes in the direction of the cougher. "Juveniles." He continued addressing the youngest employees, "Beer's judged on five categories. I don't care if you think it tastes good. That's not the point. It has to adhere to the standards for the name it's given."

The cougher coughed, "IPA!" again, to a chorus of sniggers and snorts.

Arthur inhaled deeply, as if this was childish and below his dignity. "In five areas you'll judge: appearance, aroma, flavor, mouthfeel, and overall impression. You noobs can't be expected to know an English IPA has different characteristics than an Imperial IPA, but you can assign number values to color, head retention, and clarity, as well as carbonation levels, aromas, and flavors. If you feel like you must write the beer a love letter, do so on the overall impression space...Carl."

That was Carl's cue to serve the beers. When he got to Rory, Arthur stopped him. "Not him. I have something else for him." Arthur set a flight before Rory, shades of dark brown to orange to golden yellow.

"I'm honored," Rory said. And suspicious. *What's up your sleeve, Arthole?* Rory glanced at Carl, who shrugged.

"Your palate is too *sophisticated* for a true-to-style," Arthur drawled. "Everyone, can I have your attention?"

No one stopped talking. It was as if Arthur hadn't said a word. Dubrow put his fingers to his lips and whistled loud enough to summon all the dogs in Rootsville, and all eyes turned. Conversation ceased.

Arthur pulled something from his back pocket. A bill. "Everyone, what I've got here is a Grover Cleveland." He waved it imperially. "Anybody want to guess which bill President Cleveland is on? ...Anybody?"

Dubrow answered quietly. "The thousand."

"Right. I have here a thousand-dollar bill. And yes, they are still legal tender. I assure you, it will spend." He turned to Rory. "I challenge you to a blind study. Grover Cleveland says you can't name all seven of these beers."

Was this something Arthur did before–challenge the chemist? Could Rory guess seven beers, having no idea which brewery they were from?

"Give me the states and countries of origin."

"No."

"They're made in commercial facilities? No basements, right?"

"No basements."

If Rory didn't take the challenge, no one would hold it against him. But it would mean a thousand bucks if he won...and Arthur would eat some badly deserved humble pie. Rory was excellent at blind studies. But the odds, they were terrible.

"I don't have–" Rory began.

Arthur put up a hand. "I know you're broke, Slim. I give you a thousand bucks if you guess all seven. If you don't guess correctly, you can give me what little you have, your soul."

"You could use a soul," Rory mumbled.

Snickers and snorts, from all around the brewpub, even Dubrow.

Arthur rolled his eyes. "Joking. Did you think you didn't have to put some skin in this? Here's the deal." He slid the flight ski to Rory. "If you lose, you wash my car ten times, whenever I ask you to."

Rory made a face.

"Ten times, Slim. That's equal to a hundred bucks a wash, compared to my thousand bucks. Doesn't get any fairer than that."

Dubrow harrumphed. Staff murmured. Oh, the fun Arthole would have videoing Rory as he washed his car. And he'd no doubt find a way to make it extra embarrassing. Still...a thousand bucks. Rory could use a thousand bucks. And maybe he could do it. *Maybe.*

Rory nodded his acceptance, and Arthur shouted, "Done. We have a deal."

Rory surveyed the mystery flight. Porters could be counted on to taste or smell like coffee, chocolate, or caramel. IPAs often had a pine or citrus kick. Lagers were light and crisp with a swirl of honey on the back of the tongue. But within those broad categorizations, there were thousands of other flavors, aromas, and mouth feels, not to mention the foam, haze, and carbonation.

The staff began smelling and sipping their flights and scribbling notes. Rory set to work on his. Every so often, Dubrow looked his way. At each sip, Rory made notes on the mouthfeel and the finish, on the flavors he detected. He closed his eyes and smelled the beers, tasted them fully, then felt backward in his mind for when he'd experienced something similar. Of the seven beers, two were easy guesses. He was confident he found the Great Lakes Edmund Porter, a gimme because Great Lakes had an unidentifiable uniqueness some said came from the Lake Erie water used in the brewing process. The second was also easy. The moment he sipped Little Creatures Pale Ale from Australia, the citron notes produced by whole hop flowers brought the label to his mind: a cherub with a thug's face, holding a beer stein as large as his head.

The next golden beer was a mystery. He saved it for last.

Elysian Space Dust came to him after a few sips. Galaxy and Calypso hops with their high acidity and citrus punch were Rory's favorite, so he'd drunk enough to recognize all of them. Could a man forget the lips of his lover? The smell of her hair? Beer was Rory's love. A thousand nights spent in the study of his love yielded a knowledge deep and intuitive and truer than science. It wasn't like studying for a test. It was thirst and hunger and slaking and feasting. It came as naturally as breathing. Should one be praised for breathing? People were amazed by Rory's beer knowledge, but it was love, plain and simple.

The next three beers proved more of a challenge, but eventually mouthfeel helped him come to a decision, and he wrote his guesses down, kept them concealed. Telling whether a beer was top fermented or bottom fermented was easy. Ales were top. Lagers, bottom. But throw in a thousand other variations like cooking time and temperature, added spices, type and blend of hops...and there were always beers so similar it would be a 50-50 chance to guess correctly.

That mysterious, golden beer he could not place.

He asked for more.

Dubrow finished his guesses and came to sit beside Rory, asked to see the notes he made and his guesses, how he came to his conclusions. "I want to play too...Arthur, give me that flight. Let's see if I agree with our newest chemist."

Arthur bristled but got to pouring. "Here you are, sir." Arthur set the flight down and addressed Rory. "How's it going, Slim? You stumped? I think I'm going to inherit a soul today—and a car washer. Carl, play 'The Devil Went Down to Georgia,' will you?"

Rory narrowed his eyes. He knew the song. "I *am* the best that's ever been." But inside, he wondered if he could do it.

"We'll see," Arthur sneered.

The staff gathered around to see if Dubrow agreed with Rory's first six guesses.

He agreed with three of them. For three he made alternate guesses. Like Rory, Dubrow was stumped by the last beer.

"I can't place it," Dubrow said.

"It's not American. I'm getting Germany," Rory said. "Argh. Germans. So deceptive."

"You have to make a guess." Arthur could barely contain his glee.

"One more pour, please," Rory said.

"You won't be fit to drive." Carl swiped the glass and disappeared behind the bar.

"If he gets it right, I'll call him a limo," said Dubrow.

Rory took a big sip of water, threw back a handful of pretzels, and took more water. He closed his eyes and focused. Had he ever...before...

"Light to medium gold color." He held it high. "I see some clarity, some carbonation." He sipped, held it in his mouth, swallowed. "And a wonderful malt character, maybe a little bit of spicy hop character...but now...okay. I'm definitely somewhere in Germany."

The staff cheered him on, hooting and hollering. Someone shouted, "Clairvoyant!"

Rory pointed to his temple and to his mouth. "All the crystal ball I need. I'm getting impressions of pale malt...pilsner...Munich Helles? ...umm hmmmm...a grainy sweetness. The bitterness is restrained." He set the glass down with a confident smack. "The carbonation tells me it's lager. Doesn't have enough snappy bitterness to tell me that it's a German pils. No. I'm going with Munich Helles. Munich Helles it is."

"Final answer?" Arthur eked out the words.

"Final answer."

"Arthur?" Dubrow questioned.

Arthur's eye twitched. His sideways glare said he was as angry as he was beaten. Out of his back pocket, he pulled the thousand-dollar bill. Cheers went up all over the taproom. Dubrow looked at Rory with undisguised awe. "Call the man a limo, Arthur, and put it on the company credit card."

Chapter 4

RORY WOULD GLADLY GO back in time and lose the tasting challenge, would throw it on purpose. A thousand bucks was not worth Arthur's venom. In the week since the tasting scandal, Arthole-engineered daily pranks, like using a tack to punch a pinhole in the top lip of Rory's Starbucks cup. Or he filled Rory's desk drawer with fish flakes—and a dead sunfish. Or Rory's computer mouse wrapped in spoiled bacon. They usually involved food, and succeeded in yanking Rory's guts into the bottom of his thoracic cavity. Arthur managed to video Rory's reactions and send them to him. That smarted worse than the pranks themselves.

Having had his fill of shame, Rory decided to give Arthole a taste of his own medicine. A teeny tiny chip of dry ice in an Eppendorf tube and...BOOM. The fright would (hopefully) make Arthole shit himself right there at his desk. *Thank you, chemistry.*

Rory munched on a sour cream donut and listened for Arthole's annoying voice say, "Good morning, Candy." The receptionist's name was not Candy. Every day Arthur had some almost-inappropriate comment on her dress, her hair, her "athleticism." *Gag.* With ninja speed Rory didn't know he possessed, he trucked it down the hall to Arthur's office, stashed the tube, and returned to his own office. He was full of delicious *schadenfreude* (which tasted better to his soul than even Thigh High donuts). He set a timer for ten minutes. He need not get up. The sound would carry.

A delightfully loud half-pop-half-boom and Arthur's scream were music to his ears. Would Arthur guess it was Rory? Maybe. But Rory didn't seem like the vengeance type. Not even to himself.

The Eppendorf tube day was one of the best days Rory ever had at Telluric. Rory felt like he'd aced an exam. He was as blissfully full as a man who'd eaten a dozen donuts. Arthur went home early and without a word to anyone. Clearly, dishing it out was his jam, not taking it.

Whenever Arthur played a prank, he would quip, "It's a joke. What? Can't take a little joke?"

How'd you like them apples, Arthole? Take that joke.

But the next day, Arthur bounced back to his annoying self.

"Slim!" He cracked up, thinking himself wittier than God. Arthur strode the entire facility calling out, "Slim! Slim! You of all people shouldn't be this hard to find. Where are you?"

Upon finding him, Arthur stumbled and grasped the corner of a doorway and gritted his teeth, pretending it cost him great effort to not be sucked into Rory. "I...can't...hold...it. The planet's gravitational force is sucking...me...in..."

Rory rolled his eyes and responded, "What do you call a man with no arms and no legs, hanging on a wall?" It was a terribly stupid and overused joke, but still. It was insulting. And compelling: the idea of Arthur with no arms and no legs, pinned to the wall, begging Rory to help him down.

"What do you call a chemist who needs to crawl inside the Belgian fermenter because maintenance didn't show up? Slim. That's what. Hope you have a raincoat. It's wetter than a—well, it's hot and yeasty and wet in there. You hear me? You'll have no idea what to do with a space like that." Arthur gave his snifter glass an erotic lick and took a gulp of coffee stout.

"What—what?"

"I dropped a screwdriver into the Belgian."

"So. *You* get it."

"I would, but..." He looked at his chest, then his groin, and puffed up. "Too large to fit in that hole."

A brewpub line cook walked by the lab and called out, "That's what she said."

"She did say that, didn't she?" Arthur quipped. "I don't have to get in there because I'm your boss and I'm telling *you* to get it out. Perks of power, Slim. Perks of power."

Rory was tongue-tied.

"What are you waiting for? Get in there."

"Uh...no? And you're not—technically—my boss."

Arthur glared. "Actually, I'm claustrophobic. That's why I need you to do it. There. You happy?"

Rory didn't have a raincoat. He'd never gone inside the fermenter before. No one did. They were enormous and could—in theory—fit even a man as fat as Rory inside, but there was no need. Arthur could not be serious. Claustrophobia?

It was difficult to read Arthur. Was he showing a vulnerable side?

"There was a problem with the CIP. I was trying to fix it and I dropped the screwdriver." Arthur lowered his voice, "We need to get it out before Dubrow finds out. He'll have your ass." The CIP was short for clean-in-place. Essentially a custom-designed shower head that blasted water everywhere.

"*My* ass? I don't think so."

"You're in charge of making sure the equipment is clean. It wasn't. That's why I had to take the CIP apart, because you dropped the ball on maintenance."

"Bullshit."

"Says *you*. Who's Dubrow going to believe?"

"But...what about a server? Surely it would be easier—"

"Look, Dubrow's going to be here any minute. It's a quick job. I was joking about the raincoat. I even emptied the fermenter for you. Just watch the sides. They're slick. Hurry, okay?"

Rory climbed into the steel tank.

"You should wear a rubber," Arthur teased.

Same cook. Must've had bionic hearing. Walked by again. "That's what she said."

Rory rolled his eyes. The darkness temporarily blinded him. He felt around for the screwdriver, located the CIP at the top where the pipes poured the wort and hops into the fermenter. The CIP was a steel implement, of generous phallic shape and size with a two-inch ball on the end. The ball was where the water jetted in all directions, acting like a dishwasher anywhere it was placed. A hose ran high-powered water through the CIP and could clean any shape or size container. That was why no one ever had to climb inside a fermenter to scrub it down. A perfect, if expensive, cleaning system.

As his eyes adjusted, Rory's mind tried to grasp what he *didn't* see and what the implications were: no screwdriver, anywhere. Thinking he understood what Arthur intended, Rory reached for the CIP to uncouple it from the hose.

Too late.

The CIP came to life, blasting water on him from every direction. Even the fizzing sound of water rushing and splashing the sides of the steel drum didn't mute Arthur's laughter. The water mixed with the yeast left in the tank and made foam. Rory stood there for a moment, paralyzed.

And angry at himself for letting Arthole dupe him, again.

Worse, as Rory leaned out the hatch, dripping and foamy, he saw Dubrow, frowning. Wearing his three-piece suit and Converse sneakers, Dubrow pointed at Rory with his snifter glass of water and lemon, his face pinched as if he'd sucked on said lemon.

Arthur had run off.

"What are you doing, son?" Dubrow asked.

What could Rory say? Arthur forced him into the Belgian fermenter? Only an idiot would be inside the fermenter. And an idiot would let Arthole convince him to climb inside the fermenter. He had no good answer.

"Well?" Dubrow pressed.

"I dropped my screwdriver into the fermenter and someone turned it on."

"You don't say? If you fellows spent half as much energy on brewing beer as you do on pranks..." And Dubrow gave Rory a tongue lashing and finished with the lamentation, "...how will this place ever run without me?"

Arthur captured video footage of Rory's conversation with Dubrow. He'd left his phone against a bucket full of CO2 tubes. It caught Rory's graceless fall to the slimy floor (because Arthur had removed the ladder) and Rory's deer-in-the-headlights look as Dubrow lit into him about not playing around in the lab. This was serious work and they were already behind on the TLC line and "...how about showing some intensity, Mr. Harper?! It's not playtime." Dubrow turned on his heel and stormed from the lab, not even grabbing the reports he'd come for.

The that's-what-she-said cook brought a pile of hand towels from the kitchen. Rory dried himself the best he could, but he smelled strongly of yeast. He imagined stuffing Arthur in the fermenter and turning on the CIP, filling it to the top, so Arthur would struggle to tread and suck at the couple inches of air. Arthur's arms and legs would thrash furiously until they became exhausted, and right then—of course just before Arthur gave up and died—Rory would drain the fermenter and Arthur would emerge, soaked and humiliated, to a room full of laughing colleagues. In the daydream, Dubrow laughed loudest, slapped Rory on the back, and told him how funny he was.

Justice was served.

In Rory's imagination.

Chapter 5

The end of summer heat was in full force, and the cicadas' electric yammerings could be heard even though Rory had his air conditioning blasting. He could no longer count on his fingers how many mornings Arthur had cut him off on the turn into Telluric. Rory was jealous of Silas, who had only a week left in his internship. He'd miss the kid though…

…And there was Arthole, waiting in the berm like usual, and when he saw Rory approach the intersection, he entered. It had gotten so Rory let him go through, even if Rory had the green arrow. Because if Arthur was sitting at the intersection, and Rory's arrow turned green, Arthur would run the red light. "What? You don't like playing chicken?" he'd quip on the way into the brewery. "You're no fun."

Arthur rolled up to the intersection and waved Rory through. Drivers behind Rory saw the way was clear. Rory could make the left turn yet sat there holding them up.

They beeped.

Rory inched forward.

Arthur inched forward.

More beeping. Some even from behind Arthur. He didn't care.

As Rory executed his left turn, Arthur gunned the gas, barely missing Rory's car. It was almost as if Arthur wanted a crash. No. He believed he could outmaneuver anybody. Chicken was a way to prove it.

Rory snapped. He couldn't say why. Just that he was tired of starting his day by having the shit scared out of him before he finished his commute. The many intersection offenses reached a critical mass, and Rory barreled into the parking spot next to Arthur, stormed the Trans Am, and banged his fist on the hood.

Arthur's jaw dropped. "Dude. What's your problem?"

Rory could barely keep from a full-scale fantod. "*My* problem?" He banged again.

Arthur slipped out of the car and checked the hood, ran his fingers along it and put his eyes at the surface level to detect dings. "A little immature hitting my car, don't you think?"

"Oh you are a sonofabitch."

"And calling me names. What are you, five years old?"

Rory slammed his fist gavel one last time and left without another word. How Arthur, who started the whole thing and was entirely unreasonable and vile, could turn the tables on Rory...well, it defied sense.

Rory stomped to the kitchen. Someone had brought those little muffin quiches to share. Thank God. They were arranged in a pile on a decorative plate. Rory swiped a bacon cheddar and a sausage pepper.

Mr. F instantly began his little feed-me dance where he "wagged" his tail and put his mouth to the water's surface. Mr. F's vase now had bright gravel and a fun little chest of gems and gold and silver coins. Watching his fish (*his*—Rory fed him) make parabola circuits around the vase always brightened Rory's mood. Whenever he went into the kitchen for coffee or a snack, Mr. F's tenacity for life taught Rory to be likewise.

And another thing they had in common: Mr. F wasn't exactly slim these days, either.

Rory touched his finger to the glass and sighed. "You're lucky. All you have to do is eat and swim."

"Good morning, Mr. F...Good morning, Rory." Silas' inclusion of Mr. F made Rory smile.

"One more week and you're off to college."

"I can't believe summer's over," Silas touched Mr. F's vase. "I should get a fish for school."

"He's always hungry," Rory joked. "Like me."

Silas' face wrinkled into a funny look Rory couldn't read. The intern stared into the tank, ran a finger along the bottom where flakes collected. "He'll eat until he explodes. Fish are like that."

"Oh. I didn't know," Rory said.

"That's okay. Why would you? But you won't have to clean his tank so often if you feed him less. He's cool with it, trust me."

At least Silas didn't make a fat joke.

Rory enjoyed teaching Silas and the other interns to do the cell counts and Co2 tests. His yeast was robust (like him, Arthur said). A reliable in-house source of yeast would make Telluric even more profitable. Dubrow had asked Rory whether yeast expansion was a possibility, and Rory was presently figuring out that yes, it was. Rory could produce the extra yeast, but they needed to monetize the used-up product, as opposed to throwing it out. Could Rory find a local farmer to sell it to? He was sure he could. That was today's task.

"The yeast counts are up," Silas said proudly.

"You read my mind," Rory patted his shoulder. "Great problem to have: extra yeast. I'm off to solve it." On his way out, Rory grabbed the only quiche flavor he hadn't yet tried, cheese scallion.

Rory lost no time in contacting a local farmer. Was he interested in the worn-out yeast in exchange for a monthly quota of beer? A savvy move. On a previous occasion, Rory had taken note of the farmer's belly (so like his own) and put his money on the idea that beer would be the best trade. Or free meals at the brewpub. The farmer either ate like a king, drank like one, or both.

"The wife, she'll be none the happier, but I like it," the farmer admitted.

Aha. The wife. Keepers of health. Roadblocks to fun.

Rory's wife—should he find one—would support his love of beer and be a beer drinker herself. Girly girls didn't do it for him. He wanted the woman who would join the stein-holding contest at the German club, who wasn't afraid to climb onto the benches and do a shot ski. Although Rory could no longer trust the bench to hold him for said shot ski. Still. That type of woman. The one who didn't cut her spaghetti noodles. Who reached out to pet a groundhog or allowed a dragonfly to land on her skin. That one.

The farmer agreed to take their used yeast. It was excellent fertilizer, he admitted.

Pleased with himself, Rory took the elevator down to the brewpub and poured himself a snifter of Sunnylicious to celebrate.

"You get laid, or what?"

Augh. Arthur.

"Huh?" Rory stammered.

"That smile, it's bigger than a plumber's ass crack. What're you so happy about, Slim?"

"I got Perry Flanders to take our yeast, almost for free."

Arthur rocked back, awed. He recovered. "Yeah, well don't let it go to your head. You still can't drive for shit."

The intersection, always the intersection.

Carl came by Rory's office before lunch. "Arthole's in an unnaturally good mood, right? Any idea why?"

"'Candy' gave him the time of day?"

Carl laughed.

"I lost my shit on him this morning," Rory admitted.

"I want to hear. We can sound off about Arthole over lunch, right?"

Rory met Carl in the lunchroom and recounted the morning's run-in with Arthur. And how he "punched" (his word) Arthur's beloved Trans Am. He didn't say how hollow the victory felt, though, because he wanted to feel good for a minute, and Carl seemed to like the idea of Arthole being mad over his Trans Am.

"Amenth and hallelujah!" Carl gave Rory's back a chummy slap. "He needths somebody to tell him off. I think we should video you banging on the hood of his car. We'll send it to him."

"Me? Why not you?" Rory unwrapped his hoagie, took a bite.

"No, no, I got a better idea. We should video you taking a dump on the hood of his precious Trans Am, right on the golden eagle. You can bounce up and down, like you're having a fit, right? That would be–" Carl looked over Rory's shoulder and stopped. His eyebrows knitted. His mouth pulled into a frown.

"What?" Rory asked.

"Where's the fish?"

Rory spun and almost fell out of the chair. Sure enough, Mr. F wasn't in his vase. Everything else was in its place, the water, the gravel.

"Did he jump out?" Rory wondered aloud, unable to keep the panic out of his voice. "He couldn't have, could he?"

Carl checked in the sink, on the counter. He got down on hands and knees and checked under the lip beneath the lower cabinets.

Rory pulled out the garbage, his heart sinking. No dead Mr. F on the top of the trash. Rory sniffed in case he'd fallen beneath other trash. No fish smell, either. "What the hell? Where could he be?" Rory asked, hoagie forgotten.

Carl patted Rory's shoulder. "Sorry, pal. I know you liked him. He probably died and someone flushed him."

"But I saw him this morning. He was fine."

From outside the kitchen, a snigger. Arthur.

"Hello? Arthur?" Rory called out.

No answer. Rory and Carl looked at one another. Arthur knew the whereabouts of Mr. F.

Carl stood and called out to a retreating Arthur, "Hey, you know what happened to the fish?"

Arthur ignored the question. His mocking laughter died away.

Carl sat down. "Bastard knows what happened. Mr. F probably died and Arthur flushed him."

"I hope he died *before* Arthur flushed him," Rory said.

Rory wanted to go home, but nobody went home over a dead fish. He excused himself and returned to his desk, trying to lose himself in emails and reports, but he had to repeatedly corral his mind back to work when it strayed to a dead Mr. F. He tried to convince himself it was no big deal. Mr. F had a good life, longer than he should've, considering he was bought to be swallowed before Rory was even hired.

After work, Rory joined Silas and Carl and some of the lunch servers who'd finished their shifts. The employee taproom also functioned as the private party room, an intimate, gaily furnished area with plush furniture and square tables that could be pushed together to accommodate large groups.

"Anyone know what happened to Mr. F?" Rory asked, even before he'd sat down with his glass. He'd helped himself to a 9% Imperial IPA, not in a snifter as it was usually served, but in a lager stein–enough beer to make Goliath tipsy. The IPA was to help him manage his emotions.

Servers looked at one another, each shrugging. They eyed Rory's choice of drink and glass.

"Awwww, did the poor little thing die?" Asked the server who bought him originally. "He was a fighter. He cheated death once, but you can't cheat it forever."

Rory took a big gulp. "Yeah, I know. I just wanted to know who found him. He seemed fine this morning."

"We can get another. Those things are a dime a dozen," another server said before she was elbowed in the ribs.

"Shhhh. He liked Mr. F."

Carl held up his glass. "To Mr. F, who had a long and happy life, especially after Rory came to Telluric. May he be swimming with the angels."

Everyone toasted Mr. F.

The next day, Rory continued to ask around. Who found Mr. F?

No one.

The interns, the cooks, the salespeople—no one admitted to finding a dead Mr. F and flushing him. There was one final person Rory did NOT want to ask. But because he liked Mr. F and was crazy-curious, he did.

"Maybe he took a vacation," Arthur, who could barely contain his snorting, offered. His hand cupped his mouth, and he bent double as if he'd said the funniest thing. "You need a vacation, Slim. From eating. Wait. You ate him, didn't you? You're trying to cover it up by asking around. You fattened up the little guy and then...pop." He made as if to throw back a pill.

Why had Rory bothered? He wouldn't get a straight answer, but what he was sure to get (and what he got) was assholery. Later that day, Rory received a text with a link to a video from an anonymous sender. Probably a scam. He didn't open it. A few seconds later, his phone buzzed again. Same text link to the same video. A third came. A fourth. Rory powered off his phone and worked a while. When he finished his yeast counts, he powered his phone on and was astonished to see the caller had sent the link over twenty times.

Done for the day, Rory cleared his desk and logged out of his computer. The sheer number of texts unnerved him.

Carl must've heard him getting ready to leave. He called out, "Have a beer to wait out the traffic?"

"Yeah...one minute." Rory held his phone, undecided. He silenced it. At that moment, another text came in with the link. All were from the same phone number, not in his contacts.

"Screw it." Rory had an iPhone. They almost never got viruses, unless the phone was jailbroken, and his wasn't.

He clicked the link.

Instantly, his throat closed. His heart hammered.

It was Mr. F, swimming.

As Rory watched, the frame panned back, and it became clear where Mr. F was swimming: the etch marks of one cup, two cups, the smaller increments of ounces.

Mr. F was in a glass blender.

Chapter 6

Before Rory could pause the video, the blender roared to life with a metallic shriek. Orange, foamy water with little white flecks licked the sides with each pulse of the motor. The orange broth had an odd, horribly beautiful iridescence produced by the milling of Mr. F's scales.

Rory's stomach lurched. He picked up his pace to hopefully get past the receptionist's desk before he hurled. He shifted to a run when he realized there was no stopping his stomach. His belly would not be told what to do. He searched for a trash can, even a recycling one with a little hole. He'd gladly put it there. But noooo. Nothing but marble floor, overstuffed leather chairs, and oak tables with replicas of beer bottles or crystal Telluric logos. He. was. going. to. puke.

He could bend over and let his stomach empty onto the waiting area. It would splash on his pants and shoes, and the receptionist (head in phone by the blue glow on her face) would call one of the brewpub workers to come clean it.

Or he could hop on the elevator and disappear. Thank God she didn't acknowledge him. For the first time, he was grateful to be fat and unremarkable.

Phone still in hand, Rory slammed the elevator call button so hard he jammed his finger. His stomach heaved. He squeezed himself off. Pursed his lips. The force below pushed up, up, up, and just as the bell rang that the elevator car was there, he puked into the empty side of his backpack, the side that didn't contain his laptop. Still puking, he shuffled inside. Puke splattered his phone screen.

He pressed *G* and wiped the phone on his pant leg. He sniffed. So, this was what the inside of a stomach smelled like. Rory held up his backpack, expecting to see it dripping. It wasn't. An accidental glance at the phone screen almost made him lurch again. He was about to power it off when a wiry arm shot in between the closing elevator doors, a fist with painted fingernails. The doors bounced off the arm.

Noooo.

Rory smashed the door-close button, hoping to override it. Pushed "G" several times, insanely wishing it would shut, arm be damned.

The door opened.

Delene Dubrow stood before him.

Head down, hair in her face, the arm not stopping the door was plunged into her purse, rooting around. When the doors sprang back, she breathed a sigh and smiled at Rory before her face wrinkled a little. She hesitated, then stepped into the elevator, still focused on finding something in her purse. That was the only reason she didn't see him frantically trying to close the door on her arm. Delene Dubrow, Benjamin Dubrow's daughter. Her long, wavy hair curtained much of her face, but he recognized her from the pictures in Dubrow's office and all over the brewpub.

"Hello," he croaked casually. It could be, someone else puked in the elevator and had already gotten out. He wondered if he had any vomit on his face. To wipe it would betray him.

From her purse Delene pulled a clear plastic band that looked like a piece of telephone cord, the ancient kind that hooked to walls. She bent over and shook out her tresses, and with hands as rapid as an artist's, she whisked it up with the little cord and piled it on top of her head. One stray piece fell into her face. She grabbed it and tucked it away.

For the first time, she looked at Rory.

"You the tasting wizard?"

"Er..."

"The one who never guesses wrong."

Rory arched an eyebrow.

"I mean, Dad says that." She blushed. "You're the true-to-style guy, the one who stuck it to Arthur."

"Yeah, I guess that's me."

"Dad thinks you're a genius. You managed to embarrass Arthur, twice. I'm sure that's a record."

"He's gotten me back, I assure you." Was the elevator even moving? Rory prayed she wouldn't put out a hand to shake.

"Dad's hard to work for," she said. "He makes you work your ass off for that one compliment, doesn't he?"

Rory wanted out.

She continued, talking almost as if Rory weren't there. "He expects the best, always. No down days. No half-assing anything, am I right?"

And with Rory's big ass, half was almost always plenty. Working for Dubrow was not easy, no. But he made great beer, and he was generous with his staff, which smoothed out the rest. Yes, although Dubrow worked him like a Hebrew slave, Rory found he greatly admired the man.

"He does have high standards," Rory admitted. To keep her from seeing inside his pack, he clutched it to him, pressing it closed. For once, he was glad for his big belly.

The elevator stopped on the brewpub floor, and kitchen staff and servers entered, pushing Rory and Delene to opposite sides.

Sniffs. Gags. Someone grumbled, "What the hell?"

Rory shook his head, as if he, too, was disgusted by whoever would do such a rude thing: puke on the elevator and stink it up. The pack was nestled between Rory's girth and the wall. Rather than meet any eyes, he looked through the people to Delene's shoes, her legs. He was curious about the daughter of Dubrow. She brought the energy of a river and the scent of flowers and coffee into the elevator. She wore athletic shoes, cut-off jeans, and a black tank top. Her legs were tanned, suggesting she was the outdoorsy type. He'd have thought Dubrow's seed would be more vogue. Oh, but couldn't the elevator car move faster? Would puke leak out the seams of his bag?

The elevator emptied, and Delene caught Rory staring at her legs. He almost explained he was looking through them, but that sounded ridiculous, even in his head. He reddened and looked away, exited the elevator quickly, ahead of her, which he chastised himself for doing. Not exactly chivalrous, but in his defense, he did have a sack of puke in his hands.

"Nice to meet you," she called out.

Rory waved (he hoped heartily) as he slipped into a maintenance closet. "You too."

He set the backpack on the sink and pulled out his laptop, surprised and grateful for the waterproof material. The laptop was safe. His pens, thermometer, and gum were fine, too. The side he'd puked into was where he kept his lunch. Having left it half-eaten on the table, the side was empty. He dumped the puke in the sink drain used for cleaning out buckets and mops. A forgotten pen fell into it. Damn. He tweezed it in two fingers and threw it away.

After scrubbing his hands furiously, he examined his pack. It was a total loss. He stuffed the whole thing into the trash can. Maintenance workers were used to gross things. Still, he apologized to whoever would inherit this mess.

The orange image on the phone was still there.

Arthur.

How could he? The man had no heart. He wasn't human. Most people had a good streak and a bad streak, but Rory could find not a thread of good in Arthur. (Okay, so he got results in the brewery.) Only psychos killed small animals. That was one of the tells. A sparkly, painful feeling had landed in Rory's solar plexus.

Rory peeked out the door to be sure the way was clear before he walked to his car. A Jeep was parked next to his. A woman wearing the exact same outfit as Delene Dubrow leaned over, pawing in the glove compartment for something. Rory wanted to turn back and wait until she'd gone. He didn't want to have to talk with her anymore. Would she notice he was shy a backpack, that he held his laptop under his arm like a book? She might put it together. Augh.

He hopped in his car, pretending not to see her.

"Oh, it's you," she said, as his door slammed shut.

He rolled the window down. "Everything alright?"

"I can't find my keys."

Rory attempted to heave himself back out of his car, an embarrassingly green Chevy he'd been meaning to trade in, but the thing never gave him any problems, and with Arthur playing Chicken every chance he got, Rory was hesitant to get a car he loved. The bite of the seatbelt reminded him he was buckled. He released it, stepped out, and sent the phone flying from his lap. He bent to pick it up.

There was Mr. F again on the screen, bright orange water.

Mr. F deserved justice. Rory could actually—not just in his imagination—make Arthur pay for his crimes against humanity and fish. Rory was a chemist, after all. He understood the properties of substances and could find the right one or a mix of them to give to Arthole.

A potion came to mind.

It had come to him before, but he'd pushed the thought away as childish. Only a coward did what Rory was considering. It was like putting tacks on somebody's chair. But what if the person deserved the tacks? What if tacks were all a person had at his disposal, being unable to (fine, unwilling) to fight openly?

Rory picked up his phone and pocketed it.

Arthur was going to get *his* guts blended. The whole grand scheme of it fell into Rory's mind like a gift, and he accepted it, turned it over and over to make sure it would work. Yes, it would. Arthur wouldn't ever know he'd been served a plate of *fuck you*, but Rory would, and the thought of it gave Rory a small amount of satisfaction.

Delene Dubrow's Jeep roared to life. She must've found her keys while Rory was inside his own head. He waved a goodbye, but she didn't see.

Chapter 7

Rory made two stops on his way home from Telluric. One, to the office supply store for a new computer case. And two, the pet store. He bought a new fish, a betta fish, and brought him to work. Enter: Bruce Lee. Bettas were Siamese fighting fish, the males known to fight each other to the death, which was why they came in tiny little bowls, one per bowl. Rory's Bruce Lee was a deep plum color with ruby red fin tips and a stunning iridescence. He'd heard bettas didn't enjoy the cramped bowls they were sold in, so he took Mr. F's vase and lined the bottom with black opal confetti glass. The effect was stunning.

The real Bruce Lee—the man—was from Hong Kong, not Thailand, but what did it matter? Bruce Lee was a fighter, and Rory's Bruce Lee would be a fighter, too. If something happened to him, Rory would buy another. And another. Arthole would not beat him. Maybe Rory would take up Taekwondo again, earn his black belt. He considered the hours it took to perfect the forms, the kicks, the blocks, the strikes. The sparring. And the boards. Rory did not go looking for pain, even if it was beneficial. No. It was easier to give Arthur the anonymous smackdown with no sweat from Rory, no one to know.

He began a devious internet search, his gaze often flitting to Bruce Lee. No matter how fashionably decorated the vase, Rory could not be there 24-7 to make sure no one put Bruce Lee in a blender. Was Arthur stupid enough to do the same thing twice? Then what? Rory would go to the police with: *Hey, I've got two dead fish.* That'd bring the full fury of police muscle to bear on Arthur. No, the way to keep Bruce Lee safe and get justice for Mr. F was to strike a little fear into the arrogant Arthole. Arthur was going to pay for blending Mr. F.

Blind study day.

Arthur-pays-for-his-crimes day.

Rory gets the perfect, *anonymous* revenge day.

Rory had to walk a long hallway, feeling eyes on him. Could they see the bulge in his pocket? He tried not to worry at it as he'd been doing all morning. The bag of Senna capsules served as a stress ball while he talked himself into going through with it. What could go wrong? Nothing, that's what.

At the end of the hall stood Arthur and a glut of execs, sales reps, and VIPs from other breweries. They looked in Rory's direction, and Arthur motioned to him. As he approached, he heard: "This is our newest chemist...and elevator counterweight."

They responded with polite, subdued laughter reserved for inappropriate jokes.

"Hello, Slim."

The baggie of shit-inducing capsules felt oh so right. He squeezed it with one hand and shook with the other. "Rory. Nice to meet you."

"Slim here would love to join us for lunch, but he's busy running our study today," Arthur said.

This was news to Rory, but rather than give Arthur any satisfaction, he smiled.

Rory breathed a sigh of relief when the lot of them stepped into the elevator and left.

For the blind study, it was Silas' job to remove the bottle labels and assign them numbers. Silas and Rory would be the only ones who knew which number corresponded to which product line. With Arthur out to lunch, Rory and Silas could work in peace. He was already ordering pizza in his mind. And choosing his after-work beer.

Rory had enough Senna capsules in his pocket to clean God's colon, and he had to figure out how he'd stir it into Arthur's beer flight. The oaf always made a speech about the lab's doings on these occasions, what new recipes they were kicking around, what celebrities had been spotted with a glass of Telluric to their lips. On the enormous bar screens, Arthur would show the same pictures every time. Brad Pitt with a pint of TLC. Jennifer Hancock's larger-than-life smile as she toasted with Dubrow. Even Elon Musk was known to partake of Telluric's unique brews—clandestinely because he was launching his own Tesla beer. Arthur would play video clips: brewery spoofs where Rory was the star, like the fermenter cleaning. Dubrow chuckled at the image of Rory climbing out of the fermenter, looking like he was being birthed, slick and miserable. Weren't Telluric's staff having the time of their lives, laughing at Rory? Never mind the fact that Dubrow had been furious about the fermenter incident. Now, as everyone guffawed, Dubrow looked around and smiled. Points for Arthur. There'd be no stopping his bullshit now.

It made Rory want to Senna him to death. Was that even possible? Death by diarrhea? Sure, sure it was. Dysentery killed lots of people. But Arthur was too healthy for that. Rory would have to be satisfied (for now) with the idea of Arthur's spasming colon fixing him to the toilet in the wee morning hours.

As Arthur enthralled the staff with beer trivia and basked in the attention like the narcissist he was, Silas poured the beer. This was by Rory's design. If Arthur suspected someone of tampering with his beer, it wouldn't be Silas. Rory and Silas knew who was getting what beer, but the tasters didn't. Each participant received a beer flight, a set of various five-ounce beer pours. Flights ranged from four flavors of beer to eight or even more. Wooden skis were made to hold the glasses in line. Before each flight, Rory placed a grading form. The first beer was the easiest to guess, so most everyone guessed correctly. What flavor were you drinking? Write it down. One or two flavors would be hard to guess. The idea was that, as soon as Arthur was finished riffing, the beer would be poured, fresh as could be.

Rory sent Silas to the supply room for more forms (Earlier, Rory had made sure they didn't have enough forms). The moment Silas was gone, Rory dumped the Senna into Arthur's flight and stirred. He was rinsing the spoon when Silas returned. Kid was lightning. Each beer had Senna leaf extract, so the flavor would not stand out in one.

The beautiful thing about Senna was its bitter taste mixed well with first-pour hops. Arthur bragged he liked the bitter IPA. No hazy. No citrus. The Senna would go down easy. And in a couple of hours, when Arthur was home playing his dumbass puerile video games, he'd feel an urge. And the urge would turn into giant hands squeezing out his large intestine as if it were a stress ball. Or a dishrag. After a night of Senna leaf, Arthur would be ready for a colonoscopy. Rory smiled. Arthur would wonder if he'd accidentally got some of the poison meant for the bottling test, that when he'd used the pipette to inject a few drops into the beer during the bottling process he'd not washed his hands. Maybe he'd wonder if he'd ingested some cleaning agent. Or got a bad burger or chicken breast. Or, maybe he'd consider Rory wasn't the lamb he played at being, that Arthur had woken the tiger, so to speak.

The servers working the dinner shift had come early to take part in the tasting. The first batch of Roctober Birch would be consumed publicly as well as some recipe ideas Rory put forward and one Arthur submitted.

Bruce Springsteen played from most speakers. Dubrow had a second set of speakers playing a recorded loop of busy kitchen: dishes clanging, sinks filling with water, the sizzle of meat hitting a hot pan, the scratch of a shaken pan over the gas flame burner, laughter, and the quiet buzz of production. This was Dubrow's idea of how to use sound psychology to influence behavior, specifically, to make people consume more alcohol. People naturally liked beer they'd consumed in positive environments. And while The Boss was the main musical accompaniment, the background joy of cooking sealed the deal. That, and the decor of the tasting room. Telluric had been a brewery before prohibition, then an ice-packing plant, and then Telluric. The original upstairs bar was kept intact. It included the bullet holes from some long-ago brawl. Dubrow had the original bar stools copied by a local woodworker, the original oak bar refinished by the same. The glass behind the bottles was original too.

Dubrow was busy charming several businesspeople who managed or owned local restaurant chains. He made gifts of Telluric coasters, glasses, and swag wear. In return for deeply-discounted product, the owners would put Telluric on draft in their establishments. Bottles and cans were great. Draft was better. Dubrow called Rory over to his table.

"Here." He handed Rory a sampler glass of honey-yellow beer. "Tell them what it is." Dubrow faced his guests. "Watch this. He never misses."

"How do we know he wasn't told?" one asked.

"Pine Hour," Rory said without a trace of doubt.

"You give him one," Dubrow challenged. "Grab one from the fridge in the lab. There's a hundred different kinds in there."

The skeptic set off to the bar. He spoke briefly with Silas, who led him presumably to the lab fridge. They returned with a glass for Rory. The beer was more amber and hazy and had a finger's worth of a foam head. The aroma gave it away.

"I can already tell you this will be a space hop beer."

The rep pursed his lips but couldn't help giving away that Rory was correct. "That narrows it down to thirty of the beers you have back there."

Rory tasted.

Arthur wandered over. Of course he did. To watch Rory and try to jangle his nerves. "Slim never strikes out," he said. "Except with the ladies."

Rory gave Arthur the stink eye and continued to feel the beer, taste it. "I didn't strike out with your mom," he surprised himself by saying.

The table roared.

"Cable Car."

The sales rep pulled out the bottle. "It *is* Cable Car. Glad I didn't bet against you."

"Now if you'll excuse me." Rory bowed. "I must get back to serving."

Dubrow nodded in appreciation. "Silas, would you be so kind as to bring us another round, please?"

The whole time Rory was drinking, Arthur hadn't taken a single sip. Now, he tipped his glass. Rory could practically hear the epic chords of "300 Violin Orchestra" play as the golden liquid went into his enemy. Enema, Arthole? As Arthur drank, Rory stared at him deeply, hoping to introduce into Arthur the idea that would flower later, that he would suspect but not be certain Rory was behind his bowel explosions, that

Rory had gotten him good. Like Mr. F couldn't be proven Arthur's doing, but Rory knew it was. So it would be with the Senna.

Why would Rory want to do such a thing to Arthur? In retaliation for the fish? But what fish? There was no proof Arthur had anything to do with Mr. F's demise. And there'd be no proof Rory had a hand in Arthur's diarrhea. Oh, he hoped there'd be a blowout right there in the taproom. More likely, it would take effect later. So Rory wouldn't have the satisfaction of seeing his face? So what? Arthur hadn't seen Rory's either. He'd sent the video and let it be. Touché, Arthole. Touché.

Rory watched Arthur for any sign he recognized a difference in the flavor of the beers. Nope. The dumbass. He tossed them back and declared his favorite: Mystic Moment. Rory poured another Senna flight and had Silas serve it to him.

In all his days at Telluric, Rory had never felt more powerful than he did at that moment. *Justice was blind* went the saying. Impartial. Objective. Anybody who'd spent time with Arthur would know that this justice, although not served within the normal channels, was of the purest, the most righteous kind.

After throwing down several thick, syrupy stouts, Rory felt the fuzzy glow of happiness. It didn't hurt that he knew Arthur would be clinging to his toilet bowl any time now. He'd put the rest of the Senna beer beneath the bar as if it was his glass and he'd be back for it. He set it next to the liquors because that was where he usually set his belongings. Silas was talking to him, and he couldn't justify why he'd throw perfectly good beer down the drain. Servers would assume he'd forgotten about it, and it would be tossed out at the end of the night.

When Arthur asked for a snifter of Magic Moment, Rory poured him a third Senna Special.

Have some cold revenge, Arthole.

Chapter 8

Occasional hangovers could be expected when working in a microbrewery. Rory's aching head told him perhaps he overdid it last night. But the pain didn't stop him from glorying over Arthur. No matter how awful Rory might feel this morning, it was a certainty Arthur felt worse. So sure was Rory about the state of Arthur's digestive tract, he didn't bother looking for a Trans Am at the intersection and pulled into Telluric like he owned the place. Ahhhh, the bliss. He parked his car in one of the two spaces Arthur usually did.

In one arm Rory balanced his usual Friday treat of a dozen donuts plus a dozen more because he felt very *Caesar* this morning. Very *I-just-did-that.* The idea of Arthur making love to his toilet bowl was buzz enough to make Rory skip across the parking lot. He sang ZZ Top in the elevator, not caring who heard.

The elevator doors opened to the endless ringing of the phone and to Anne (Arthur's "Candy"), the receptionist. A tissue obscured her pretty face. She blew forcefully into it and didn't rush to grab the phone, so Rory reached over the desk. "Telluric Lake Brew Works. Can I help you?" he asked, feeling chivalrous.

She looked at him with grateful, wet eyes.

Ken, one of the interns was calling in "sick," which translated: I had too many beers last night at the tasting. Rory told him to enjoy the day off and be careful of IPAs in the future. He scribbled a note for Anne to pass along to human resources. Rory wasn't the only Telluric employee who'd had a few too many, and yet here he was, not calling in sick. Noooooo. Not on a day when Arthur would be out. Would be home. Shitting his brains out. Mwah hah hah.

The phone rang again. Anne ignored it a second time.

"What's wrong?" Rory asked, letting the box of donuts tip a little.

She buried her face in her hands and sobbed, said something Rory could not even guess at. The phone rang and rang, grating Rory's nerves. Somebody from the brewpub finally answered it.

Rory handed her a fresh tissue. "I'm sorry. I didn't catch that. Do you need to go home?"

"He's dead." She shook her head and spat the words, trying to deny them.

"Arthur's *dead*?"

Her face screwed up in confusion. "What? No. Not Arthur...Mr. Dubrow."

"Dubrow?! What happened?"

"I don't know. I just found out he's gone. How can he be gone?" And she took refuge in her tissue again.

Dubrow...dead?

Couldn't be. Could. Not. Be.

Rory spun on his heel. This was inconvenient, if karmic, timing. God wanted Rory to feel remorse for what he'd done. The Almighty couldn't just let Rory have his day in the sun. Noooo. *Vengeance is mine,* sayeth the Lord. Rory took what belonged to God when he put Senna in Arthur's beers. He wasn't a particularly religious man, but the oddly-timed circumstances made him question whether invisible, divine machinations were at work.

He shook his head. "I'm jumping to conclusions," he gasped, clamped his mouth, and scoped the hallway, relieved no one was nearby. Had he said that out loud? His mind raced in circles into the memories of the evening. No way could Dubrow have gotten any of the Senna beer. Rory'd been careful, so careful. Not that he believed the Senna could truly harm anyone, and never, no never *kill* someone. It was a laxative. Dubrow dying on the night Rory poisoned Arthur was a fluke, was all. A terrible coincidence that took up residence in Rory's guts and kicked and screamed. Even if Dubrow keeling over had nothing to do with the Senna, Rory's prank would be found out. How would that go down, Rory spiking beers with Senna? He'd lose his job for sure and maybe go to jail. He'd meant no harm. Only to Arthur.

Wait. Was Arthur dead, too? What if something went wrong, like he'd measured incorrectly? He was a chemist. He knew what he was doing. A moment ago, he was glad for Arthur's absence. Now, he worried.

Had Dubrow gone to the ER with stomach pains? Had Arthur? Was a morgue doctor doing an autopsy and finding a belly full of Senna at this moment? And...*dead.* A man was dead, and all Rory could think about was if he'd be caught in his Senna prank.

"You're a horrible person." Out loud, again. He clapped a hand over his mouth.

He spun on his heel and rushed to the taproom to make sure his Senna had been tossed down the sink. With all the "celebrating" he'd done last night, the gloating, he wasn't sure he'd disposed of the evidence. Because last night, it wasn't evidence. It was a little well-deserved revenge on Arthur.

At the taproom door, Rory stopped dead in his tracks. Had he seen any police cars outside the brewery? He wasn't paying attention. But there, sitting in a booth along the back wall was a plainclothes policeman typing away on a laptop (he could see the holster and the badge on his belt).

"Can I help you?" The cop didn't look up.

For a second, Rory considered turning and fleeing the building, driving until he was out of the state. His mind tried to work, to find an answer to the question—what was the question again? Oh yes. Could he, this officer of the law, help Rory? Help him into the back seat of a cruiser? Into a jail cell? He considered laying it all out, admitting he was concerned he'd accidentally had something to do—*something?* Okay, admitting *the teeny weeny chance he may have accidentally killed Dubrow when all—ha! ALL he'd meant to do was poison his co-worker, Arthur. Arthole, and he deserved it, Your Honor. If you knew Arthole, you'd find me innocent...*

"Er...I left my coffee mug behind the bar." Rory said.

The detective's fingers flew on the keyboard, making little insectile clicks. His frown deepened at something or other on the screen.

Rory needed one look at the sink behind the bar, to make sure the Senna glass had been put in the dishwasher and not, as Rory feared, left on the counter.

"Do you mind if I grab it?" Rory asked.

An arched eyebrow, a deepening frown, but still no eye contact.

"You hear the news?" The detective finally looked up from his laptop.

Rory nodded solemnly, thankful he didn't have to speak. He didn't think he could.

"So I won't say, 'Good morning' because it's not, especially for your boss who also happened to be an acquaintance of mine. I'm Detective O'Deens. Where did you say your coffee cup was?"

Rory's tongue was a dry, dead leaf. "Behind the bar...I think."

Detective O'Deens scrutinized Rory in a way that made him feel naked. There was no coffee cup behind the bar. Anybody could mistakenly think they left one, though. It was a perfectly legit reason to come running to the taproom the moment you heard your boss had died.

"It'll be at least a day before you get it back. I'd suggest making do," O'Deens said.

"Okay...but why? Is the brewpub a crime scene?"

O'Deens looked at Rory as if he were an imbecile. "I didn't say it was a crime scene. I said you'll have to make do. Someone died here."

"Dubrow died here?"

"I don't think he meant to."

Rory turned to go, couldn't retreat fast enough.

"Wait," O'Deens demanded.

Rory turned back slowly. In his soul, his hands were in the don't-shoot position.

"Those for me?" O'Deens shot Rory a toothy smile. "You shouldn't have."

"What?"

He nodded at the box of donuts. "You know how we feel about those things." He winked and pretended to shoot at Rory with his finger. "Mr...?" He looked at Rory over his glasses in a way that demanded Rory provide his name.

"Harper. Rory Harper. I'm one of the–"

"Chemists. Thought so. Don't leave town or anything, okay?"

Rory gulped.

"Joking."

Rory didn't think he was, though.

"Jokes aside, don't talk to your colleagues until we have our rap session, ten-four?"

"Uh-huh."

Rory didn't eat a single donut, though six of them were French crullers. He left them on the kitchen table. By the time lunch rolled around, O'Deens still hadn't left Telluric. The waiting was going to kill Rory for sure. Through the walls, he'd heard the detective talking with Carl. It sounded like the teacher from the Peanuts cartoons: "Whah-whah whah-whah whah."

Silas walked past his door.

"Psssst," Rory made the sound as loud as he dared.

Silas' head popped back into the door frame.

Rory motioned him inside, mouthed *oh-my-God* and whispered. "How did Dubrow seem to you, last night?"

Silas didn't take a seat. He combed his hands through the curls in his bangs and gave a sad, helpless look. "I don't know. Fine...I guess. He drank a lot, but he always does. He even drank the flight of beers you had me pour for Arthur."

It was Rory's turn to gulp. He had to, or he might throw up. "Oh," his voice was choked. "Arthur didn't drink his second flight then?"

Silas shook his head.

"What was he drinking?"

"I don't know."

Rory stared at his computer screen and re-played last night's tasting. When had he last seen Dubrow? He was cleaning up the tasting notes, looking at them, filing them by flavor. Dubrow and the owner of Heartland Heat were talking at a two-top in the corner by the bourbon barrels. They had beer flights before them, and Rory specifically could recall an image of Dubrow holding a sample glass, studying it in the light. Dubrow looked to be in perfect health. Rory had gone to make copies of the tasting notes, put a file on the table beside Dubrow, and left. Dubrow was thick in conversation and hadn't even acknowledged Rory, which was fine by him.

Arthur, on the other hand, had a pinched expression when Rory handed him the tasting notes. Rory had decided it was that look right before you excused yourself to use the toilet. The look he, Rory, put there. And still, to be sure Arthur got his just desserts, Rory had served him another Senna-spiked flight.

"Here you go, Boss," Rory said as he handed Arthur the IPA flight. He'd never called Arthur "Boss" before. Where had that come from? Likely from the dense, dark hedge of vindictive camouflage. Like drawing out the "Your Highness" right before plunging in the knife.

An image flashed in Rory's memory. At Dubrow's table. A flight of the same colors of Arthur's last pour, the one full of Senna. The sweaty glasses. Had it been the wrong flight? Had the Senna somehow gone to Dubrow, and harmless beer to Arthur? Silas' words gnawed at Rory: *He drank the flight you had me pour for Arthur.* Rory wanted to dispel that possibility. He reached, but the arms of his mind were too short. No matter how hard he concentrated, he couldn't be sure of the flights, the timing. Dubrow was dead, and Rory had been serving poisoned beer. Those two facts were too proximal.

Silas and Carl were some of the first staff to leave the tasting, Rory remembered, and he had no buddies to sit with. Drinking alone was out of the question. Staying any longer, alone, would be out-of-character for Rory. So, he committed Arthur's pressed lips, twitching neck muscle, and slightly popping eyes to memory and wished everyone a good night. He dumped the Senna beer down the drain on his way out.

Certainly, he did.

Did he? He had been drinking. He couldn't recall.

Rory poisoned Arthur, and Dubrow was dead. It didn't make sense.

Rory's mind returned to the present and his gaze landed on Bruce Lee. The Siamese fighting fish was giving him the stink eye, he swore it.

"Oops. I forgot to feed you. It's been a rough day." Rory sighed. "I wonder, does Arthur even know yet? No way he came into work today." He dropped in a pinch of the little rock-like food and watched, transfixed. Bruce Lee was famished.

Rory put his face close to the glass and addressed Bruce Lee, "How you can eat on a day like tod–"

"I thought I told you not to speak to anyone."

It was O'Deens, leaning on the door frame, a wry smile playing on his lips but not reaching his eyes.

"I..."

"You don't have a sense of humor, do you?"

"Uh, my boss died?" Rory said, unsure if this O'Deens was intentionally trying to unsettle him or if he really was trying to lighten Rory's mood. He could imagine the police report on him: *Suspect showed no remorse for his boss's death.* Rory didn't trust cops and their verbal judo. They had one objective: compliance.

"My old friend died, and I still have a sense of humor."

Did he think that was a point of pride? "How'd he die?" Rory ventured.

"I'll ask the questions first, ten-four? Then you can have the conch shell."

"The what?"

"*Lord of the Flies*." O'Deens rolled his eyes. "No one reads any-more. Forget it. Me first on the questions, then you. Ten-four?"

"Sure."

Rory had read *Lord of the Flies* forever ago, but he was a few steps behind O'Deens, who had already launched into his first question. The questions came as rapid fire, one after another, until Rory's brains were scrambled eggs and he wasn't sure of anything. O'Deens had asked at least five times what time it was when he went home for the evening. Finally, Rory answered, "The same time I told you the other four times. And I didn't check my watch. I didn't know my exact moment of departure would be required of me."

O'Deens chuckled. "Just making sure you're sure."

"Do you do this to everyone?"

"Are you asking if you're a suspect? Because that's awful defensive of you."

Rory snorted. He'd had about enough of this O'Deens and his mental sparring.

"Yes, Mr. Harper, I do this to everyone. Like I said, Ben was an old family friend. I'm here to make sure he went out singing the 'Hallelujah Chorus.'"

Rory breathed what he hoped was an unnoticeable sigh of relief.

O'Deens shook his hand and was almost out the door when he turned back. "One last thing. When I came in, you were talking. To your fish. You said something about your colleague Arthur being absent today. What was that about?"

Heat engulfed Rory's ears. An invisible boa constrictor had settled around his neck. "We were drinking last night. The tasting. He had a lot. Of product. I mean, beer. I figured he might not make it in. Like...Ken. Ken didn't make it in. The internist, he called in this morning, sick. But we all know what it really is."

"Hangover?"

"Right."

"But *you* made it in."

"I ate a lot of carbs." Rory's pat on his belly was his witness.

O'Deens made a note in his little pad. "I hope you don't mind. I took a French cruller. You know us cops and our donuts."

For a guy who lost a friend, O'Deens didn't look shaken up. He and Dubrow must not have been close. Or perhaps, like Rory, O'Deens' outside didn't match his inside. A poem from Rory's bedside anthology rattled around in his head, like an earworm. No matter how he tried not to think it, there it was: *Wilt thou forgive that sin where I begun? Wilt thou...*

Could O'Deens tell? Could he see the guilt?

After O'Deens left, Rory practically ran to the brewpub. He couldn't wait to talk with Silas and Carl about their O'Deens talks. The detective was using the reception area to interview—that's what he called it, not interrogate—the serving staff who had been working yesterday evening during the tasting.

Silas looked ill. He looked as bad as Rory felt. Rory patted the kid's shoulder and plopped into a seat.

"This is a joke," said Carl. "Dubrow had a heart condition. He was fat—no offense, Rory—he had a heart attack. I don't know why anyone would think otherwise."

"How do you know it was a heart attack?" Rory hoped his voice didn't betray his excitement at the idea of cardiac arrest.

"Wife's a paramedic, remember? She says Dubrow had all the signs of a heart attack. Overweight, his hand was clenched in a fist over his heart—they see that a lot. His face didn't show signs of stroke. No blood. No bruising, other than where he hit the floor, right?"

Arthur put his head between Carl and Rory.

Rory stifled a scream.

Arthur looked like Jack Nicolson in *The Shining*.

Rory was both startled and relieved. Not dead, then, but Arthur should be home, shitting himself.

"Unlessssss," Arthur hissed like a snake, looking like the picture of demented health, "what if someone told the cops he suspected foul play."

Carl leaned away from Arthur. "You called the cops? Why?"

"I didn't say I did. I said, 'What if?'"

Rory couldn't understand. Why was Arthur standing there, looking as smug and hydrated as ever? And he stared Rory down, a challenge in his eyes. Rory wasn't imagining it. Arthur was messing with him.

"Hey, Slim. You parked in my spot."

"You were...uh...late."

"Had some trouble exiting the throne room this morning, know what I'm saying?" Arthur let that fact settle. "You're almost out of beer. Can I bring you another?"

Carl's and Silas' jaws dropped. Arthur would never stoop so low as to serve someone. The malevolence in his voice was unmistakable. He reached for Rory's glass, but Rory held it to his heart, unwilling to hand it over.

"No? You don't want another beer? You're always getting beers for everyone, and it's high time I get *you* a beer, Slim."

"Really, no. I'm good. I'm going home anyway."

"If you say so." He winked archly and was off.

"What was that about?" Carl asked and drained his glass.

"Fucking weirdo," Rory said, hoping they couldn't feel his freaked-out vibes.

Silas shifted the attention away from Arthur when he announced, "That's it. I'm having a beer. Dubrow made it his life's work to create great beer, and that life needs to be toasted. You're not going home, are you, Rory? C'mon, remember Dubrow with us. He'd want you to."

So Rory drank to quell the rising angst in his throat. As the beers went down, his anxiety did, too. Replaced by a fuzzy idea he could do nothing to stop whatever forces were at work. All he could do was drink beer with his friends and try to stay in the moment. Everyone was acting out of order today because it was a fucked-up, horrible, no-good day. Silas was drinking. Arthur was serving. Rory was fasting. And Carl, he downed beer after beer and shook his head sadly. Everyone was jolted by the idea that the great Benjamin Dubrow had fallen.

Chapter 9

Dubrow's grave was in the new section where the gravesites were sparse, the ground patiently waiting for its occupants. To get there, they passed through older sections of the sprawling cemetery where tired-looking gravestones leaned or lay in pieces, their etchings no longer discernable. The original church property overlooked Nob Lake, but the trees had grown, obstructing the view. A nearby basketball court had a lively game going. The players didn't seem to mind the rain. There was the unmistakable slap-slap-slap of sneakers, the pound of a ball on court, the shouts to teammates.

Rootsville. Wet. Gray.

Like Rory's soul.

You died, and they still played basketball. It didn't seem fair.

Summer was dying, too. The cottonwood trees had long ago lost their fluffy nose-itching bits and had begun to shed the gnarled, leafless sticks that, to Rory, looked like enormous Grim Reaper fingers scattered over the grass. Last night's thundershowers had pulled them down. Today's rain was the steady, never-ending kind that made Rory yearn for an afternoon nap—for dry socks and a stout beer. Spongy earth licked his shoes and leaked into the seams as he made his way to the gravesite. Rory scanned the groups of mourners and stood in the place he felt most invisible.

Nothing could be done about his decision to attend. He was here. Might as well embrace the moment. An appearance at the boss's funeral was the reasonable response of an upright, morally sound and caring employee. And although being here, graveside, was the absolute last place on earth Rory wanted to be, not to show would cause suspicion because if he were innocent, he'd come. Simple as that. Do the actions innocent-Rory would do. Every move he made since the "accident" was the result of a long process of strategic internal questioning (to avoid external questioning): How would the action look to a watching world?

Rory's thick hands shook uncontrollably. He stuffed them in his pockets, willed them to stop. They wouldn't cooperate. His whole body trembled like an idling semi-truck, and he was sure it was a spectacle, screaming his guilt to the innocent mourners all around him. As more people showed up to the gravesite, Rory inched further backward, often knocking his belly or bottom into grief-zombified people paying their respects to the late Benjamin Dubrow, CEO of Telluric, beloved father, entrepreneurial genius, Dionysian, crotchety boss, wholly undeserving of death-by-Senna.

"Sorry," Rory mumbled. Stepped aside. Bumped another person.

"Sorry."

"Sorry."

He couldn't allow his quaking hulk to get too close to anyone. But if someone did notice his butterfly hands or quivery lips, Rory had a story prepared: hangover. He had too much product last night at the staff's celebration of life for Dubrow. Silas' idea. Once that boy got a taste of good beer, he was *in the club*. He'd slur-shouted while holding a glass toward the heavens that Benjamin Franklin was NOT blaspheming when he famously said, "Beer is proof God loves us and wants us to be happy." Kid couldn't try enough flavors.

"Beer is God's drink," Silas had said. "I can't believe I missed it all this time."

Rory had told him how lucky he was to have blown right by the piss-water most collegiates drank, that he had gone straight to the good stuff. Like your first cup of coffee being Starbucks dark roast. Or your first chocolate being Godiva. Everything else, ruined.

But there wasn't enough beer in the world to make Rory happy.

Not enough beer to wash away the guilt. Rory felt sure his guilty soul stuck out from everywhere. He tried to soothe himself with the idea Dubrow's death had affected everyone in strange, unexpected ways. That didn't mean the staff were guilty of murder.

Just him, maybe.

Silas had admitted, once he was thoroughly pickled, that he took his first drink in order to rid himself of the image of his boss, dead behind the bar. Silas hadn't seen Dubrow's corpse literally, of course, but the idea... The brevity of life had a face now. Dubrow had died on Silas' last day of work, and Silas needed help processing the shock of it before he headed off to Cornell where life would become considerably more worky. He planned to drink large quantities of delicious beer while he had the chance. Cornellians, he had slurred, had a reputation for flinging themselves off the tall Ithacan bridges to a merciful end to their excruciating studies. The college responded by installing nets below the bridges. Silas said the beers were like nets. They'd save him. But he wouldn't make it to the funeral, he'd said, he had to pack.

Rory had seen through that; the kid didn't have the stomach for a funeral. "No need to remember the boss, dead, in a casket," Rory had said, "Better to remember him in life."

Carl had said open caskets were gross, like looking at a person naked. People had no business looking at dead bodies, according to Carl, and when he died, they'd better cremate him. As Rory recalled, everyone had strong opinions on what to do with their dead bodies, all shared around the table last night in minutia and with the help of beer. Rory had claimed cremation as his pragmatic choice. Who was strong enough to carry Rory's coffin? Superman?

Today, Carl was nowhere to be found. He hadn't shown up to the mass. Rory wondered if he'd come to the gravesite.

Should Rory be here? Or did showing up make him look more guilty? He'd come to this hateful ceremony to ensure he looked less guilty. Oh, he couldn't make a decent decision. His brains were pickled in guilt and beer. His belly grumbled, but food repulsed him.

Arthur had lied about calling the cops. Being his usual asshole self, he had wanted to stir the pot. But Arthole's strange behavior had Rory on eggshells. He would not allow himself to relax, even though O'Deens had declared Dubrow dead of natural causes. You couldn't trust detectives. They were always angling. O'Deens said there were no suspicious circumstances, no persons of interest, no reason to believe there'd been any foul play. Sure, some people hated Dubrow, the detective said. Poor guy was rich and powerful. And in business, sometimes you had to piss on the little people. Or piss them off. Whatever it took. Dubrow was a savvy businessman, and he had an empire to show for it. O'Deens had made the round of questions to satisfy his own curiosity, Dubrow being a family friend and all, but as far as the detective could tell, old Benjamin Dubrow had died because his heart gave out. He'd had a lot of beer at the tasting, and it was his time. The coroner agreed. Case closed.

But O'Deens didn't know Silas had served Dubrow a flight of Rory's Senna beer. Or that Senna had over two hundred drug interactions.

And an autopsy had not been done. Because of that, Rory could not be certain he had not inadvertently caused Benjamin Dubrow's death.

Rory had to be careful with everything, most especially the expression of his face. To prepare for this moment, Rory had stared at his reflection in the bathroom mirror, rehearsing his lines. "I know, I know. I can't believe he's gone. Damn tragic. He seemed so healthy."

That was an entirely true statement. Just...Rory believed he might be the one who killed him. That part he omitted. That was the lie.

Best lies...mostly true. Best lies...mostly true. Best... A mantra Rory had repeated to himself over and over in the days since the accident, trying to stifle the poem by John Donne: *Wilt thou forgive that sin where I begun?* —Best lies...mostly true— *Wilt thou forgive that sin through which I run?* BEST LIES...MOSTLY TRUE... He chanted to himself in order to focus on whatever task needed doing or to have the next "natural" conversation. Hopefully, the pounds Rory had shed wouldn't show in his charcoal suit because anything out of the ordinary was bad for him, he decided. Rory couldn't help it he wasn't hungry. His belly was full of guilt.

O'Deens was, of course, at the funeral. Rory almost bumped into him, as both were keeping to the outside of the crowd, under the radar.

"Sorry." It came out choked and an octave higher than he'd meant. Could O'Deens divine guilt from that? Wasn't that what detectives were trained to do? Spot guilt a mile away?

Rory's wing-tip oxfords were slathered in mud. The women had to walk on the balls of their feet to prevent their high heels from being sucked right off. Two little girls dressed in matching black dresses had backs spritzed with mud. They must've run from the car to the gravesite. O'Deens' shoes were unscathed. Rory considered asking him if he also walked on water, and if so, could he change the weather for them? A little sun, perhaps? A few degrees cooler? But that would put him as a thing in O'Deens' mind. And Rory didn't want to be anywhere near O'Deens' mind.

"No worries...Rory, is it?"

"Uh-huh."

"Good of you to come. So many people lack etiquette." He sniffed and nodded in the direction of the coffin. "Makes me want to pass on the beer." His eyes dropped to Rory's girth. "I got to wonder how many years it took from him."

"Beer? Well, yes...it's unhealthy. All things in moderation." Rory shook O'Deens' hand and moved away, pretending to see someone he knew.

The pallbearers were an eclectic mix. Several were robust, bearded men with beer-loving bellies. One young, strapping man sported a long ponytail at the nape of his neck. A young boy about ten or so danced alongside the coffin, corralled by Delene Dubrow. Her long, coffee-colored hair veiled half her face. She wore a long-sleeved, simple black dress that hinted at her athletic build and black Converse sneakers—in honor of her father? They certainly didn't match her dress but were a nod to the man who cared little for fashion rules and preferred to blend sophistication and hipster. That unlikely union of uptown and back alley was what made his beer great. Every social stratum agreed: Telluric was the best.

The boy "holding" the casket in front of Delene was more theatre than help. His limp hand lay over the bar, lightly touching it. His little legs kept threatening to trip Delene or the man behind him. Rory wondered if a casket had ever been dropped before, or if he was about to witness it. The strain on their faces made it clear that navigating the muddy cemetery was a last sacrifice they made for Dubrow. Superman? We need you here.

What did Delene feel, exactly? Her manner radiated willpower and doggedness. Her eyes were puffy but clear. The coffin was obviously unwieldy. It still felt impossible his boss lay inside that ornate and cumbersome box.

A lone soprano stationed on a folding chair beside the grave tent strummed a guitar and sang a sad rendition of Don Henley's "Fields of Gold." As the pallbearers and altar boys passed, the scent of expensive perfume mixed with the fresh flower arrangements and incense. Each potent smell competed with the others as if to overpower death with a cloying fragrance. The faux grass had a rubbery scent that bloomed when many people stepped upon it. The funeral director had the presence of mind to gently shoo the boy back so he wouldn't trip the pallbearers. He took the boy's place as pallbearer and helped guide the casket onto the metal stand. It settled into place with a somber thunk. As a consolation, the director gave the boy the wreath to lay upon the top. The little boy's face broke into a smiling sob. His two front teeth were missing.

Rory did that. Rory made the boy cry. Rory was to blame.

Did it show?

How could the accident have happened? Rory had been sure, sure as the sun was yellow, the Senna went in Arthur's glass, not Dubrow's. And he was even more sure that the amount wasn't enough to do any more than keep that thieving, conniving bony-balled asshole, Arthur, glued to his toilet for a day or two.

But Silas had switched the flights. And what if Rory had measured wrong or read wrong or...or something? It gnawed at Rory, the coincidence of it. Deep down, he believed he was a murderer, that he, not a heart attack, was responsible for Benjamin Dubrow's death. Senna, when it interacted with medications for edema, could cause heart failure.

And while Rory couldn't ask about Dubrow's medicine cabinet, he learned Dubrow had been on a slew of medications.

Through the cluster of mourners and standing before the casket, Rory found Delene Dubrow. Her gaze was fastened on him to the point he turned to see who might be behind him, who she might be looking at.

No one. She looked straight at him. What to do with his face? Why was she staring him down? Did she know? It got so awkward he made a small wave. Was that what innocent Rory would do? He was losing his grip on what innocent Rory would do.

She didn't respond. Her eyes were shiny with tears.

Through him was where she looked.

What a relief. How he wished everyone would look through him until Dubrow's death was a dim memory. Nothing to see here, folks.

The priest invoked Dubrow's own sense of humor when he said Dubrow was, "in Heaven, in glory, and that, with Dubrow in Heaven, the angels can wash their ambrosia down with some wonderful beer. Jesus makes the best wine, but Benjamin Dubrow makes the best beer."

In response, there were subdued funeral chuckles.

"You can laugh," the priest said. "Benjamin Dubrow would want you to. Rootsville lost a pillar. We lost a friend, a father, a benevolent man. Be sad for yourselves, not for Benjamin Dubrow. For he is toasting with Jesus."

Rory could not conjure that image, no matter how hard he tried. Jesus was not Dubrow's type. Too understated. Wore sandals, not Converse.

Rory caught sight of Arthur wending his way through the crowd, parting it like the sea because of the enormous dog on his leash. What was he doing, bringing a dog to a funeral? Arthole didn't allow his lateness or the dog at his side to stop him from getting the front row on the casket. He stationed himself beside Delene Dubrow, and with a curt and solemn nod, greeted her. She returned with the same gesture, but reached a hand down and played with the dog's ears. The dog—some sort of German shepherd mix—nosed her hand. Seeing the three of them in a row: Dubrow's daughter, Arthur the asshole, and his stately dog, Rory had an idea. Here between two innocents—the dog and the daughter—was Arthur. And while Arthur deserved to drink a little Senna and shit his brains out for the requisite two days, Rory's vengeance had somehow been thwarted. He tried to deliver a blow, anonymously, and he'd become the angel of death. But the key word was *anonymously*. A new idea formed, a strategy to take away Rory's guilt, to distract him from himself. This new, ingenious plan would also ease Delene's pain.

Rory would change his tactics. He'd work under the radar, anonymously, doing good deeds. Rory could become an angel, period. A good, anonymous angel to the person he'd most heinously wronged.

Delene Dubrow.

Delene hung her head, the thick tresses curtaining her face. With one hand, she gently took the little chubby hand of the boy beside her and gave a comforting squeeze. With her other hand, she continued to pet the dog. The dog gave Delene a measure of comfort. Wanting ever more of that, Rory imagined giving Delene scores of dogs, of her petting them and laughing and forgetting all about her pain. Rory couldn't bring Dubrow back, but he'd atone by doing whatever he could for Delene Dubrow. He'd learn about her and figure out what he could do to bring her joy. He would show her the world wasn't a horrible place, even though her father was dead. Rory would make it his mission to bring a smile to her face.

Arthur stared. Rory came out of his reverie to the hard eyes of his nemesis, the one who should—if there were any justice in the world—be inside that coffin. Rory glanced away, but instantly brought his gaze back and squinted like Clint Eastwood. He thought of Mr. F as orange water, and of Bruce Lee, still alive and gloriously swimming in his vase. How would Arthur like it if someone blended that majestic dog of his? Not that Rory ever would. Animals couldn't help it if they loved assholes.

The priest finished his sermon, and several family members took turns sharing moments from Dubrow's life.

Rory heard none of it. He was too busy planning his penance.

The priest gave the benediction, and mourners turned to go. Rory couldn't be a spectacle, couldn't stay overly long at Dubrow's grave. With a last hateful glare at Arthur, he turned and walked away, holding his head as high as he dared. The dog barked for the first time in the ceremony, but Rory didn't look back. He'd come to the funeral, paid his respects. He'd devised a plan. It could get him in trouble and was maybe a little stupid, but he could already feel his heart become unfreighted at the idea of doing Delene Dubrow a good turn.

Chapter 10

Rory reclined on a bench outside Delene Dubrow's place of employment and considered what an enigma she was. It wasn't too difficult to find her on social media. She wasn't a selfie person, which was both refreshing (her modesty) and disappointing (Rory wanted to see her). Her feeds were shares of children and their accolades. An eight-year-old and his father fashioned plastic grocery bags into sturdy, reusable totes and donated the proceeds to the local K-9 program. Another story she shared was about a student who hiked the Appalachian Trail in sections over the summers. Chapman Elementary School had the highest-ranking students in state proficiency scores, she'd hyped.

And...?

At first, Rory didn't understand why a single woman was so pumped about this or that kid's performance in a spelling bee. Or by what kid received a full ride to Harvard. Delene was one of those who had a tidy social footprint, as Rory liked to think of it. Not vomiting anger into cyberspace. No shares of plates of food or pictures of her in front of an exotic beach. She didn't use her space to promote political agendas. The only causes she shared were some GoFundMe campaigns for families with critically ill children.

Puzzling.

Until he landed on her LinkedIn page and solved the mystery. Delene was a second-grade teacher at Chapman Elementary School, where he now waited for school to let out. He rustled the crispy leaves with his feet, enjoying the crunch and the earthy scent they released. According to an article shared on Delene's profile, she had jumped out of an airplane wearing a Winnie the Pooh suit. This was her part of a bargain if the students of Chapman Elementary collectively read a million pages in one year. The picture of her skydiving was so endearing, he printed it out and put it on his refrigerator.

What a kind soul, this Delene Dubrow.

And Rory had taken her father from her.

No putting that egg back together. All he could offer was penance, in the form of anonymous kindnesses.

Rory's plan required the help of one of Chapman Elementary's stellar students, a kid under the age of ten, preferably. Because kids wouldn't remember (he hoped) the details of his face and because he wanted—no, he *had* to see her face when she opened the card, Rory had a small pair of binoculars in his pocket. The kid's job would be to give Delene the card.

The end-of-day bell blared. The front doors exploded open, and a swarm of little people rushed out onto the sidewalk. After perusing the grounds for the perfect accomplice, Rory settled on a freckled boy with a pirate swagger and a mouth obscured by a gum bubble.

"Hey is that Miss Dubrow over there?" Rory knew it was, but he needed an in with the kid.

The kid popped his bubble and wrinkled his nose, but didn't answer. Well-schooled on stranger danger, apparently.

"Can you do me a favor?" Rory ventured.

He blew another, bigger bubble until it popped.

"Run this envelope over to Miss Dubrow Tell her to open it, see? Like it says on the envelope here: O - P - E–"

"I'm not dumb. I can read."

"But tell her to open it, okay? Here's ten dollars."

"Why don't you take it yourself?"

"I'm...shy."

The kid wasn't buying it. "I'm not supposed to take stuff from strangers."

"That only applies to candy," Rory said. "And when strangers ask you to get into their vans."

"What?"

"Never mind. You're safe, see? You got a good head on your shoulders. Don't ever go anyplace with a stranger. And I'm not asking you to—look, you can trust me, kid. All I need is for you to deliver this card." He waved the ten dollars like a flag.

The boy shrugged, swiped the money. "Okay." Off he went, crumbling the bill in his fist, skipping a little and crunching the maple leaves littering the sidewalk.

Convinced Delene's happiness would cure his guilt, and although it was a risky maneuver that could get him recognized, Rory planned to observe her opening his card. He ducked behind the building and removed his fake eyebrows and mustache then donned a ballcap and changed his coat. Transformed, he sauntered back the way he came and took a seat at one of the benches that offered a view of the front of the building. Delene had gotten down on her haunches and was having a conversation with a little girl, being careful not to touch her. Touching was not allowed, not like in his day when a teacher could not only touch you but could, without repercussions, take a two-foot-long wooden paddle to your backside. In Rory's day, teachers could high-five, hug, and yes, spank. This Delene, she did what she could. Got down on the little one's level and gave the child her full, empathic attention. The girl hitched with sobs.

Delene said something and offered a tissue. The little girl nodded, and as they stood, Rory's messenger ran to them and held out the envelope. He pointed in the direction Rory *had* been in, where no one presently was. Delene squinted and when she saw no one acknowledging the delivery, bade both littles to accompany her to one of the busses. She ushered the crier onto the bus and gave an encouraging wave.

She held Rory's messenger back and frowned as she gave what Rory supposed was the stranger lecture. She waved the envelope and—again Rory guessed—asked where he'd gotten it. After another look around, Rory's messenger shrugged.

Victory?

Delene canvased the schoolyard and parking lot and even landed on Rory for a second. He made sure he was looking away. Out of the corner of his eye, he could see Delene point him out, could see the boy shake his head.

Victory.

The little messenger ran off to his own bus. Kid was smart enough not to show her the ten bucks. Hmmm. He'd go far in life.

Delene held onto the envelope but didn't open it.

Damn. Defeat.

Rory changed back into his original disguise and walked the sidewalk that hemmed school grounds, hoping he'd see Delene as she walked to her car, after the kiddos were on yellow busses or picked up or well on their walking way. She'd gone back inside the school, so maybe she already opened the card. Maybe when she exited, there would be a bounce to her step, a mysterious smile playing at the corners of her lips. Maybe she'd look to heaven and shake her head in wonder at the anonymous act of kindness.

A rumble in Rory's stomach reminded him he hadn't eaten today, again. So far, he'd lost eighteen pounds since Dubrow's...accident. Rory was still technically fat, but his body seemed to be sloughing away before his very eyes. All desire to eat had died with Dubrow. Rory's love of beer, too. The servers at the brewery had started noticing, which was bad. Any change was dangerous and could draw suspicion. Instantly Rory's mind went to the day O'Deens had "just stopped in for a beer," how he questioned the servers as to exactly when Rory Harper had begun to lose weight. The detective, knowing the science behind guilty consciences, would connect the dots, and bam: Rory'd be discovered. The servers smiled and made jokes about Rory "getting shredded" and asked who was the hot lady in his life? Rory would redden and say nothing. Why was staying under the radar so hard? He was a fat guy, a lab nerd. But he was getting thinner, and change drew attention.

Food and beer disgusted him now, even donuts.

His shoe caught on a block of sidewalk pushed up by roots and obscured by leaves. He stopped his fall with his hands, but one of his eyebrows fell off. He only knew because the second eyebrow almost fell off and dangled into his eye. Reaching to fix it, he felt his other side and realized it was gone. He backtracked, swirled the dead leaves in the spot where he fell, and found it. Careful to face away from the school building, he pressed the eyebrow back on, feeling the grit of little stones. His palms were red and scrapped, and he blushed, feeling foolish. The fact that he was here to do a good deed wouldn't protect him from the cosmic justice of falling and busting his skull open right in front of Chapman Elementary School as he paced the grounds.

At the end of the street, he turned back and walked at a crawl, feigning a fascination with the squirrels in the locust trees. He could only "happen to stroll by" the school so many times before he'd look like a stalker. *Was* he a stalker? Stalkers had bad intentions. His were good. Besides, he didn't even want to talk to her. Ever. Just wanted to know he'd done her a good turn. To make her smile. For some reason it was important he see—not just her smile—but see the smile *he* put there.

The overgrown forsythia bushes at the end of the street were full of those little speckled birds that squeaked obnoxiously. They traveled in large flocks, and any tree they overtook quivered with their frenzy.

Rory nodded a greeting to a stooped, white-haired man walking his little dog.

"C'mon Bruster. Leave him alone," the man scolded his terrier. The little dog was interested in Rory's ankle. In tasting it. Rory tried to gently dislodge Bruster and his plenty big enough sharp teeth.

Delene finally exited the building. She had a backpack slung over one shoulder, and her heels had been replaced with black Converse sneakers. Her hair, previously down, had been whipped into a slap-dash chignon on the top of her head. He thought he'd be able to tell if she'd opened the card, but nothing about her gave away her state of mind. A purposeful, but not euphoric, stride. Her face in her phone. A frown of concentration. Even so, she didn't trip over the place where the concrete buckled as Rory had. She made her way to an old model Jeep Rory recognized. It had a vanity plate: TCHEVRY1.

Rory's breath hitched.

She pulled out the envelope and swiveled it in the sunlight coming through the dashboard window.

Yesssss. Open it, Delene.

Rory had to get closer, see her expression. He stood and managed to free himself from Bruster. Was that tearing fabric he heard? Maybe. Who cared? He made as if he were walking home. The parking lot fronted Fair Road. It was reasonable his house could be any of the bungalows in the crisscross of residential streets surrounding the school, which would give him reason to be walking by her car, right then. But what if she remembered him from the funeral? Or worse, the elevator? But he had on his mustache and he decided it was worth the risk to catch her in the act of opening the envelope. He didn't want her to see him, to suspect her father's employee of being the gift-giver because that would invoke the question: why? Why are you, a stranger, giving me gifts? That's creepy. Are you a creep? A murderer?

Rory saw exactly how the line of reasoning would go, should he be caught watching her, now.

She put the envelope to her nose and sniffed. Frowned. Looked again.

Please. Open. It.

Maybe Rory didn't deserve to see her smile. He was twenty feet from the car, would pass it soon, and once past, looking back would invite suspicion for sure. The man and Bruster, the ankle-eating terrier, was coming his way. All gazillion birds lifted off at once, and it was as if the red-leafed bush threw off a cape of black. They hovered and darted and shrieked before settling upon their limbs once more, deciding the terrier's yips were harmless. Ten feet away from her Jeep. Rory purposely looked at the bush. To look in her direction, to make eye contact right now, would draw suspicion. He decided to give himself one glance. Only one because that would be appropriate eye contact for a stranger walking by a woman who was in her Jeep. One, because anyone would be curious. A movement in his peripheral vision—her holding up the card or just the shape of a person sitting in a car—could draw anyone's attention. That was what normal looked like, and Rory was playacting at normal. Doing a great job.

Five feet from her car, he looked. Right at her. The perfect distance. The driver's side window gave a clear view. He could see the different shades of coffee in her hair: black, sweet cream, milk. Her petite, catlike nose and high cheekbones, her long neck, and cords of muscle sloping, disappearing inside her windbreaker. Some might call her pretty.

The card was open. She bowed her head. Her hair veiled her face completely. She'd taken out the ponytail.

Damn.

He had to keep going. How he wanted to stop and watch. Or ask, did it make her day a little better? Give her some comfort? The card was blank inside, except for what Rory had written. The outside was a picture of a path through woods in fall, a shaft of sunlight cutting through the trees ahead. He'd thought hard about the card. What it communicated. Flowers and hearts, they said things he did not want to communicate. That was stalker shit. But he wanted her to know someone was looking out for her, that someone wanted to be the sunlight in her day. That someone was very fucking sorry he accidentally killed—*stop, Rory.*

He had written: *The loss of your father is not forgotten.*

Inside the envelope were two tickets to see the Van Gogh exhibit at the art museum and a gift card for lunch at downtown's most opulent four-star restaurant, the Marble Room.

The question was, who would Delene take with the second ticket? For some reason, he cared. He wanted to know who would accompany her. He wished he was better at this private investigator stuff, that he could tail her or bug her phone so he'd know who she invited and when she went. He wanted to shadow her.

But only in the friendliest, non-stalker, non-creepy way. He couldn't talk to her, and he couldn't get enough of her. Not because he was smitten, he told himself. The reason she occupied so much of his mind was that Rory couldn't do enough good to make himself feel clean. She was the object of his obsession, the way out of his guilt. He thought it would feel good to deliver the card, even if he didn't see her reaction. Now that the deed was done, he wanted more, to witness her enjoying herself. It wasn't enough to imagine her appreciating *Starry Night*. He wanted to see her eyes light up at a painting or at a steak or lobster or whatever food she loved. He had to know: what food *did* she love? He wanted to see her eat a piece of cheesecake. Or a donut. Did she like those things? It became clear, in order to be her angel, he needed more information.

More than food, he wanted to be an angel to Delene Dubrow.

Chapter 11

Rory could not believe how many people were awake at this unholy hour. He wormed his car around runners and spectators in Rootstown's business district. The obliterative night sky was still in full control of the city, but the hustling crowd wore reflective shirts, vests, hats, the whole don't-run-me-over wardrobe. They jostled one another and spilled onto the streets, jockeying for the sidewalks. As sleep-deprived as Rory felt, these pre-dawn runners had better fear his slothful reflexes. If one of them walked in front of his car, splat.

What was wrong with these people? They were running to the start of a marathon where they'd RUN some more, the commensurate 26-point-something fucked-up miles. You'd think they'd walk to the start, save energy. Nooooo. They were bouncing around, some of them, like Tigger on Red Bull. Smiling. It was five-thirty in the morning.

One of these masochists was Delene Dubrow.

She did this. For fun. That's what he'd overheard, anyway, which was why Rory, sleep-deprived, showed up. Delene had mentioned the upcoming race, posted a link to it on Instagram. A friend asked in the comments if she was going. She was. And bam. Rory, not sleeping, struggling to wend his car through apocalyptic numbers of pedestrians at an obscene hour.

Anyone of them could be her. He squinted. He searched. He imagined her tossing her hair into that messy nest she wore piled on her head. Or maybe she'd slick her hair back tightly, a more pragmatic choice for race day. And what would she wear? Many of the women in all shapes and sizes wore sports bras and shorts. Mostly eye-scorching neon.

Rory had read everything he could about Delene Dubrow, trying to ferret out who she was and what sort of things she'd like. He knew he was acting like a stalker. (Could one feel like a stalker and not technically be one?) For today's stalking, he'd bought a pair of aviators and a ball cap for the local baseball team he actually thought sucked, but he didn't want to be caught wearing one of his own ball caps. He even bought a jacket, a Carhart knockoff. How these nutjobs were warm enough in shorts and bras, he didn't know.

Once Rory got close enough to the course, the streets were closed to all but foot traffic. He had to circle back and try for a space again. This time he took the first space he found, in front of a laundromat. As he stepped out, his foot met something soft and yielding, accompanied by the blow of a sickly scent. The laundromat windows spit a filmy, flickering light, so he chanced a look down.

An emptied ashtray, or, based on the number of cigarette butts: plural, ashtrays. A bar full of chain-smokers joined forces and dumped their butts right there in the street because the garbage can right beside the laundromat door apparently wasn't convenient enough.

"Nice," he mumbled and followed the crowd.

October downtown was a vortex of bitter winds that bit through his jacket and jeans. Rory had all his fat that should've kept him toasty, but there was less and less of it every day, and he wasn't accustomed to the new, less-padded him. Losing weight affected him in unlikely ways. He no longer held cement blocks on his arms and legs and had pared inches of concrete from his midsection. Sometimes, though, he expected there to be more mass, and the lack would unbalance him.

Every so often, he passed rows of port-o-johns with lines ten-people deep. What was the deal? And he realized too, he'd never find Delene Dubrow in this crowd. There had to be thousands of people. He'd imagined a marathon meant a few hundred string bean types galloping along the street. The pictures showed a bustling crowd, sure, but he thought that was marketing, not reality.

Wrong.

And another preconception shattered by reality: many of the runners were overweight or older than Rory, who was winded by the time he found a suitable place to watch the send-off. A covered bus station with a bench would allow him to scan the runners as they went by. And, luck of luck—a homeless man and his shopping cart of plastic bags, tent poles, and pillows got up and ambled away, leaving it available. The street was packed with runners from one side to the other, so he'd only see those closest to his side of the street. The sidewalks were jammed with folding chairs and blankets. Not even space enough for him to wedge himself into a sitting position on the curb. Never mind the fact that levering himself up from said curb would be ungainly at best and impossible at worst. *I've sat on this curb and can't get up. Can I get a forklift?*

From somewhere ahead, energetic music blasted. Rory checked his watch. Six o'clock. Everywhere runners stretched, pulling yoga positions on the yellow street lines, grabbing streetlights and using them for barre stretches. Some were dressed in full-body costumes. A chicken. A prisoner in stripes. A honeybee. A poop emoji. How would they run in those things? A man painted like Braveheart bashed Rory in the shoulder as he ran by shouting for his friend to wait! Wait for him!

Oblivious.

"Sorry," Rory snarked. "Didn't see you."

Kids of all ages had been sprung from their beds to hold posters and be dragged along by parents with a scouting eye, trying to find the best position to watch mommy or daddy. Cowbells jangled. Girls giggled. Lithe-footed runners pushed baby strollers. You knew a runner by the square number they wore on their chests and their neon shoes.

"Who you watching?" asked a lean man who looked to be a handful of years older than Rory. He had a friendly, soothing voice and towed three little kids, each with a helium balloon in one hand and a powdered donut in the other. Superdad.

"Uh, no one," Rory answered.

Superdad's brow furrowed. He let down the box of donuts he'd started to offer. Rory guessed that was a stupid answer because who in their right mind would come to a marathon to watch no one?

"I mean, I'm here to get motivated," Rory patted what was left of his belly. "I need to get in shape, and I thought it'd do me good to watch one."

Superdad softened, brought the box of donuts back up to an offering position. "You probably don't want one of these, then," he said.

Rory did, actually.

He'd left without breakfast, thinking he wouldn't be hungry so early, but the walking and the frenetic spirit had greased his appetite. And the red smear on the kids' faces told him the box contained jelly-filled. He welcomed something with the viscosity of jelly or—*please*—cream.

Rory took the most bulging donut, hoping it was chocolate-cream-filled. He realized this was the first time he'd salivated since Dubrow's accident. He also realized he always characterized it in his mind as *Dubrow's* accident, as opposed to *Rory's* murder or *Rory's stupid fuck up*. It was Dubrow's. Dubrow owned it. All this philosophy while the chocolate cream and powdered sugar slid placidly down his throat. That he was alive to enjoy donuts while Dubrow was entombed six feet under made the sugar turn a little sour.

"My wife's trying to qualify for the Boston." Superdad beamed and jutted his chin at a glut of serious-looking runners behind the starting line. Presumably, one of them was Supermom.

Rory had no idea what that meant, qualifying for Boston, so the dad gave him a quick tutorial in all things marathon, including the excrement he might see running down the legs of runners who didn't thoroughly purge at one of the port-o-johns. The dad himself had run a half-marathon and acutely remembered being passed by a grey-haired woman with a trail of brown running down her leg. She wasn't embarrassed in the least. And she had beaten him to the finish.

"The clock doesn't stop when you do," Superdad said, "Qualifying times don't care if you missed the cut-off because you made a pit stop."

Rory, mouth full of powdered sugary fluffy-chocolate-filled donut, tried not to gag.

"Oh, sorry. Not used to filters." Superdad gestured toward his flock. "Kids."

What sort of person signed up for this?

Delene Dubrow.

Delene was here to hurt herself, so he wondered, did she too have some dark secret? Had she done something for which she felt the need to punish herself like this? She was becoming more and more of an enigma. Her old man had tons of money. And now it would be hers. She could do anything, have her fat frozen off. Why would she choose to do something so obviously painful?

Rory smile-grimaced at Superdad and choked the sticky bite down.

"Well, now that I've ruined your donut..." The dad saluted him and moved off with his little band. "We'll get a great shot of Mom from over there."

The announcer called for all runners to report to the starting line and continued to count down how many minutes until the race started. People filed into corrals based on the time they expected to run per mile. Some runners–pacers, according to Superdad–held tall flags with minutes per mile. Runners who expected to run at that pace were gathered around them. The announcer assured the runners their chip would activate when they cleared the starting line, that they should run at their designated pace and not slow the faster runners, not glut the starting line. Between announcements Rocky Balboa music played. Eminem. Metallica.

An emcee thanked various sponsors and made remarks about determination and grit. "The Star-Spangled Banner" poured forth loud and clear. Everyone stopped and gave the moment to the American flag undulating from the boom of the emcee's crane bucket.

A gun went off, startling Rory. His body instantly went into the ready stance of Taekwondo, fists up, legs apart, knees bent. And then he straightened, hoping no one noticed the complete idiot he was.

Thousands of sneakers clapped the streets to the song "Eye of the Tiger." Kids squealed at their parents. Cowbells clunked. Rory's heart chased the speed and spirit of so many people setting off to do this hard, hard thing he could not imagine doing. He smiled in spite of himself, popped the last of the donut in his mouth. The best bite, mostly chocolate cream.

Since Dubrow's death, he had lost nineteen pounds. Eating any food during his workday at Telluric was unthinkable. The moment Rory crossed the threshold into Telluric, his appetite left him. Standing here, watching more people than he thought existed, all running—literally running—toward their goal, was the happiest Rory had felt since the...accident. *Dubrow's* accident. And he'd felt hunger to boot. Although he didn't achieve his goal of seeing Delene, he thought maybe there was something to this running thing.

Maybe he'd try it, for laughs.

As the runners thundered by, he found himself wishing he were in the pack, that he'd done whatever one does to arrive at this anointed place. The crowds cheered them forward. Shoes drummed the ground. The music made him think he could do better than he'd done so far, that he could be strong. "One step at a time," the announcer rallied them, "all you have to keep in mind is that one step, the next step. YOU CAN DO IT!"

Like he was talking to Rory and not to the runners.

Rory found himself cheering right along with them, telling strangers they COULD DO IT!

He was sad to see the last of them pass by, but the map he'd been given suggested locations to see the runners at various mile markers. Rory hadn't intended to watch anything other than the start, but it was so exhilarating, he wanted to see what these crazies looked like after nine miles, after fifteen. What did they look like crossing the finish? And Delene, what would she look like? Exultant? Relieved? Pained? He found himself trying to imagine those expressions on her beauti—on her face.

At the five-mile mark he stationed himself in a modern bronze sculpture of what looked like a flame folded in half, several stories high. It offered a perfect view and had a little dip he could settle into. Sometimes he clapped and cheered. Mostly he watched in silent awe.

A messy brown chignon dashed by. The familiar hairstyle was attached to wiry shoulders, a tanned back wearing a black tank top and American flag shorts. Delene? A patriot? He jumped from the sculpture, pushed his way through the crowd, and trotted beside the runners, keeping the woman in his sights. Some spectators cheered him on. They thought he'd joined the race. Maybe he had.

Ahead of the woman-who-could-be-Delene was a pacer carrying a tall flag emblazoned with the numbers 10:55. Whenever he lost Delene, he found the flag and re-found her. He lumbered behind, half-hoping she'd turn around and half-revolted at the idea of her doing so. For a while the curiosity numbed him, but it didn't take long for Rory's legs to burn with the bites of a million hornets, for his lungs to feel so hot and horrible, fire was surely about to spew from his wide-open mouth. He gasped and hissed and slalomed to a halt. He bent over and gulped as if the air by his knees was more oxygen-rich. Salty sweat burned his eyes. Everything burned. This was hell. When he could finally straighten, the 10:55 flag and the woman with the patriotic shorts were both gone.

Because it was painful and because it allowed him to search for Delene (in case the woman who got the whole ball rolling wasn't her), Rory did that same run-gag-stop routine seven more times. Seven, because he had to choose some number and he'd heard it was God's favorite number, the Earth made in seven days and all that. He would've finished the rest of the race in that fitful, unathletic manner, but he was here to do a job, to plant Delene's gift. Who knew how long it would take him to comb the area for her Jeep? According to the internet, the average marathon time was four and a half hours, but some runners were at it for eight hours or more. Eight hours! –spent feeling like a dying dragon.

Two hours later, thoroughly disgusted with the heat-producing sunlight, the sewer smell of city streets, the sheer number of cars-not-hers in the world, and the burn in the soles of his feet, Rory found her jeep. She'd parked in front of a little strip mall that had seen better days. The store windows were frosted in grime, obscuring the insides of an abandoned computer repair shop and psychic reader. The third storefront, the Cathedral of Life, had man-sized handprints, zigging lines, and expletives traced through the film, suggesting somebody had done something in there recently, but it was neither glorious nor religious.

The familiar license plate made him smile. TCHEVRY1. He hightailed it back to his own car, barely feeling the fires in his thighs and feet now that success was within reach. Driving to her car was a lot easier than walking. From the cooler, he grabbed the dozen roses and placed them on her windshield with a poster sign he'd had printed. He was a *Star Wars* lover. *May the course be with you!* the sign said. Technically, the sign would be best shown to her while she ran, but Rory didn't like any of the other signs. They were dumb. Things like *All Toenails go to Heaven.* What did that mean? And *Worst Parade Ever.* And *Don't Walk. People are Watching.* Rory's original thought was to have a sign printed that said simply, *Great job, Delene!* But the salesgirl at the printing area said it "showed lack of imagination" when he asked what she thought of that idea. She told him to google marathon signs, which he did, and to his delight, the *Star Wars* one came up. He tacked the corners of the sign under her windshield wipers and set the roses against it. They looked bright and cheery and would make Delene smile.

Should he stay and watch to make sure the roses weren't stolen? How great it would be to watch her discover the gift. He searched for places he could hide. The stores near enough to her Jeep had a narrow door and stairwell that must've led to the businesses on the second floor. Although he would have a perfect view of Delene coming toward her jeep, Rory was wary of stationing himself on the stairs. He feared getting stuck, had visions of the fire department coming with the jaws of life to extricate him from the narrow doorway. Having lost weight, it was less likely, but he stayed away just the same. Why invite karma? Besides, the area didn't give him warm, fuzzy feelings. Maybe it was because, like New York, some streets you didn't walk if you could help it, like 145th to 170th, if you wanted to get from A to B unscathed. He knew what streets to avoid in New York, but not here.

Rory got back in his car and circled the block around Delene's jeep, waiting for someone to free up a space. Sweaty, stumbling, or limping runners started to appear on the streets. They wore silver garbage-bag-looking things over their bodies, clasped by shaking hands. All smiled triumphantly. These were likely half-marathoners or 10K runners. Rory found he was jealous. He wanted whatever they had inside themselves–discipline? –fearlessness? –that bade them run and earn those exhausted, triumphant smiles and papery silver wraps.

A group of runners, all of them retirement age, walked toward an SUV a few spaces behind Delene's jeep. They laughed and shared how their bodies, especially their feet or knees, felt at this or that mile. One woman held a banana to her lips and was about to take a bite when some punk appeared out of nowhere and smacked it from her hand. It flew into the street and landed on a sewer drain.

"Now that was uncalled for," said one of the men, but with little conviction.

"Fuck off." The scab didn't even turn his head, just kept lumbering in the other direction.

"Here, I didn't eat mine." The man handed the woman his banana.

The parking space the group had vacated would be the perfect vantage point to see Delene. Rory quickly did a U-turn and put on his turn signal, claiming the space as his.

As he put the car in reverse, a foul pack of youths lurched into the spot, cutting through to cross the street. He waited, foot on the brake, for them to pass behind his car. Clearly for this crew, jaywalking wasn't a paramount offense. Stones were warmer and more welcoming than those ashen, pierced, and tattooed faces. As Rory stared, one flicked a lit cigarette at his driver's side window. Rory winced reflexively. From behind, a horn blared. Someone else dived into the spot on an angle before he could reverse.

"You must hail from New York," he muttered, then gunned his car away, not entirely satisfied by the tire-squealing furor he left in his wake. He continued around and around, and had almost given up when a rabbit-like woman in a matching sweatsuit got in her Subaru and took off, freeing the spot across the street, catty-corner from Delene's car. The perfect spot.

Rory managed to parallel park without getting a cigarette butt thrown at him and got comfortable, trained his binoculars on the sidewalk approaching her car from the direction of the finish line. Oh, to see her break into a smile at the poster. Her smile had become his sustenance.

A stray thought occurred to him. Was she running with a friend? A man? Her Facebook picture was just her, but what if she was in a relationship–what would her partner think of a dozen roses on her car? Rory hadn't thought everything through, and now that it was do or die, he questioned whether this anonymous angel thing was a good idea. What if she was creeped out by a dozen roses from an anonymous giver? What if she thought it too stalkeresque?

Was he too stalkeresque?

As he second-guessed his decision, the clutch of thugs returned. They shoved one another and cackled. Rory instantly worried for the gift. They looked like the types who'd knock over a kid's sandcastle, the sort of person who slept gun in hand, and generally had a beef with the world at large. After all, swiping a banana from a woman's hand was reflexive. The kid didn't even think. Just: *f-you, world.*

In the gaunt, pierced, and inked-up faces, Rory saw his own pain, exponentially multiplied. Just as Taekwondo forms were meant to teach muscle memory, a self-protective reflex against attackers, so these kids had their own set of horrible forms, perpetrated against them over and over. They'd taught their lessons well. That banana-holding woman represented women in general, and women in general were probably based on the youth's mom, and the youth's mom likely hadn't asked whether he'd be home for supper. There would be no supper. He, and they, lashed out at a world that had done them wrong. White walls or pristine bridges or train cars without graffiti were an affront to the chaos within these youth. So they made the outside match the inside with acts of art or destruction, depending on the moment. Rory had taken his revenge out on the wrong person, too.

One kid pushed another into Delene's car.

The panic alarm went off, and they laughed, not at all deterred. One boy wearing a black trench coat flicked the head of one of the roses, sending petals flying like confetti, but the bouquet, other than leaning deeply, was unscathed. They moved on. Eventually, the car alarm silenced.

Rory breathed a sigh of relief.

The roses looked nicer standing up, wedged in the windshield wiper. Leaned askew, it could almost be mistaken for someone having thrown the roses willy-nilly, that maybe somebody repurposed the whole thing, the sign, the roses, everything. Like it was coincidence, and not for Delene, specifically. That would not do. It was important to Rory that Delene feel special, that she knew someone cared about her, about her grief. She had already inspired Rory—she and those overweight runners.

If they could do it, so could he. Baby steps. How do you eat an elephant? One bite at a time. Arthur's insult came unbidden into Rory's mind: *And you would eat an elephant, wouldn't you, Slim? You look like you've eaten several.*

Rory put Arthole out of his mind.

Before he forgot how glorious this whole marathon thing was, he would sign up for a 5K. He was already picturing himself breaking the finish line ribbon, hands in the air, athletic Rory, smiling Rory, a Rory who hadn't killed anyone by accident. But no way did he have the energy to do any more running today. He'd run off the chocolate cream donut and could feel the caloric deficit eating away at his core. It was a good sign that his hunger returned. A sign he was on the right track.

The Sharpie was still in his glove compartment. He checked the sidewalk in both directions and, once he was satisfied Delene wasn't approaching, got out and fixed the stems, placed them carefully in a line pinched beneath the windshield wiper. He wrote her name in the corner of the sign, so there'd be no question it was for her. D-E-L-E

A scuffle of feet behind him.

The thugs.

All their dead eyes on Rory. For the second time that day, his body instantly took the ready stance of Taekwondo.

They laughed.

Rory expected villains to say things like: *Well, well, well, what have we here, boys?* Or: *Not so fast, mister.* Or they'd demand his money or wallet or the watch he wasn't wearing. These were the cliché ways Rory expected to be jumped. His hands balled into fists, but he didn't know which direction to go first. He was a red belt. He'd sparred multiple opponents simultaneously, but this was real, and there were too many of them.

What happened was a silent grab. They worked together seamlessly, like they did this every day. One put a fist in Rory's stomach so hard, he thought it would go right on through. The breath burst from his mouth in an involuntary scream. Two others held each of his arms in vicelike grips, wiry men much stronger than they looked. Others circled, smacking his belly or his face or the back of his head. He must've dropped the Sharpie, because one of them drew with it on Rory's own arm: a heart with the word MOM inside it.

"You can have my money," he managed, once his breath came back. He'd not gotten in a single punch or kick.

"Do we look like we need your money, you fat fuck? I'm insulted."

Another breath-stealing punch to his stomach.

"Who're the roses for, eh? Your girlfriend? Just look at these cake tits." He swatted Rory's chest. "Maybe if you was running instead of spying on us, you wouldn't be so fugly."

"I wasn't–"

A punch to his face. His cheek on fire.

They swiped Rory's sign from her windshield and played tug-o-war with it until it tore, sending both boys on their butts, each with a piece. They ripped it into smaller chunks, bunched the posterboard into balls, and chucked them at Rory's face. He was so mad about the sign, he barely heard their insults or felt when the posterboard struck him.

One took the bunch of roses and put them to his nose. "Mmmmm...smells like my lady's cooch." He pushed the roses at Rory's face and suddenly dropped them. "Ouch. Fucking things." He sucked on his finger. Blood drops studded his grimy palm.

Rory sneered. This was *Schadenfreude*–the same feeling that had him putting Senna in Arthur's beer. The kid didn't miss Rory's smile, though, and jammed his knee squarely into his balls.

Pain bloomed like a mushroom cloud, rising to his belly and taking ever more territory in his bowels. The simultaneous urge to paint the thugs in vomit and also defecate on the sidewalk overtook him.

"Cry baby, cry!" one thug taunted.

Was he crying? Electric pressure sliced a frontier path through his body, starting between his legs and finishing in his head, where dizziness reigned supreme.

Another surprise. His arms were dropped, as if by mutual agreement, and a force struck his knees from behind, sending him to his back in half a second. The back of his head on the sidewalk: a grand slam followed by fiery throbbing. Still, his crushed testicles pulled his body into fetal position. His bashed skull meant nothing in comparison.

But they wouldn't let him stay there.

"Get him on his back. Hold his arms. Out, you know, like Jesus."

And they did. Like Jesus.

Rory tried to yank his arms free, but they kneeled on each hand, crushing them into the sidewalk with their kneecaps. One of them had a cigarette dangling from his lips. The long ash broke off and the wind carried it away. He sucked on the cigarette till it glowed, blew smoke in Rory's face.

Coughing was the least of his worries.

The one who started the whole thing, who Rory figured was the leader, said, "Dirk, you gotta hold his mouth open."

Oh no... Rory kicked his legs and torqued the lower half of his body until the leader stomped on Rory's genitals.

"You gonna choke him to death with your cock or what?" Even the one named Dirk sounded uncomfortable. The ghouls crushing his hands made low, growling sounds that might have been nervous laughter.

Rory clenched his jaw.

"No, you dumbass. Open his mouth. And don't let him bite you."

Dirk dropped to his knees, put one knee on each side of Rory's head and squeezed. With his fingers, he made a peace sign.

"Stop fucking around, Dirk," the leader said.

"You don't know shit," Dirk answered.

Before Rory knew what hit him, Dirk's two fingers had been shoved into each of his nostrils in the most exquisite agony he'd ever felt in his life. Fireworks went off behind his eyes and nose. His head pitched back forcefully, and his jaw dropped away.

Looming over him was the leader. He held the dozen roses in a tight, thorn-biting grip that no longer bothered him. He lifted the bouquet high above his head, as if offering them to the heavens, presenting them to the sun. For a second, Rory didn't understand.

Until the thorny stems were driven deep into Rory's open mouth, down his throat where the taste of magnets was a viscid, choking flow.

The youths swiped the sign and scattered, leaving Rory alone. Rory rolled to one side and gagged. He stared at the rusty rocker panel on a pickup truck and waited to lose consciousness, prayed it would happen soon.

Chapter 12

Three months later.

Snow swirled inside as Rory entered Moon's Martial Arts studio. He shook flakes from his hair and stomped it from his feet, waiting for Leslie to bow him in. He'd been held up by traffic, so he'd texted and asked her to start the class without him. At the door's jingle, twelve preschoolers in three perfect rows turned and broke into smiles at the sight of Rory. He stood and waited. And waited. Blackbelts bowed fellow blackbelts into the dojang as a sign of respect. The only one who didn't look his way was Leslie, the blackbelt who was supposed to bow him in.

Three months earlier and still visibly bruised from the marathon assault, Rory had showed up at Moon's Martial Arts to reacquaint himself with his lost knowledge of Taekwondo. The woman who greeted him was Leslie. Her face was a mirror image of his own: a puzzle of bruises and swelling that had yet to be put to rights. Like Rory, Leslie came to Moon's on the heels of an assault, and Moon thought they would make excellent sparring partners. When Moon learned how skilled Rory was, he asked them both to help teach the youngest students.

Everyone knew, because Leslie made sure of it, she was a broken thing. She was ever down, so don't kick her. Translation: don't have a problem with her, no matter what. Leslie coped with her assault by divorcing her abusive husband, reviewing her Taekwondo forms, and packing her heart into an icy shell. She was a dedicated teacher and held the students to the highest standards, but she not-so-secretly harbored disdain for even the youngest boys, especially when they displayed a whiff of conquistador bravado. She squashed that spirit with venom.

Moon had asked Rory to be the yang to Leslie's yin. The class didn't necessarily need both teachers, but Moon believed everyone should have a chance to become a better version of themselves. It helped to have someone to emulate. Moon hoped Rory's friendship with Leslie would melt the snow and had told him as much.

"You've got...humility. Leslie will take to you like white to rice haha."

Like white to rice.

What would Moon say about them, now?

Arthur had kept Rory after hours re-doing the yeast counts, and the traffic was heinous. If not for Rory's New Yorking, he would've missed the whole class. He deserved a medal from Leslie, not this outright disrespect.

Leslie ignored him. To the class she barked, "Again. Again. We're teaching your body to respond to a threat."

Rory's body hadn't beaten the threat at the marathon, but that was because his skills had been rusty. And, five on one.

Remembering, he absently rubbed his throat. The gang of kid-thugs who nearly killed him were never found. Fine by him. He, a murderer, was still at large, and—thank you, thugs—he would never again be a soft, easy target. The marathon was his failed act of kindness toward Delene Dubrow. He lost consciousness on the sidewalk, choking on a dozen red roses, and he woke in Mercy Hospital with his worried parents leaning over him, his mother dabbing her eyes with a tissue. What was Rory doing there, in that part of town?

Watching the marathon.

His mother cried and thanked God for the good Samaritan who had found him and called the ambulance. *Who was it? Please, God, not Delene.* But his parents didn't know who called 911. When they arrived at the ICU, their deeply medicated son made no sense. The intake nurse got the story from the first responders, who said whoever made the call had left. Rory's parents stayed in town for two weeks and nursed him back to health. The Taekwondo was his dad's idea, but Rory agreed because of how pathetic his response had been. In the face of danger, Rory had neither fought nor flown. He'd been easy prey. Well, easy prey no longer. After getting his ass handed to him at the marathon, Rory decided he would train himself for fight or flight: for fight with Taekwondo and for flight by running races.

And here he was, taking crap from his co-teacher.

Rory cleared his throat as a subtle communication to Leslie. He remained at the door until it became awkward. Obviously, she knew he was there. Rory cleared his throat again.

Still no bow.

He knew what this was about. Oh, he knew.

Continuing to ignore Rory, Leslie moved across the mats toward a little girl, Clarice, and lifted her leg to illustrate the correct angle of the roundhouse kick. Clarice was a newish student who was athletic but had bad body habits because she brought the flair and mindset of her other sport, dancing, into the dojang. Her arms were all flowy like noodles, and she was more concerned with grace than power. Because she was so flexible, Clarice was often picked to demonstrate the location the leg should be at its highest point, though in truth, it was only meant to be at that height and position for a split second. Clarice cringed and uttered little whimpers as Leslie adjusted her and casually spun her around like they were on a turret so the class could inspect what was the correct placement. Leslie talked over the girl's murmurs and over Rory's throat-clearing.

A blackbelt in attendance bowed in any blackbelt who entered the dojang. Period. So he'd passed the test only a week ago, taking him from red belt to black. So what? Rory had broken his requisite boards. He'd put in his time and taken his bruises. After the assault at the marathon, breaking boards was no big deal. As Leslie's *uke*, he'd been thrown a hundred times by Leslie herself. With, he suspected, more roughness than was strictly necessary. Leslie was a brick house; some would call her attractive. Her face was permanently lined in grit or scowl, depending on her mood. Even her hairstyle reflected her personality, with the jet black, bladed mess that brought Edward Scissorhands to mind.

All this resentment because Rory had turned down her offer to have a drink.

Rory could feel his ears get hot, the blood in his veins get angry. He deserved for her to stop what she was doing, face him, and bow him into the dojang. Whatever her personal feelings, instructors were not to bring conflict into the dojang, and never in front of students.

At Telluric, Rory put up with Arthur, who thought himself Caesar Telluric now that Dubrow was gone. The dojang, once Rory's happy place, was souring because of the drama with Leslie. Sure, he could slink off to the coat closet and pretend he didn't notice her disrespect. He could, but after the day he'd had with Arthur—getting cut off at the intersection and the "vanilla" cupcakes that turned out to be filled with mozzarella, marinara sauce, and garnished with red pepper flakes. After Arthur rode him like a bitch all day about the diacetyl infection found in the Hoptober Ale, Rory had eaten his daily quota of shit-pie and would take no more.

He opened the door and shook it violently, ringing the bell far louder than if the door just closed. Snow blasted him.

That stopped everything.

Even Leslie stopped talking. Still holding the leg, she turned toward Rory and gave a half-assed bow. Half-assed because she didn't drop the leg and place her hands at her sides, as was tradition. He was supposed to bow back.

Rory stomped over to Leslie and stood between her and the class, his back toward the students. Through gritted teeth he told her: "I've got the class now. You're dismissed."

In a near-shout, she said, "Dismissed, eh?" To herself, theatrically: "Wait. This sounds familiar. Oh, right. You dismissed me *before*. Said I wasn't your ice cream flavor, like I'm nothing more than a dish." And with her last words, she brought her foot up in a lightning-fast roundhouse kick like the one she'd just explained. Whether she meant to connect with his face or to stop her foot short would never be known.

Smack.

Rory went down.

Moon was there in half a second. "Leslie! Out!"

Tears were ready to spill over her eyes, but they were cold. Ignoring Moon, she bent toward Rory. "You don't deserve *any* ice cream." She left. Didn't even put her shoes on, just walked out of the dojang and into the snow, barefoot.

Moon helped finish the class. Over the course of the evening, a bruise formed in the well of Rory's eye. As the students filed out, Moon told him to ice it. Rory tried to wave him off. Moon wasn't a fly; no one waved him off. In the empty dojang, Rory reclined on a wedge mat and held the ice pack to his face.

"Ice cream flavor? What's that about?"

Rory squirmed, wishing he could be Bruce Lee in the vase on his office desk or a fly on the wall or one of the gazillion stars in the night sky, anything and anywhere but where he was.

"She asked me out on a date. I said no. She gave me attitude and I told her she wasn't my flavor. That's it."

Moon slapped his thighs and laughed.

"Would you be laughing if a man had kicked me in the head?"

He laughed harder. "If a man asked you out, and you told him he wasn't your flavor—yes...I laugh."

Rory smiled, and it hurt his swollen face.

He couldn't believe Leslie had walked out, shoeless. How had things gone so wrong between them? Rory had put up with her Vesuvian moods day in and day out, and rather than his companionship being a sort of cast that would allow her heart to heal, Leslie got it into her head Rory was attracted to her. In sparring, touching happened. Breath mingled. Sometimes silliness occurred, and they had a laugh or two together. According to Leslie, Rory was her only "friend." She put a lot of emphasis on *only*, which had confused Rory. He held space for her little fits and rages and simultaneously over the three months, Rory had transformed from an unsure, chubby red belt into a composed and sturdy first degree black belt.

And Rory couldn't deny the man in the dojang mirrors was not the same as three months ago. Not that he saw Casanova staring back, but the fat that once obscured him was pared away by running, Taekwondo, and the guilt he still nurtured for what he'd done to Dubrow. Rory was shocked Leslie had asked him out—shocked *anyone* would ask him out. Had he been prepared, he would've let her down easier, he told himself, as opposed to the awkward, "Er...no?" he had blurted reflexively.

Leslie's reaction was a startled and dazed silence as if she'd been physically slapped. She fled the dojang.

The next morning Rory had tried to smooth things over.

"Leslie, about last night–"

She put her palm to his lips like she was stopping traffic. "I know, I know." She patted his lips seductively. "You were caught off guard, and at first I was hurt, I admit, but then I thought about it." She shrugged out of her work pants, covered by the dobok, the white robe-like uniform. "And I realized you're intimidated by me.

She had missed Rory's grimace.

"I outrank you," she said.

"So?"

"So you're jealous."

Had he any emotional finesse, Rory would've let the moment go, let it slip down the silent black hole like he did with Arthur, with all the witty come-backs that never made it out into the cosmos. He was a first-degree blackbelt; as a third-degree black belt, she ranked higher than him. Who cared?

It was all the times he'd kept his mouth shut, both with Arthur and with Leslie, and even with his parents. It was like the words banged against the back of his throat, and this time—just this once—they would not be locked up. So it was, without thinking, he had said, "Leslie, if you were an ice cream flavor, I wouldn't pick you. It's that simple."

She had burst into tears and left. Rory had to teach her class alone. And then she took a page out of Arthur's playbook and made it her mission to ruin Taekwondo for Rory. A smirk here, a snort there, not hearing him when he asked her a question.

And tonight, not bowing him into the dojang, kicking him in the head.

"Donut?" Moon offered. He was addicted to Thigh High donuts, consuming them at all times of the day. After the students left for the evening, Moon often closed out the night with one or two of the donuts Rory had turned him on to. The only sound was Moon's chewing and the electric purr from the street lamp outside. Everything else was muffled by the falling snow.

How had Rory become a dog everyone felt they had the right to kick? Arthur was one thing. But Leslie? Because he turned her down for a date?

Moon sighed. "I thought if she got strong and fit and made some friends, she'd lose that chip on her shoulder."

"She's an angry woman," Rory answered.

"She tries to make up for being bad by doing good."

Wait. Was Moon talking about Leslie or about him? He'd traded his fat for muscle, his lethargy for running. He'd become a most excellent employee both at Telluric and Moon's and tried to be a good friend to Carl and a fastidious teacher at the dojang. The good deeds he did, the "good" life he tried to live, if it didn't undo his most terrible deed, nothing could. What was Moon saying—that doing good deeds was futile?

No.

About that, Moon was wrong. It was as simple as this: On some karmic level, Leslie could tell Rory deserved a kick in the head. Not for rejecting her. That was *her* reason. Rory deserved it for Dubrow. Rory had stopped doing good deeds for Delene, and because of that, he was due for punishment. Rory's anger subsided and he began to feel a little empathy for her. Like Rory, Leslie keenly felt the world was against her, and she swung at her shape-shifting nemesis without focus. Like Rory had with Arthur. Like the thugs at the marathon who clobbered away at anything within range. When Leslie'd swung her foot for the roundhouse, she was kicking every man who had ever hurt her.

"What's going to happen to Leslie?" Rory asked.

Moon was thoughtful.

Rory cleared his throat, wondering if Moon had missed his question. "What'll happen to Leslie?" He asked again.

"Maybe she'll teach somewhere else."

"You mean, Leslie's fired?"

"Of course."

"You weren't trying to make her case, just now?"

"Sure, I was making her case. But her case not strong enough." He shook his head sadly. "What kind of person drops somebody in front of kids?" Moon said. "Our students are watching, too, and they need to learn that actions have consequences. You can't hurt somebody and get away with it."

Rory thought of Delene Dubrow. Moon's words made her crash into Rory's heart like an uncaught football pass. He hadn't thought about her because he'd been distracted with his Taekwondo and running. Getting kicked in the head, literally, made him want to re-double his efforts of atonement, to focus his goodwill. He'd be smarter this time. More careful. He'd done Delene only a handful of kindnesses, had given her cards and specialty coffees, tulip bulbs, and one all-expense paid night out on the town. He'd screwed up at the marathon, but still, he was a better man for it. Failure was only failure when it stayed down and didn't learn from mistakes. If Rory was anything, he was a learner. This time with Delene it would be different. Leslie had done him a favor. She'd gotten him back on track.

Chapter 13

On April Fool's Day, Rory reclined on the bench in front of Chapman Elementary School. It was time for the students to be released. The double-wide snake of yellow school busses lined the circular drive. Crossing guards paced their corners and waved at passing cars. The bell went off and the front doors exploded open. A tide of laughing, cavorting children spilled onto the sidewalk. Papers launched and fell like extra-large pieces of confetti. A teacher corralled the horde with threats delivered through a bullhorn. Some were named: "Slow down, Sean Grace! Paul Loomis, hands to yourself. Krista!" (Apparently Krista needed no surname, was infamous enough, and should know better.)

Rory shouldn't be there. What was to be gained? He didn't have a card or a gift for Delene. Or a plan—yet. He was mulling over his options and found he wanted to see her from a distance. Maybe the tilt of her head or the swiftness of her steps would tell him how she fared. Like a house one moved out of, you wanted to see what it looked like after the passage of time. And also, Rory didn't have anything else he felt like doing. Nothing sounded good. Not even beers and pizza at Telluric's competition, Sassy Hop. Some of the office staff were meeting there. He'd taken the day off so he wouldn't be in Arthole's vicinity on the most prankiest day of the year.

Following several more teachers and waves of students, Delene walked in the midst of what had to be a kindergarten class, her palms barely touching the tops of their little heads as if they were half-grown sunflowers.

Some people clearly loved their jobs.

Rory resisted the urge to pull out his binoculars. At a hundred feet, he couldn't see the exact color of her eyes. Or the set of her jaw. It was hard to say for certain whether she was at peace or pressing her grief down and soldiering on. He quickly squashed an unwanted fantasy of rescuing her from a school shooter, him throwing his body over hers and taking her bullet. The last thing he'd see would be her grateful face. He'd die redeemed.

The bowing and slight creak of the bench alerted him that someone with no personal space boundaries had sat beside him. The bench wasn't long enough for strangers to double up, even with Rory's leaner frame. Not willing to meet the intruder's eyes, Rory noted the shoes were Vans, the latest trend. The pants were skinny jeans, but the legs were long and adultish. The legs thrust out in a territorial "V." Also creepily familiar.

"What's up, buttercup?"

Fucking Arthur. He'd followed Rory. Even for Arthur, that was creepy. Rory tried to come up with a clever comeback, but he wasn't quick enough. "What? No Slim?" was all he could manage.

"'Slim' doesn't fit you anymore." Arthur turned toward him and leaned in. "Registered sex offenders aren't allowed within five hundred feet of a school."

Rory snorted at the stupidness of the comment.

"Don't worry, I won't tell on you," Arthur whispered.

"You're not funny." Rory stomped off.

Arthur giggled and got in step with Rory, which with his long legs took him half a stride. "It's a joke. What? Can't take a little joke?"

"I guess not," Rory said through clenched teeth. He had to lead Arthur away from the school before he recognized Delene Dubrow.

"Where're you going?" Arthur asked, "What're you doing here? You never take personal days. You got stage-four cancer or something? You've lost weight. Even the servers noticed."

Arthur's tone was deliciously envious; there was that.

Just yesterday, while grabbing ice from the bar, Rory heard the servers talking about how "smokin' hot [he (Rory!?) was] under all that fat and who would've known?" They were rolling silverware, and laughing about Rory-the-eye-candy, and Arthur, ever-not-working-and-of-course-drinking, stood next to them shooting the breeze. At hearing his name, Rory had strained to hear the rest of the conversation through the wall.

"I saw him at Moon's." Cinnamon had a note of awe in her tone. Cinnamon was a single mom who worked lunch shifts while her son was in school. "He doesn't look like a pussy to me, Arthur. He looks...available." She made a sexy meowing sound.

"Rory's a blackbelt," Diana chimed in. "My Eddy loves his class. Rory used to be a little...soft. I'll give you that, but he's changed. I don't care what you say, Rory's turned into something *fine*. You're jealous."

"He's a skinnier loser," had been Arthur's response.

Fine? Rory?

The idea of jealous Arthur plus onto-his-Senna-prank Arthur?

No.

Though Rory enjoyed the lab and Carl and the smell of yeast and the creative aspect of crafting beer, he could lose Arthur in a New York minute. There were other breweries he could work for that didn't have guilty memories attached to them, but Rory thought he might want to try something different, something totally unrelated to beer. He couldn't un-kill Dubrow, but he could devote himself to a higher purpose. What career could atone for his crimes? Logger? Roofer? He could hold the stop/slow signs at construction areas—road construction workers had a high death rate. He'd give it some thought. The idea of working anyplace Arthur wasn't was sounding better and better.

"No seriously, bro," Arthur said, a little breathless because Rory was practically running. "You on a hunger strike or something?"

"No."

"Don't keep secrets, it's bad form. You find some magical way to lose all that weight? Watching you over the past months, it's like watching a glacier calving. You know, when those enormous blocks of ice fall into the water? Hans was on a diet, and he got so hangry and mean."

"Coming from you, that's saying something. What can I say? I don't get hungry like I used to."

"That's like saying, 'I don't get horny like I used to.'"

Rory gave him a sideways look and decided not to answer. Who followed people like this? Besides himself, but his reasons were noble.

"You out of goldfish to blend that you need to follow me?" Rory snapped.

"I deny any involvement in the stupid fish."

"He's not stupid. Mr. F is smarter than you."

"*Was.* Was smarter."

Rory gave him the finger.

"Now that was uncalled for. My feelings are hurt." Arthur intentionally stepped on a caterpillar crossing the sidewalk. "Like you never ate a fish. You don't eat clam chowder? Sure you do. Or, you did."

"What are you, my mother?"

"Hell no, I'm way more attractive. You've been acting weird—weirder than normal—ever since Dubrow kicked the bucket. Like right now: You don't have kids. Why are you leaving work to sit outside an elementary school?"

Rory froze. Except his heart—his heart stormed off into a sprint.

"Want to know a secret?" Arthur looked around theatrically as if to make sure no one was listening. "I don't think Dubrow died of natural causes. I think he was poisoned."

Rory felt himself reflexively gulp. "That's absurd."

"Alcohol is poison to the body," Arthur said.

Rory rolled his eyes.

"Maybe somebody roofied him," Arthur said. "Who would do that?"

Rory found his brains. "Dubrow was overweight and had a heart condition."

Arthur went on as if Rory hadn't spoken. "A man doesn't become as powerful as Dubrow without making enemies. I can't count on my fingers how many people have benefitted from his departure: competitors, disenfranchised suppliers, disgruntled ex-employees—hell, even Silas was about to have a come-to-Jesus meeting for messing up that batch of Ever Ale."

"Enemies do not murderers make." Rory was pleased with his witty retort. He continued walking. He'd not give Arthur the satisfaction of showing emotion, although a cramping in his gut had begun—not hunger, tension.

Arthur went on. "The detective, what's his name? O-something. He said Dubrow's glass—the last one he ever tipped to his lips—had Senna residue in the bottom. Now what do you make of that? Weird, huh? Like you."

"Why would O'Deens tell *you* that?" Rory's throat constricted, squeezing his last words into quietness.

Arthur shook his head. "No. Wrong question. You're supposed to ask me, 'What's Senna, Arthur?' Because Senna's not clove or mint. It doesn't belong in a glass of beer."

Rory winced. It would look defensive to insist he knew what Senna was. Silence would look guilty as well. Everything looked guilty. Because he was. All he could think to say was, "So I know my herbs, so what?"

Arthur grabbed Rory's arm and yanked him to a stop, gave a challenging glare. "Quit the bullshit. You've been acting weirder and weirder since Dubrow kicked it."

"I don't know what you're talking about." Rory cringed at the squeakiness of his voice, the frailness he felt. He was a blackbelt. A swift roundhouse kick to Arthur's head would show who was boss, here. But no. Even with all the training in the world, Rory could not raise a hand to Arthur, not like this, not on the sidewalk mere yards from Delene Dubrow's school.

Enough time had passed since Dubrow's death. Rory could quit Telluric without it looking suss. It was the only way to get Arthur off his back.

Chapter 14

IT TOOK LONGER THAN Rory expected to find a new job, but it was worth it to get away from Arthur, who lorded his power over Telluric and especially Rory. Until the board decided how to restructure the company, Arthur was the de facto president. Talk about absolute power corrupting absolutely. The last straw was the innuendo about Dubrow's death not being an accident and being followed to Chapman Elementary. *Stalk much, Arthole?*

Rory took a totally worth it pay cut to get out of the beer business. He accepted a job as a summer school teacher in, of all places, Delene's district. However, his assignment was at the high school and she didn't teach summers, so he never saw her. Because of his background in chemistry, he taught mostly math and science courses. When the students tried to jangle his nerves, he kept them in line with teenager kryptonite: embarrassment.

"Can you go to the bathroom? I don't know. *Can* you?" Or "Miss X, kindly bring your little toy to my desk...yes, I mean your phone." Or "Mr. Y, I find your laughter distracting. Please, come here to the front and teach us about terminal velocity. No, I'm not joking."

Rory styled himself a Godfather summer school teacher: good to you so long as you didn't cross him. Then, watch out. He'd made enough examples out of a few bad seeds that his reputation kept the majority of kids respectful. It could've been the black belt too. He didn't mention it, but Moon taught some of his students. It went like this: one day as Rory took attendance, a kid in the back slumped at his desk, long legs thrust out. He raised his hand.

"Yes?" Rory eyed him.

"You teach karate?"

"Taekwondo."

"Whatever. That's cool. Cooler than this." And to his classmates, he said, "Dude taught Dennis how to ki—"

"Okay, thank you, Mr...."

"Tullio."

And he was known. And respected. When Moon learned Rory had quit Telluric, he offered some hours of administrative work. Plus, for any new students Rory brought into his classes, he'd be paid a percentage. Between teaching school and teaching Taekwondo, Rory paid his bills.

Sometimes internal district communications mentioned Delene's school. That always made him smile. Teaching gave him a sense of purpose and satisfaction, like he was heaping good onto the scales of his life by building into the next generation. Plus, no Arthole. Bruce Lee was safe on Rory's kitchen counter. Rory could almost thank Arthur for pushing him to quit Telluric. And bonus: he could keep up on Delene's workplace activities. Arthur claimed O'Deens knew about the Senna, but that had to be bull because there had been silence from the detective. But Arthur knew. Somehow, he knew, and that was why he didn't drink it. What he didn't know was how the Senna got there. Did he suspect Rory? Did it matter? Rory quit Telluric and his days of getting bullied by Arthole were over.

Today was a darkly special day.

Starting with a ten-mile run, Rory pushed himself harder than usual. Appropriately, he took a turn through the cemetery to say *hi* to Dubrow and apologize for the gazillionth time. All the kindnesses in the world wouldn't give Delene her father back. Running himself to death wouldn't either, but one pain numbed the other. He lengthened his stride, one of several ways to increase speed. He switched his music to Metallica. "Unforgiven" seemed most appropriate today. Breath raked up and down his throat as he begged his lungs for more oxygen; the flame in his quads and the pounding on his feet were sweet penance. Gravestones judged him as he passed.

It had been exactly one year since Dubrow died.

A movie, *Seven Pounds*, gave Rory another idea for how to be a good person. Will Smith played a man who accidentally killed his fiancé in a car crash and who atoned for it by donating bone marrow, a kidney, and finally killing himself to donate his heart. The first two were reasonable. Why had Rory not thought of it? The National Kidney Registry tab was open on his laptop at home. The run was so he could think it through one last time, but what was there to think about? He had two kidneys and needed only one. A kidney could save a life. Today was the perfect day...

He slowed to a walk, considered taking a drink from his water bottle and decided against it. Dubrow couldn't thirst, but Rory could, and he deserved to. Earthworms, maybe the same ones that slithered on Dubrow's coffin, were squirming over the asphalt walkway, pushed out by last night's rain. He tweezed them with his fingers and tossed them back into the moist grass. They wriggled to be free of his grip, not understanding. With each worm he flung to the grass, he said under his breath, "It mattered to that one...it mattered to that one."

Too many earthworms littered the sidewalk, and he would never save them all. What did it matter?

"It matters to that one," Rory said again, smiling.

Dubrow was buried in the outer edge of the cemetery, where the graves were sparse.

"I'm sorry," he choked out, stopping at Dubrow's tombstone. He curled forward, gulped air, then stood upright and clasped his hands behind his head to open his lungs. The thought hit him. Dubrow could not open his lungs, could not want for air, for beer, for the sunshine on his face or the pavement's smack on his feet. Dubrow was gone to a place Rory didn't know. A wish would creep in. Rory wanted so badly not to be a murderer. He could practically feel the devil on his shoulder, the pointy snake-red tail and the horns. *Your fault,* so said the devil. Arthur didn't put the Senna in Dubrow's beer. Rory did. Yes, it was meant for Arthur, but if a bullet is meant for someone else, does it matter—in the moment it tears the flesh, stops the heart, kills the brain? The deed was done. By Rory's hand. And a year had not been time enough to soothe his conscience. The little deeds for Delene were temporary consolations.

Kidney donation to save a life. Surely that would take away his guilt.

Since watching *Seven Pounds,* which was the weight of an average human heart, Rory donated blood regularly—double red because it helped the most people. He'd mailed several more cards to Delene and planted petunias in her yard while she was on vacation. It was night time, and he feared the police, but in the morning when he drove by, he was happy with the effect. He sent an anonymous donation for a new gaga ball pit for Chapman Elementary to replace the one that had been stolen. And he was actively trying to figure out his next anonymous angel move. Running was where he had his best thoughts.

The marble was smooth on top of the gravestone and had watermarks from the rain. Benjamin S. Dubrow 1951-2023. Rory crouched beside the stone. He whispered. "Not a day goes by I don't wish things were different, that I hadn't...I can't–"

An unexpected throat-clearing launched Rory standing and startled him so he toppled backward over the tombstone. Luckily the grass had grown soft around it. Still, his face took a smudging of dirt and bits of freshly cut grass. He swiped at it as he recovered.

Delene. Dubrow.

A knit brow. Curious eyes.

"You okay?" she asked.

Had she heard?

The thought of sprinting away made his legs twitch. He forced himself to adopt a casual stance. "Oh. Didn't see you there. Yes. Fine."

"You worked for Dad. Rory, right? I almost didn't recognize you. You're half the man you used to be." She smiled slightly, intending it as a compliment.

He'd lost over a hundred pounds in the year since Dubrow died.

Could he pretend to be someone else? Rory? Rory who? No ma'am. I've always been this thin, and I never accidentally poisoned your father.

"Hi. Yes. I used to be much fatter. Er, I..."

"What are you doing here?"

Confessing. "What am I doing here? Well, I come here to remind myself of the brevity of life? Your father's death was unexpected. I—it changed me." *All true.* "I come here to meditate on what's important." *Also true.*

Delene placed a bunch of lavender flowers on the top of the stone and sighed. "Me too. I come once a week or so, to talk with him. At him."

Rory smiled at her attempt at levity.

"You visit Dad's grave?" she said. "That's the sweetest thing."

Yes, the sweetest thing. It's definitely not me readying myself for our confrontation in hell.

"I run by the cemetery and sometimes I stop in. I'm too out of breath to do much talking."

"You must live close by."

"I'm on Lindsay Drive."

"That's a ten-mile run, at least."

And because he was a Delene Dubrow groupie, he knew running would interest her. And funnier still, he'd gotten into running because of her. *How about them apples, Delene?*

She continued. "I run, too. Not as much lately." She waved a hand around at the graves as if they could explain her lack of energy.

Rory knew he stood and stupidly stared at her, but words were not coming. Would she see through him, know he knew about her running already, down to her pace and finishing place in races? All online. You only had to know where to look.

"I should get back into running," she continued. "My mind was clearer." She surveyed herself. "I was—"

"You look great," Rory blurted.

She closed her eyes and smiled, as if willing his compliment to latch onto something inside her. Rory got a jolt of elation. His (true) compliment had made her smile. The thought that he could do a direct kindness and participate in the delivery, to not watch from the shadows as she unwrapped whatever deed he'd done for her, was intoxicating. Part of him—the dumb part—wanted to sit her down right there on her father's grave and pour out the many wonders he'd learned about her over the past year.

That was impossible and would ever be. Rory would know Delene the way one "knew" the constellations. From a great distance.

He found his voice. "How's Telluric doing? I see their beer everywhere, even in the grocery stores. I don't partake as often." He patted the place that used to be an enormous belly. "But they're still my favorite when I do."

"Right. I got into running so I could drink my fill of beer," she said. "Not exactly holy motivation, but it worked. Dad's rolling in his grave over some of Arthur's strategies in the brewery. Dad never wanted our beer in grocery stores, but Arthur's idea of canned pints put Telluric back on the map." She massaged her temple. "Can't say I enjoy his company, but he was Dad's right-hand man and he knows the business inside and out."

At her mention of Arthur's name, Rory felt his pulse quicken, his face twitch.

"I always felt like he chose Arthur the way a person chooses an attack dog. And he kept him close, but leashed," Delene mused.

A flicker of heat began at the base of Rory's neck. The old rage popped up like a jack-in-the-box.

A crunch of gravel announced cars coming into the cemetery, going toward a fresh grave lined in faux grass and shaded by a tent. A hearse and a solemn train of cars passed. Rory was grateful for the distraction. He used it to compose himself.

"We used to call him Arthole," Rory said, "Remember how he never used anyone's real name? I came up with that one, Arthole."

"You!? The chemists still do this funny accent whenever they talk about him–when he's not around, of course. I think they all fear him."

"Do they talk like thith?"

She laughed. "Yesth. Exactly."

"He called me 'Slim.'"

"And now, it's true. Joke's on him." She laughed but when her gaze fell back on the grave, her joy was clipped. "Today is...one year."

Right, that's why I'm here. He should've known Delene would come today. But the day had many hours. What were the chances of them running into each other? As if the idea of kismet had struck her, too, she brightened.

"Hey...want to grab a cup of coffee? I'm off work."

"You have the whole summer off," he said.

"What?"

And he realized his mistake. How would he know she had summers off? Sprinting away felt like the best course of action again, but before his body could hijack the moment, he took a deep breath and reminded his prefrontal cortex how him fleeing would appear to Delene Dubrow.

"Your license plate. It says 'TCHEVRY1.'"

She visibly relaxed. "I want to...what did you say? Consider the brevity of life, what's important."

Rory looked around, as if an excuse for not going to coffee would present itself.

"It would be a nice distraction—I mean, you're not *just* a distraction—but it would mean a lot to me...if you don't have any other plans?"

"I'm a sweaty mess." There. A good excuse.

She dismissed him with a wave. Then she shocked him by leaning in and taking a whiff. "Smell fine to me...and you can run home from Holy Grounds. Unless you're busy?"

Donating a kidney, yes. "Sure. I have some time before I have to log in for a meeting." He did not say it was for his kidney donation health consultation. "Coffee would be great." Great? How about mind-blowing?

Rory was going to have coffee with the woman who'd occupied his mind every single day for the last year.

Delene ordered a red eye and turned to him. He realized he didn't bring his wallet on runs, which meant she'd be treating him to a coffee. With her presence blotting out his experiential reality, he wouldn't taste the drink anyway, so he ordered a dark roast coffee, about as hum drum as an order could be.

He thanked her awkwardly, and they found a table.

"Tell me a story about Dad." Her rapt attention mixed him up and emptied his mind of everything but her eyes.

"He...he once had a limousine drive me home from a tasting."

"I remember, the beer tasting, the thousand bucks." Her face lit with recognition. "Dad told me about it. Dad was all about success, but it had to be honest and sweaty. A win couldn't be lucky or easy or—God forbid—treacherous, *that* Dad could not respect."

Rory spoke into his coffee mug. "Arthur didn't like me much, after that." And before that, but who cared?

Delene swatted at the idea of Arthur. "He hates everyone except Hans." She brightened. "I'll bet you didn't know this. My dad made a mean cannoli."

Rory blinked. "He didn't come off as the domestic type."

"And he was a tiger mom before the word was coined. After mom died, he threw himself into two things: the brewery and me. He pushed hard, sometimes too hard, and it frustrated me right up to the moment of whatever breakthrough only Dad could see coming." She laughed, but it didn't reach her eyes. "I use Dad's strategies on my students, and it's like I can feel him smiling."

She cried silently into both their beverage napkins and had begun to wash her sleeve across her face. Beautiful.

Stories about Dubrow made her cry happy tears, and she almost fell off her chair when Rory told her about Arthur and the fermenter and how her dad had caught enormous Rory trying to pry his soaked self out of a fermenter. Rory pretended he thought it was funny, too, although even with the passage of time, it wasn't. He feigned only casual interest in her every word, in the sights and sounds of the moment. He acted as if he was not keenly aware of the smooth wooden chairs, of the way her hand curled possessively around her coffee mug, the steam rising up and away until it didn't exist anymore. As if her eyes weren't deeper than the cosmos and her laugh wasn't the highest order of music. Just another day. Like any other day.

He pretended everything, really, except for the feeling of being enchanted. This, Rory decided though it lanced him, would be their first and last time together. He could not be her friend while secretly being an angel to Delene Dubrow. He simply wasn't that good of a liar.

Chapter 15

"I UNDERSTAND YOU'RE INTERESTED in becoming a Good Samaritan donor?" the nurse asked, thumbing through Rory's screening results.

Him, a Good Samaritan.

"Yes."

"Why do you want to donate to a stranger in need of a kidney?"

"Er...because I have an extra."

The screening nurse let out the tiniest laugh-snort. "I never heard that one before."

Rory smiled sheepishly.

The young, blue-haired nurse leveled a solemn gaze at Rory. "This operation isn't without risks. They're small, but they exist. Are you aware the kidney could be rejected?"

If any would be, mine would.

"Yes, I'm aware," Rory answered. He spun a story of a friend at UC Davis who died of kidney disease and could've been saved if a match had been found. Satisfied, the nurse checked the box. His interview was followed by several more screening interviews and pages upon pages of questions, blood screenings, and a psychological test he was delightfully amazed to pass.

And just like that, Rory would donate a kidney.

"Mr. Harper, how are we feeling this morning?" Nurses always used the pronoun *we*. Why did they do that? As if whatever Rory experienced, she did too, simply because she put herself in the equation with a plural pronoun.

"Like I'm light one kidney," Rory muttered.

The third-shift nurse asked the question in such a way that it was clear *we* were doing fine. And *we* didn't need anything. Rory's was a non-directed kidney donation. He thought he might expect the same hero treatment as when he gave blood. A *thank you for your service* wouldn't hurt. A little *you're the best*. It wasn't like he was giving a cup of sugar.

Someone forgot to tell this nurse what a Good Samaritan he was.

He didn't know the nurse's real name because her lanyard was caught in her ample cleavage, stuck like a book marker. It looked like it might be Rachel, but her mannerisms were all Ratched. She had the thickest, longest black hair Rory had ever seen, and her face had a smattering of dents leftover from puberty, he guessed. Maybe she was bitter about her bad luck with the gene pool. But she'd be pretty if she didn't scowl. He wanted to tell her that. Smooth skin was overrated. Smiles weren't.

"Jokes aside," the nurse frowned and gave him a sideways glance. "How are we?"

"We're fine," Rory lied.

Truth was, his bladder felt full. The collection bag was mostly empty. He suspected there was a crimp or some other problem. It was 6:45 AM, which meant the day nurse would be arriving soon. She would have more of a bedside manner. Medusa would have more of a bedside manner.

Ice-cold hands took his pulse. "Sixty-t—what's this!" Nurse Ratched held up the empty bag.

Rory felt guilty for his bodily functions.

She pressed his bladder. A blade of pain followed by a wet warmth gushed between his legs. "Oh we are NOT fine, mister." And she reached under his bed sheets and did some terrible things with her cold hands that yanked way up inside and also relieved him at the same time.

"Now I have to change your sheets."

Rory hoped she didn't have children.

"Hello?" Delene Dubrow's merry face popped into view from behind his door.

Rory snatched the sheets over his legs to hide his ugly hospital socks, and other things.

"You able to have visitors?" She tipped a bouquet of lavender toward him.

Nurse Ratched answered, "Just a minute. He wet the bed."

Rory pulled the sheet over his face.

Delene waited in the hall until Ratched left the room then entered with a lively, theatrical step, a flushed face as if she'd run that morning, and bright, playful eyes. She glossed right over the bed-wetting thing.

Rory wanted to explain he hadn't wet the bed, that it was Nurse Ratched's fault. Instead, he said, "Hello?" The question being, *What are you doing here?*

Delene set the arrangement on his bedside table. "I hope you don't mind me showing up out of the blue. I was out."

"Not at all." *Lie, big fat one.* "Lavender. Are you trying to tell me something?"

"Oh, because I put these on Dad's grave? No, I just love lavender. It grows wild in the field behind my condo. Your neighbor told me you were here. It's altruistic of you to donate to someone you don't even know."

"It's nothing."

"Nothing!? The world needs more people like you. You're either a saint or crazy."

"If it's between those two–"

"You make me want to be a better person, Rory Harper. That's why I came. Okay, initially I came because I found this in my car." She held up his GPS watch. The little band that held the strap in the hole was torn.

He'd wondered where his running watch had gotten to.

She continued, "I was going to leave it with your neighbor, but he told me where you were and what you were doing, and I had to come. I had to see you. You visit my dad. You give your kidneys away. You're too good to be true."

Don't you know it.

"If you need anything when you get out of the hospital, anything at all, don't hesitate to call or text. My number's in the card."

Rory would make sure *not* to need anything.

Day two home from the hospital, Delene showed up at Rory's door.

"Er...hi," Rory greeted her.

She thrust an aluminum tray toward him. "Dad's lasagna recipe. And cannoli."

Rory stammered a thank you, but he didn't cross the threshold or let her in. The awkwardness mushroomed. Oregano and garlic emanated from the still-warm offering. He balanced the tray in one hand and gripped the doorknob with his other.

"And here." She held a bottle of red wine and a paper bag. Her eyes flickered beyond him.

"You didn't need to do that," was all he could manage.

When the polite time for asking her inside had long passed, she set the offering on his doormat and stepped back. "I guess I'll be going. You did a brave and generous thing, donating a kidney."

Rory swallowed, relieved she got the hint. "Bye. Thanks for the dinner. Very thoughtful of you."

Delene took a few steps away then turned back and asked, "Why'd you leave Telluric?"

The million-dollar question.

"You were one of Dad's shining stars, went to UC Davis—best beer-making college around, and Dad loved your recipe ideas. Why'd you leave?"

"Honestly?"

"No. Lie to me. I love lies." She toed a weed in a sidewalk crack.

Rory arched an eyebrow at her sarcasm and decided the best lies were mostly true. And she *had* asked him to lie to her. He'd oblige. "Without your father there, the environment wasn't a place I enjoyed."

"Environment. You mean Arthur?"

Rory shrugged. She didn't exactly lead with shallow conversation, did she? "I wanted a change, that's all."

She made a little sound, like she didn't buy it. "What do you do now—when you're not jogging or donating a kidney?"

"I substitute teach, usually at the high school. And I teach Taekwondo to preschoolers."

"How cool is that? Can you show me some moves?"

He looked at himself, at his PJ's and slides.

"Right. I mean when you're recovered."

This moment, her standing on his sidewalk about to walk away maybe forever, gave Rory a twisting in his chest, like when he was offered his first beer. He knew he shouldn't, but he craved a sip of the mysterious, golden substance that would supposedly make him happy. Many good times followed that poor decision. Right now, he wanted her. She was mysterious, golden. Before he could think another thought, he opened the door, glad his apartment had improved from his Telluric days. He had furniture and even some decorations, mostly nature pictures he took and had printed onto canvases. How surreal to have Delene Dubrow cross his threshold. What would someone do who wasn't infatuated with her, someone normal who hadn't killed her father?

"Can I offer you some coffee?" he asked.

"Sure." She gave a slight bounce. "I thought you'd never ask."

As he opened a cabinet, his eyes fell on his refrigerator, to the newspaper article picture of Delene jumping out of an airplane wearing a Winnie the Pooh costume. He dropped the canister and threw open the freezer door, simultaneously crumbling the paper in his palm. He pretended to look for something in the freezer and then closed it—he hoped—nonchalantly.

Delene righted the coffee can, which luckily, hadn't opened. She hadn't seen.

"Cream? Sugar?" Rory slipped the balled-up article into a drawer.

They settled in on each end of his couch.

"Tell me about your mother." He'd meant to start with more appropriate topics like a normal person, but the Pooh picture stole his composure.

She made a face.

"Oh. Sorry." Rory squirmed and stared into his mug for a response. None came.

Delene sighed and—before he could take back his rude question—she answered. "Mom died when I was eighteen. Cancer."

"Augh."

She waved it off. "Dad threw himself into the brewery even harder after that, almost like he had a deadline to meet. We both became obsessed with distractions, me with getting into college and him with building Telluric. Dad had heart problems, and when Mom died, he got so bad I thought I'd lose him, too. I think, when he looked at me, it was hard for him not to see Mom. He said I looked like her."

"She must've been stunning," he mumbled, more to himself than to her.

Her silence became a living thing.

He glanced up to see she wore a wide, grateful smile. "What?"

"You're something, Rory Harper."

"You don't know the half of it," he mumbled into his mug.

"I'd like to. Know, I mean. I'd like to know you more." She stumbled over her declaration. "Would you ever consider a running partner?"

Part of Rory wanted to jump at the thought of running beside Delene, of knowing her for real, as opposed to knowing her covertly. But the other, rational part said he ought to get her the hell out of his living room and out of his life as quickly as possible. Befriending her was dangerous on so many levels. He'd never be able to be himself, never tell her all that was in his heart. What she saw when she looked at Rory was an altruistic kidney donator, when the truth was: it was penance.

But what a drug, the heroic way she saw him. He wanted to be the person Delene Dubrow saw, for real. She was definitely interested in spending more time with him. This female attention was foreign. Rory didn't know what to do with it. He didn't want Delene to become a Leslie experience, where his big mouth got him a roundhouse kick to the head. It was better to keep her at a distance than to get on the dead-end street that was any sort of relationship with Delene Dubrow. The safe thing was to tell her he ran alone. But what a drug, the heroic way she saw him.

"Depends," Rory heard himself say with a bit of flirtation. Like he was Casanova. Where did this come from?

"On?" She asked.

"Your running pace." He smiled.

"Eight minutes, flat."

Rory knew, but he pretended surprise, and he didn't need to pretend to be impressed. "You'll have to slow it down for me, Usain Bolt."

She laughed at Rory's reference to the greatest sprinter of all time. "Have you ever run a marathon?"

"I'm signed up for my first. I'm not going to lie, it looms."

"Oh, this will be great fun. We can train together."

They shared Delene's lasagna. Afterward, they talked about their college days, about good and great beer. Theirs was a swift and deep encounter, like a spade cutting through soil.

It was the end of Rory doing anonymous good deeds for Delene Dubrow and the beginning of the most vile, sophisticated lies of his life.

Chapter 16

RORY AND DELENE SPARRED on the patchwork rubber mats at Moon's Martial Arts. They had the dojang to themselves, the students and Moon having gone home. Rory had a set of keys so the instructors could practice late into the evening if they wished. Delene was a quick study; Taekwondo complemented her running goals and helped her overall balance, flexibility, and strength. Not to mention she'd be able to defend herself.

After an evening spent corralling six-year-olds, Rory had adrenaline to use up. And he enjoyed the time sparring with Delene, who had proven to be an excellent running partner and an even better friend. How he called his life *living* before her, he didn't know. He understood why Delene's students adored her; her passion for excellence was contagious. Whether Taekwondo or running, Delene brought all of herself.

"She works harder than any of the guys," Moon had said, and Rory winced at the backhanded compliment while agreeing with it.

When Rory and Delene trained together on long runs, she did most of the talking, which his burning lungs appreciated. He gulped air and tried to stretch his stride. She showed him how to do tempo runs, and he showed her "fartlicks," which were a type of brutal sprints. In German: *fartlek* meant speed-play and involved alternating fast and slow paces. Whether or not the exercise complemented martial arts, Rory didn't know; he just enjoyed saying "fartlick." And he certainly enjoyed speaking it more than doing them and waaaay more than completing Delene's Satanic tempo runs, which were fartlicks on steroids. The goal, she said, was to build the heart rate up to race pace and let it cool down again. But Rory said the goal was a heart attack. She'd smile and tell him he had "more in the tank" than he thought. Sometimes they did tempo runs in ladders. Climb up, drop down, then climb up again.

Rory wondered if Delene somehow knew what he did to her father, and she was trying to kill him back. But no. This sort of punishment was the secret recipe to the mind-game of marathons. You stayed in motion. Maybe you geared down, but you never stopped, not until mile 26.2.

To pass the time on a long run, she told him about the history of marathons, of the first hapless runner who died at the end of the run, after giving the good news that the Greeks had beaten the Persians. Rory knew the story, but he loved the musical sound of her voice, so he told her he forgot. He asked why the strange distance: 26.2 miles. Why not a straight 26? Or since most of the world ran on metrics, an even 40,000 meters? He felt like he got a peek at the teacher in her when she explained the race's distance changed over the years, how the London Olympic committee wanted the finish to happen in front of the royal box, so they tacked on a spin around the track. Somehow, 26.2 stuck.

He told her about the one marathon he'd watched, but didn't say it was hers, told her how insane he thought everyone was for being awake so early, for choosing to run until their legs gave out. He saw the runners' joyful, triumphant expressions and decided he wanted to feel that, too.

"That's how I feel, about you," she said.

What could Rory answer? *No, Delene. You don't want to be anything like me. That would make you a lying murderer.* Because he couldn't tell her the truth, he worked harder, ran faster. He pushed himself beyond his limits every day, savoring the pain in his calves.

He could tell Delene saw him in a certain, illusory light. She saw grit and strength, and she signed up to run the marathon with him. They crossed the finish line together: Rory on his last ounce of strength, Delene gliding along beside him. They had trained together through the fall, winter, and spring. Rory knew she wanted to be more than friends; he knew it was a bad idea. But things were slipping out of his control, and their worlds became more and more intertwined. Delene used her influence to get Rory a position as a long-term substitute in her district. They settled into a routine of dinner at each other's place, Taekwondo at Moon's, and long talks about beer and books or whatever drama was going on at their respective schools.

After the marathon, Rory took Delene out for dinner and ice cream. They kissed for the first time on the Sunset Steps overlooking the Root River while their sundaes melted, untouched beside them. She had reached over and threaded her arm through his. It was as if the energy of the river had rushed into Rory and took him to the peak of his imagination, where he saw a future he'd never seen before. *He* could be Delene's joy. He'd give his life to make hers the happiest it could be. No one would love her the way he did, that he knew without a doubt. Although a father's love was taken from her, Rory would make sure she lived happily ever after, that she smiled the smile *he* put there. He'd make her his life's mission.

He kissed her with the passion and strength of the rush she'd ignited. Gone was the fearful fat man who wanted nothing more from life than a thick, hoppy beer and a greasy pizza. Rory had a purpose, something to live for. Some*one* to live for. She taught him running, and he taught her Taekwondo. The more time he spent with her, the clearer it became she sussed out whatever good had hibernated inside of him. To hold her hand, walk and talk with her, share his workday, this was surely Heaven. The only blight on his otherwise perfect life was, of course, the Lie. If only Rory could confess his crime. His secret weighed on him, took the place of the extra pounds he used to carry, but it also motivated him to be even better in every way, as if, by loving her perfectly, he could make up for his deceit. There were cosmic scales he tried very hard to balance, but no matter how good things were going between Rory and Delene, the weight pressed upon him. Fear crouched, and he could feel the tension, feared it would eventually pounce, tear them asunder, and devour the good they had together.

He wanted to ask her to marry him.

It was the most reckless, untenable thing he'd ever devised. As he chose the round brilliant diamond ring that cost him a month's salary, he suppressed his misgivings. As long as Delene was in his life, he could face anything. But shouldn't he come clean with her? It was the right thing to do. He dreaded the storm his confession would bring. He'd explain it probably wasn't him that killed her father. The Senna was meant for Arthur, that it probably–*probably??* was a fluke coincidence that kept Rory awake at night, and he had to tell her because it was a monster in his life. A monster had led him to penance and to her and so couldn't possibly be all bad.

Could he risk losing her? It wasn't fair to ask her to marry him until she knew all of Rory Harper: the good, the bad, and the ugly. But he was no dummy to go off half-cocked and spill everything. He'd feel her out first.

But how? He couldn't just toss out: *Hey Delene, where do you see yourself as far as forgiveness goes—on a scale of Jesus to Hamlet?*

So, he waited for a conversation that would organically lead to deeper topics. The ring stayed in his sock drawer, and several weeks went by before Rory's opportunity presented itself.

One of Delene's fellow teachers broke down in the middle of a lesson and had to go home for the day. During their ten-mile run, Delene confessed her concern that something terrible must have happened. It wasn't like Melanie to run out.

The next evening when she joined Rory at his place for dinner he asked, "How's Melanie?"

"She didn't come to work again."

"Really?"

Days later, Delene asked Rory to bring over sushi because she was too tired to cook. She indeed looked ragged.

"Rough day?" Rory asked.

"I found out what happened to Melanie," Delene stared off into space.

Rory waited. When she didn't go on, he said, "Must be pretty bad."

"Her husband cheated on her."

Rory blew out the breath he'd been holding. "That's the worst suck there is."

Delene nodded, still in space.

"She catch him?" Rory asked.

Delene shook her head. "The scumbag confessed. Asked her to go on a walk. He sat Melanie down at a park bench, got on his knee like he was proposing, and told her he slept with his sales rep."

"Damn."

"Damn is right," Delene said.

"She kick him to the curb?"

Delene snorted. "He thinks he can earn back her trust. He said as much."

Rory couldn't help but see a parallel. Here was his chance. He could tell she expected him to condemn the guy. And his actions were contemptible, but here was a chance to plumb her tilt toward forgiveness. He allowed the betrayal story to hover in the air.

"Well?" Delene's indignation had teeth.

Rory knew what she expected, what she needed to hear. Any strongly-worded condemnation of *the scumbag* would do the trick.

Instead, he ventured, "Must've been hard for him to confess, knowing he'd probably lose her."

"What?"

"He wasn't caught, there's that."

Delene's face scrunched in confusion and ire. "I don't get it... *Why?*"

"Melanie's husband risked losing his wife to re-claim his integrity," Rory faltered. "He had a secret, and he came clean. I'm not saying he didn't mess up."

"'Mess up' doesn't cover it."

"But he *confessed*."

"So did Jeffrey Dahmer." With that, Delene launched from the table and took her aggression out on the dishes, clanging them and splashing her fury all over the counter and cabinets.

"Why are you doing my dishes?" Rory asked. "The whole point of sushi was because you're tired."

She fixed him with a glare.

Not only did that not go according to plan, she was more indignant than he'd ever seen her.

He let her cool down, hoping he could persuade her to see his point of view in a later conversation. They taught their classes at the dojang that evening, as usual, and he kept his distance until the students were gone and they had the place to themselves. He hoped to put off their intended sparring, as it wasn't the best environment, her being tired and infuriated and all, but they'd planned to practice for Delene's upcoming chevron test. She re-affixed her hair and tightened her belt, signs she readied herself to spar.

When she turned to face him, it was clear by the icy gleam in her eye she was still mad about the dinner conversation. She strode to him and bowed exaggeratedly.

"Ready?" she asked with mock sweetness.

"Er, no. Probably not. You're tired, remember?"

"Be my uke tonight," there was a confusing and slightly terrifying sultriness to her voice.

"You want to practice throwing me?" Rory said, "I thought we decided on forms."

"Forget it. Let's spar."

"Yes, ma'am." He readied himself. Sparring partners entered into an unspoken agreement to allow space for each to practice a back and forth, a mix of offense and defense. Hits were done with precision, not to bruise. Each person could expect a reasonable amount of mat space. Men could expect their groins would be safe. The look in Delene's eyes made Rory wonder if his groin was safe, and adrenaline put bees on his nerves. Usually, the program was that Delene's hand or foot could come at him from any direction. His responsibility was to block her attack and give her advice on form.

They did the dance of sparring, wordless, for a long time. Her anger manifested, not in a breach of contract, but as clumsiness. Poor girl was striking with her emotions, not her will. Or, trying to, anyway. A sheen of sweat glossed their faces and left sweat streaks wherever their bodies touched the mats. It was the longest running spar they'd ever done. Rory wasn't about to give up. Apparently, neither was Delene, but eventually, her thirst overcame her pride. Rory was relieved.

At a loss for how to begin, but thinking a man couldn't go wrong by leading with an apology, Rory said, "I'm sorry my response to that story made you angry."

"That's not an apology." She shot her left leg up, and her toes knocked the water bottle from his hand. A warning shot off the bow.

"I said, 'sorry.' How is that not an apology?"

"You're apologizing for *my* feelings. It doesn't work that way. How could you stand up for that deadbeat of a husband? I don't get it."

"How could you not?" he shot back.

She spun and shot out her other foot, almost catching him off guard, would've tickled his jaw had he been a second later with his block. "He. cheated. on. her."

"We were talking about second chances." He leaned back and away from the swinging paddle of her hand. "Yes, he did a terrible thing. He lied to her, broke her trust. He was selfish and thoughtless and reckless. I'm not saying the guy deserves a medal."

"That's exactly what you were saying." Delene grit her teeth.

"You know I was talking about him coming clean. I said it was admirable that he approached her and confessed, as opposed to getting caught. Most cheaters get caught."

"You talk like one who knows," she growled.

Indeed. Rory had to be careful. He was on unstable ground, possibly giving her the wrong impression about him. Murderer, yes. Cheater, not on your life.

"You are the only woman for me." He palmed her neck and kissed her deeply, taking her by surprise.

She pulled back and sent a chop to his neck he barely managed to dodge.

He circled to parry.

She tried another.

He stopped that one too and graced her with a triumphant smile.

Her inability to strike dialed up her fury. "So he does that really, really hard and honorable thing called *apologizing* for being the scum of the Earth and everything's A-okay. Give the man a mulligan. Or the Nobel Prize. Onward and upward. Love you, babe."

"Sarcastic much?" Rory side-stepped her when she tried to sweep his leg.

She used too much force, lost her balance, and landed on her butt. She narrowed her eyes. "You've been going easy on me, haven't you?"

"Why do you ask that?"

"Because I usually land *something*."

He tried not to smile but failed. He'd been allowing her to land a kick or a punch to keep her spirits up. It was also good practice for her. He hadn't meant to beat her so handily; their conversation took all his attention.

Her hands went to her face. "I'm sorry. It's just...I can't believe you feel that way, Ror, that you'd defend him."

She was the only one who called him *Ror*. He loved it. Except now.

Oh, those disappointed, hurting eyes.

"I didn't say I liked him. I said he deserves a second chance. Or should the guy roll over and die? Not try to be better or fight for his marriage?"

"He lost that fight when he made the decision to cheat."

"You're the one who says people are works in progress."

"I mean kids."

"Oh, so only kids mess up? At what age are you no longer allowed to make a bad decision? My point is, what do you do with your life's regrets? The little ones can be tucked away somewhere, forgotten maybe. But the big stuff, those things you wish like crazy you hadn't done, but you did, and even though you feel so bad about yourself you wish your heart would seize, and you know it should because of the blackness inside, but it doesn't seize. It keeps beating and beating, and you wake up every day, surprised and a little disappointed to be alive. What to do? Does this guy shoot himself in the head? Drink himself to death? Sure, some despairing people do. But *should* he? I saw one small piece of goodness in a guy who, otherwise, is a piece of shit. Don't hate me for it, Delene. Don't. Because no one's perfect, and you don't know what you're capable of. You may think you do, but you don't. Given the right circumstances, I believe anyone's capable of betrayal. Or even murder. You said he was always home alone with the kids. That's no excuse for what he did, but I see a man floundering. Nobody notices him. He feels worthless. Life primed him for this, and right at the perfect moment this—your words not mine—'drop-dead gorgeous' woman starts pursuing him, and he tries to shake her off, you know, but she's persistent. She keeps coming, and a guy's only got so much willpower. He caves. He cheats. And then he goes to his wife, begs for forgiveness, tells her how sorry he is and what a piece of shit he is. And could he please have another chance? And your response would be—"

Her leg came up, fast.

He didn't see in time to parry. Instead, he dropped to the mat a little out of control.

"I'd show him the door."

From the ground Rory asked, "No second chances?"

She extended a hand to help him up. "Ror, some things you can't come back from. You say something you don't mean. Okay. You get mad and put your fist through the wall. Okay. But cheating..." She shook her head. "There are some things you can't be sorry enough about. Once you do them, you're in the club of the unredeemable."

Unredeemable.

"The high school kid who accidentally runs over someone with his car. He's technically a murderer. Unredeemable?"

"You're trying to muddy the water. Melanie's husband is an irredeemable scumbag."

He sighed and shook his head. *Just like me.* "The best thing the guy could've done–assuming he wants to stay married—would be to end his affair and keep his trap shut."

Delene jutted out her chin. "You know I don't think that's the best way. He shouldn't have cheated in the first place."

Rory swept his leg under her and dropped her almost to the ground, caught her arm before she hit, cradled her body in his arms inches above the mat. "One of the many things I love about you, Delene Dubrow. You always take the high ground."

She searched his eyes.

He kissed her before she could say another word. What would Moon have thought about what they did in the dojang after that kiss? It was adventurous. And steamy. It wouldn't matter what Moon thought because Rory wouldn't give away his secrets.

Keeping secrets was the only way to keep everything. That was the takeaway.

Chapter 17

It took Rory several weeks after the sparring episode, as he referred to it in his mind, for him to work up the guts to ask Delene to marry him. A rational, logical voice inside his head (very soft-spoken) asked whether it was a good idea to marry the woman whose father he had inadvertently killed. But he'd see her lovely face or kiss her, and the voice was muted.

As far as Rory could tell, Delene enjoyed bringing up philosophical topics while he was otherwise engaged in trying to kick her butt in Taekwondo.

"What do you have against church?" Delene asked. "Let me guess, you think Judas should've been given another chance after he got Jesus killed?" She waited until he was out of breath and dizzy from executing several *Kata Gurumas*, shoulder wheels.

"I didn't say I was against church. I said I wanted an outdoor wedding."

Delene inserted her head into Rory's armpit and grabbed his arm, hefting him onto her shoulders. She spun with him. "You said–and I quote– 'Church is against my religion.'" She spun again and with precision dropped him into a harmless roll.

He popped up like a prairie dog. "My darling, where'd you get those guns?"

She responded with a punch aimed at his belly which he easily deflected.

"But your Jedi skills are no match for me," he teased.

Delene breathlessly explained that her father had been a tepid Catholic. Something in his past, long before Delene was born, had rubbed him wrong enough that he'd abandoned his faith. Delene's mother had cobbled together her mysticism from books, mostly the classics like *Paradise Lost, Great Expectations,* and *Anna Karenina*, but she added works like *Watership Down* (lessons on leadership from bunnies and oh, so exciting!) or Pat Conroy's *Lords of Discipline* when she was in high school and trying to define grit and strength and personal responsibility, while wanting very, very badly to drink and party and be reckless. Other moms pushed food into their children's mouths; Delene's mother was a pusher of books. Before Delene ever had a school lesson on the Civil War, her mother had read to her: *Twelve Years a Slave*, *Huckleberry Finn*, and *Uncle Tom's Cabin*.

In following her mother's lead, Delene's God was the God of *The Hiding Place*, of Cory Ten Boom during WWII, and of countless missionaries who gave up everything, sometimes their lives, in service to their God.

"Seriously, what's your beef with God?" she asked.

"I don't have a beef with God. I have a beef with organized religion."

"Why?"

"Let's see...the Pharisees who killed Jesus, the Spanish Inquisition, the popes, Jim Jones, Sam Baker...and our own Father John."

"The pedophile? Surely you want to give him another chance. I'm sure he's apologized for his crimes."

Rory snorted. "You're the one who says there are some things you can't atone for. Did you learn that in church?" Rory's vitriol surprised even him. Was it his guilt that made church an uncomfortable proposition? He didn't know, hadn't thought about it. And didn't want to.

"I told you, we never went to church," Delene said.

"So why in the world would we get married in one?"

Delene sighed and before Rory could stop her, pulled a *Tomoe Nage* on him. The move sent him flipping over her foot to his belly, landing him neatly on his back.

Rory spoke from there, mostly grunts. "I'm all for new starts, forgiveness, mercy. I'm yet to find those things in a church."

"In how many churches have you looked?"

He didn't answer her. She knew it was zero.

The location of their wedding was their second official disagreement. Rory won her over with the idea of a just-them wedding in New York's Central Park and a later reception for their wider circles of friends and family.

After their wedding vows, they had an intimate lunch at Cafe Frida on the city's west side. A limo took them to JFK airport, and from there to Aruba for a week of sand, sun, and everything hot.

It was the most wonderful, fun, and sultry, week of Rory's life.

A month after their return from their honeymoon, Telluric hosted the largest wedding reception in its history, with the brewpub and the surrounding park decked out with tables, tents, and merry finishings. Since the restaurant was closed, customers who showed up were invited to celebrate with the newly-married couple, which meant they were treated to a free meal. Not a bad PR move. It had been Rory's idea and—when Delene shared it with Arthur—he reminded her they were "running a business, not a charity."

"Exactly the time to be generous," she'd said. And because she, not Arthur, owned the brewery, it was done.

The reception at Telluric was idyllic. Candles flickered on every table against the backdrop of the shimmering lake, the sand, and the sinking sun and fiery glow of its wake. The parking lot was converted into a dance floor, complete with clear lightbulbs strung overhead. A local band played the favorite wedding songs and line dances, and the beer. Oh, the beer. Special glasses were brought in for the wedding reception, champagne flutes made thick and wide and filled with citrus, hoppy beer. All the guests toasted with a special, fruity recipe created by Carl as his gift for the couple. Delene made her way to the microphone, beer in hand.

"May I have your attention?"

The room responded by clanging their spoons against their glasses, prompting Delene to lean over and give Rory a saucy kiss. The room transitioned to whoops and hollers and applause.

Delene continued, "As many of you know, my father isn't here to walk me down the aisle. It's been two years, and I still miss him terribly. He's here in spirit, I believe. He's definitely *here*." She patted her heart. "Oh how I wish Dad was alive to share our wedding day, but I know he's watching from Heaven. He's smiling down on us because I got the greatest guy—"

Here, spoons clashed again and Delene gave Rory another kiss before resuming her speech."—Dad would agree, we're so lucky. I got one of the good guys..."

Rory squirmed, he hoped, unnoticeably. Benjamin Dubrow would be happy, so happy to see this day, she said.

Good thing the dead could only turn in their graves and do no more. Otherwise, Rory would be in trouble. Yes, sir.

Delene shared how her father was a generous man who had big dreams and bigger ideas, but he never turned away a person needing help if they were willing to put in some skin of their own. In other words, he'd give work, not hand-outs. But the most notable trait of her father, Benjamin Dubrow, was his grit. Whatever goal he had, he dug in and held on until it was accomplished. Nothing would stop him. There was no *can't* with her father, only *how*. That was Rory, too, she said, and she went on to paint the picture of Rory-the-Taekwondo-teacher, Rory-the-marathoner, Rory-the-kidney-donator, Rory-the-amazing-chemistry-teacher. Rory, Rory, Rory, the saint.

The deceiver.

Arthur snarled from his seat. It didn't help things that, according to Delene, Arthur had once asked her on a date. She had told Rory her reason for declining was that she didn't want to "mix business and family." The fact that Rory no longer worked at Telluric when they met at her father's gravesite was a sign to her. He was available. Rory had wanted to ask her if Arthur was bisexual because he knew for a fact that Arthur was into men, into some guy named Hans, but he held his tongue. Again, the less they talked about the Arthole, the better. And Rory enjoyed the idea that he got what Arthur had tried for: Delene. Oh, if the arthole only knew the truth: it was because of him Rory and Delene had met, and because of Arthur Rory had become the kind of man Delene could love. Arthur. Arthur. Arthur. He was ever in Rory's peripheral vision.

During Eric Clapton's "Wonderful Tonight," Arthur cut in on Delene and Rory.

"Mind if I take her...for this song?" Arthur didn't call Rory "Slim," but Rory didn't miss the hesitation after *her*. Mind if I take *her?* A freighted glare passed between the men before Rory looked to Delene, who nodded.

Rory reluctantly moved off the dance floor to talk with other guests. From his seat, Moon waved to him and swayed to the music. Moon's wife looked as comfortable as a wax statue. Straight-backed and pinched-lipped, she sipped water and pushed the icing around on her plate. Moon reached over to grab it, and she swatted him away. He moved on to the centerpiece chocolates, popping several in his mouth and giving his wife a brazen, chocolatey smile. The raucous affair with beer spilling and line dancing and zealous cavorting was more than Moon's stoic soul had ever experienced, more than Moon's wife could abide by, Rory figured. He thanked them for sharing the special day.

"Wouldn't miss it." Moon said. "But this cake..." and he made a double thumbs up.

"Delene looks stunning," his wife chimed in.

Rory couldn't agree more. As he watched Arthur whisper in Delene's ear and lead her around the dance floor, he envied the confidence Arthur radiated. The two of them knew the steps or knew one another well enough to make it look effortless, the twirling and the matching strides. With Delene, and only with Delene, Arthur was pure charm.

The treasure that Delene was to Rory coalesced in his mind as he watched her laugh at something Arthur said. The world. Rory had the world and he couldn't risk losing it. For Delene, he wanted to be strong and good and kind and...honest.

But that was the one thing he could not be. Just that one thing.

Delene excused herself after dancing half a song with Arthur. His shoulders slumped, and he dejectedly made his way off the floor. When he saw Rory looking his way, the set of his face changed. He strode over, took the empty chair, and nodded a greeting at Moon and his wife. He thumbed to where Delene mingled with guests. "Now that's a piece of cake." He plunged his pointer finger into someone's untouched piece of wedding cake, hooked it, and shoved it in his mouth. Icing settled on his chin.

Moon's wife pursed her lips.

Rory felt his eye twitch.

With a mouthful of cake, Arthur said, "Hey, it's couples dancing. How about you and the lady take a spin? Me and the groom have business to discuss."

Disgusted with himself for not sucker punching Arthur, Rory stood. "You know what, don't worry about it. Arthur and I can take a walk... Arthur?"

Moon nodded, expressionless.

Rory noticed Moon didn't say, *Nice to meet you.*

As they exited the tent, Arthur swiped a beer off a server's tray, and at the server's open mouth, gave a challenging stare. The server turned back for a replacement.

"I'm sure that beer was up for grabs," Rory muttered.

"*All* beers are up for my grabs," Arthur spat.

They walked in silence until they got to the lake, well away from other guests. Arthur leaned a hand against a willow tree and looked out over the water. The moon made a ghostly trail that shimmered and skipped.

"And...?" Rory had a wedding to return to. Standing in silence with his enemy wasn't how he wanted to spend the evening.

"I have a proposition," Arthur began. It was clear the words didn't want to come. "Telluric's turning around, but it's slow going, as you know. Carl's been doing your job since you left, and the interns help.

But it's not enough. We need fresh eyes, someone who knows the competition in terms of flavor, who senses the intricacies in similar hops processes." Here, Arthur stopped. It was as if it pained him to go on. "I've already talked to Delene about this, and she agreed I could ask you to come back to Telluric."

"No. No way, especially not now. I have a long-term sub contract. I'm getting my certification to teach. I don't mix business and family."

"A line conveniently stolen from your bride. She got you the teaching job, too."

"Borrowed, and yes," Rory admitted.

"She gave me the okay to ask you."

"I don't care. You asked, and my answer is no. This is the rudest time possible to ask me, but at any time, the answer would be the same. No."

"Here, I want to show you something." He pulled out his phone and held it for Rory to see the screen. The image was gold. A goldfish. In a blender.

Rory looked up, astonished. "What's this?"

"Watch."

He played the horrible clip Rory remembered. The grinding whirr of the gears, the gold flecks shimmering like some sort of magic elixir. But this video went longer than the original. The camera panned back to show a pimply kid in a pet store. He'd brought his blender to work when his boss wasn't around, whirled a piece of "product" and asked his audience to give a thumbs-up if they wanted to see more videos. The pet store also had a selection of birds, lizards, and guinea pigs. "It's an extra-large blender. They can fit," the kid said.

Rory was speechless. All this time he thought the fish was Mr. F.

"I found your dumb fish floating in his vase" Arthur explained. "I flushed him. But then I thought: why not have a little fun? I'm sorry."

"That's it? You're sorry?!" Rory's fists balled. His body electrified with rage. Everything, EVERYTHING had sprung from that one, hateful, horrifying deed Rory was sure, absolutely sure, Arthur had done. And to think, he didn't do it. Rory tried to poison Arthur because he killed Mr. F, and Dubrow had died because Rory had somehow mixed up the Senna beers. And now he was married to Delene because of it all.

That thought, that wonderful, calming thought stopped his blood from boiling.

"Why are you telling me this now? It's my wedding day."

The breeze lifted a song and brought it to them at the lake's edge, as if to confirm: wedding day.

"Because I want you to come back, to Telluric. Work for me."

"No. Never. We don't work well together."

Arthur shoved his hands in his pockets, the sound of the video clip still played. He ignored the whirr of the blender and the kid's cackle and prepubescent voice. He made an exaggerated sigh. "I thought we could do this the easy way. I apologize for misleading you about the fish, and you obediently come back to Telluric. That's how it's supposed to go. I don't beg, you know."

"I'm going back to the party." Rory spun on his heel.

"Wait. You asked why we're here jamming on your wedding day? Well, let me tell you. It's because you *will* come back to Telluric. You'll do anything I tell you. Because I have proof, Slim...of what you did to Dubrow. I told you about the Senna leaf residue found in Dubrow's drink. The O'Deens part was a lie to see how you'd react, but do you know what Senna does to people who are being treated for edema? Well, of course you know. That's why you did it. You spiked the boss's drink. And look at you, your plan to take the Telluric fortune worked flawlessly."

"I didn't— I wouldn't—"

“Tut tut tut,” Arthur made a duck bill with his hand and shut its mouth. “You and I know you schemed to get into Delene’s panties. All that matters is what it looks like, see, and it looks like motive. Detective O’Deens will agree, should he find out. It’ll look like you killed Dubrow and took advantage of his daughter’s grief to wiggle into her life. And what would *she* think?”

Rory grabbed Arthur’s shirt and readied to strike.

“You can keep her,” he quickly added. “I don’t mind, so long as you come work for me, *under* me. You keep the pretty heiress, and I’ll keep your ugly secret. Fair enough?”

Chapter 18

As much as Rory deserved punishment for what he did to Dubrow, he wasn't sure he could go through with the cutting of his vas deferens, a vasectomy. Delene couldn't know, of course. Rory picked a weekend she had an out-of-town convention for teachers. It was now or never.

After Arthole dropped the Senna bomb on Rory's wedding day, Rory was unable to perform his conjugal duties, entirely out of character for him. Perplexed, Delene had asked what was wrong, and he lied about having an upset stomach, which he did have. Lies were versatile like that. No way could he allow Delene to become pregnant, with Arthur holding their future for ransom. All along Rory believed his prank was responsible for Dubrow's demise, but he didn't know the exact chemical reasons. He still didn't, not exactly. But it seemed Arthur did. Googling Senna interactions had always felt dangerous; leaving any record of his thoughts and worries could be used against him. Even the library computers were tied to his library card, and he wondered whether his search history was kept as data and somehow tethered to him. Rather than chance leaving a breadcrumb trail of guilt, his game plan was to hunker down, wait and see if the bones of his guilt grew flesh and started dancing about for all to see.

A baby would complicate things.

The doctor explained Rory would have to ejaculate twenty-five times before he could be certain of safe sex.

"What?! Why?"

"You're not sterile immediately after the procedure," the doctor said. "It takes time to clear the pool, know what I'm saying?"

"But it can be reversed, right?"

The doctor sucked in a breath. "If you're already thinking that way, don't do it, bro."

"Why not?"

"Sometimes, the sperm builds up inside your scrotum, all those little suckers, swimming like mad and no place to go, and it can make a lump called a granuloma, which of course, we have to remove. Not a ball of fun. Get it? Ball. Of fun?"

Rory gulped. He had, thanks to Dubrow, become a student of pain. He exercised to agony or allowed his belly to hunger. He was exploring the frontier of physical discomfort, but this? Squarely outside his realm. Was he really going to sign up for this? He had never even gotten a tattoo.

The doctor continued, "If you have any doubts, you shouldn't get a vasectomy."

Rory had lots of doubts. In fact, this vasectomy was lunacy, but he wasn't ready to bring a child into the world when he hadn't been honest with Delene. He'd told himself he'd come clean before the wedding, that even though she all but stated she'd kick him to the curb for telling the truth, he'd do it because it was the right thing to do. That's what he told himself. And before he knew it, the wedding was upon them, and he hadn't come clean. And then, Arthur. Why didn't Rory run from this doctor's exam room, find Delene, and tell her everything? Because he was less afraid of having his balls cut open. She wanted children more than anything in the world. Rory would give them to her. Eventually. Once she loved him enough to not leave him over a little white lie, he'd tell all. He'd have his balls put back to rights. They'd have children and live happily ever after. Yes, they would.

In the consultation appointment when the operation was theoretical, Rory boldly declined the offer of a sedative to "take the edge off." Now that he lay on the table with his man parts covered by nothing more than a blanket-sized tissue, he asked if he could make a game day change. "And feel free to make it a double," he said. He had no idea why he felt the need to talk sports and beer and all things man, except that the colossal vulnerability of the moment needed a counterpoint. The doctor gave him valium.

Was the vasectomy a temporary measure? Or was Rory too chicken to be a father?

"Okay, here we go." A needle slipped into Rory's scrotum, and it was surprisingly painless.

"That wasn't so bad." He unclenched his teeth.

"That's the easy part. The numbing solution feels like fire as it spreads through your testicles."

Oh yes, there it was. Hellmouth gnawing on his balls. He gripped the table until it passed.

"Now you'll feel some tugging because I have to remove the vas deferens to make the cut. Normally I'd cauterize the tubes to turn your scrotum into a mini-Alcatraz, but since you mentioned some uncertainty about your reproductive future, I'm not going to do it. Cauterizing is extra insurance, and some guys like the idea of smoking balls."

"Just curious, how long do I have to wait before I get it reversed?"

"I'm going to pretend you didn't ask me that, Mr. Harper. This isn't an ear piercing."

There was no way Rory would be able to ejaculate twenty-five times before he and Delene were intimate. He'd done the research on vasectomy recovery and knew he'd want to lay in a recliner with a bag of frozen peas on his balls for a day or two, and sex was a no-no for seven days, unless he wanted to ejaculate blood. The best situation he could arrange was the Friday before Delene was to be gone at an education convention. He'd make sure to be asleep when she arrived home Sunday night. He'd stave her off and hopefully convalesce during the week of her period. But if not, he'd make sure to have some malady that would prevent their mattress romps, their trail runs, and their sparring sessions until he healed.

Rory knew God was mad at him for getting a secret vasectomy when Delene's convention got canceled. The venue had flooded, and they couldn't secure another. Unexpectedly freed up for the weekend, Delene bounced through the house and begged Rory to take a hike with her. The fall leaves were at the height of color, and she'd found a trail she wanted to explore.

What excuse could he give for not wanting a walk? He loved walks. She knew that.

"I don't know, my back's acting up," he said.

"Oh, is that what the peas are for?"

"Uh-huh." He had pushed them behind his back to hide them.

She offered to massage his back. What could he say? She hummed and straddled him, leaned down, and whispered in his ear. "I know how to take your mind off your back..."

Laying on his stomach while Delene pushed on him was his scrotum getting stung by a hundred million bees. He groaned and she misread it, dribbled warm oil on his back and followed it with erotic kneadings along his hips. The scent of cacao butter filled the bedroom.

"What about the sheets?" Usually, they put down a blanket to protect the sheets from the oil. Delene was in a rare, reckless, hungry mood. Rory had to act quickly, before she grabbed her phone and tapped the link for "Sensual Songs for Sex."

"Wow." He rolled away before she could protest, "You got the spot. I feel better. Let's hike." Rory planted a firm, promising (lying) kiss on Delene's confused frown. "I want to see this new trail."

Her joy made her easily re-directable. She had exciting news to share, and she loved to take long hikes and talk about her day or politics or books they read together. On the drive to the trailhead, she blasted the radio and sang along to "I'm Still Standing." Rory tried to enjoy the off-key warbling because it was a sign she was happy. And happy-Delene was the point, the point of his maneuverings and lies.

It took only a few minutes of hiking for Rory's balls to become the size of oranges. He resisted the urge to look at them. Please, let them only *feel* like oranges. With every passing second, he waited to hear Delene gasp and point and ask what was the matter with his man parts. It would almost be a relief. He could stop walking, pass out, and Delene would call the fire department to carry him out on a litter. But that was not to be; the narrow, root infested trail meant they walked single file.

Assuming him to be right behind her, Delene bounded up shale-studded riverbanks, calling over her shoulder the happy events of her day. She learned that the students had reached a challenging reading goal she'd set at the end of the previous year. She'd promised to skydive wearing a Winnie the Pooh suit (again—she'd done it before) if the students collectively read a million pages. Now, she was going to have to make good on her promise. Did Rory want to jump too? Several other teachers had joined in the skydiving. Delene's co-teacher said she'd jump wearing a Snow White costume. Even Mr. Seyer committed to jumping in a poo emoji suit. Delene was pretty sure it was the idea of the principal in a poo emoji costume that motivated Chapman Elementary students to read all those pages.

"But all that matters is, they did it!" She was giddy.

Rory coveted her easy strides, nodding, barely listening. He'd jump into the La Brea Tar Pits if it would comfort the horror between his legs, licks of fire with each step. He had on his tightest underwear. It didn't help.

My kingdom for an ice bath.

Delene commented on what a good listener he was as they made their way up ravines and over creeks they could bridge because of downed tree trunks. As they finished the five-mile loop, the flush of joy and the exertion made her breathless. She hugged him tightly and kissed his neck in the way that meant she wanted him. Right there, in the woods.

Noooooo.

He didn't want to deny her, ever, but he hurt so bad and he was backed into a corner.

"I'm not in the mood," he blurted.

She froze. "You? I don't believe it. *You*, not in the mood?" She cupped his balls and he thought he'd scream. A grunt erupted from him, and it made her smile. "I could put you in the mood, Mr. Harper. It's dark in the woods. No one will see."

He gulped. "I feel a little sick, is all." And it was true. Her gentle touch on his scrotum sent him into waves of nausea and made him see a few stars.

"Awww...I didn't realize."

"I thought the fresh air would make me feel better, but it's getting worse."

When they arrived home, she made him chamomile tea and gave him a fresh bag of frozen corn for his back. He pretended to place it there then moved it to his balls when she wasn't looking, all under the cover of a throw blanket for his "chills."

The postoperative oranges between his legs made sleep impossible. A hundred times he almost touched Delene's shoulder to wake her and confess. Who knew how lonely a lie could be? Each time he imagined her eyes going wide at the truth, he pulled back his hand and stared at the ceiling. Because where could he start? *Delene, I have something to tell you. I got a vasectomy because I'm not ready to have kids. Why? Well, I haven't told you everything about me that is...pertinent to having children. What? Well, I may have accidentally killed your father, and the vasectomy would buy time until I got the balls to tell you. Yes, I see the irony there. I never meant to hurt you. I'd never hurt anyone on purpose—except Arthur. He was supposed to drink the Senna, but I didn't want to kill him—only give him a case of the shits. And it went wrong, but then I met you and it went right, and now I'm not sure what's up and what's down.*

And that would probably be the moment she'd punch him in the head and leave him, never to return.

Instead, he talked himself off the ledge. So he got himself a secret vasectomy, no big deal. They were reversible. He needed time, was all. Bringing a child into the world—one so dishonest as his—was not a good idea. He wanted to give her everything, yes, but in time. Once he confessed his concerns about his role in her father's death, once she forgave him, he'd march right back to the doctor's office, have his vas deferens sewn back together, and be the most willing baby-maker in

Rootsville. It was a big disclosure, and it shouldn't be executed willy-nilly. Especially now, while he was in so much pain. He wasn't capable of stringing elegant words together, and he'd need to be in top shape, physically and emotionally, to pull off a confession of this magnitude. Never do anything in the middle of chaos. Life 101.

And it wasn't like Rory couldn't handle pain. He'd survived worse. On his past achievements in Taekwondo, he called for the strength needed to push through a covert recovery from a secret vasectomy. And by day three, he was humming the theme from *Rocky* as he loaded the dishwasher. Rory was supposed to ejaculate twenty-five times to clear out the stragglers and have his sperm checked twice after the procedure, to make sure it was a success.

Not happening.

Too likely he'd be caught masturbating, and how would he explain that away when Delene was, for all practical purposes, a nympho? Realistically, how often did the procedure *not* work?

A year later Benji was born.

Chapter 19

At first, he had been horrified when Delene told him she was pregnant. Luckily, she broke the news by placing the positive test inside his briefcase, wrapped it in cellophane and decorated it with a little bow. He found the white stick halfway through second period and thought it was a student prank. He held it up for his chemistry class and chuckled and said he was a traditional teacher and preferred apples. Who did it? he asked. No one answered. Students laughed and looked at each other, scanning for clues. Rory stared them down in turn.

"No one's taking credit? You're not in trouble," he offered.

"Why would we do that?" a student called out.

Good question.

As the class progressed, it niggled at Rory. Had Delene put the pregnancy test in his briefcase? No, it couldn't be. He had a vasectomy. And Delene was on birth control...right? He could barely finish the lecture and was so discombobulated, he confused covalent bonds with ionic bonds, going on for several minutes using the wrong terminology. He noted the many scrunched eyebrows and befuddled looks but plowed ahead, until a student raised her hand and asked for clarification.

Wait. What were they talking about? He couldn't recall.

Fifteen minutes early, he dismissed his students and hurriedly dialed Delene.

Her delighted squeal told him the pregnancy test was *not* a student prank. Thankfully, he had the phone between them, so she couldn't see his ears. Neither could he, but they were hot as hell and surely would've been questioned, and his guts said he'd better get to a restroom, pronto, because his large intestine had walked off the job. But his guts also said, wouldn't it be nice to hurl that half a sour cream donut he'd indulged in before class? Either way, he hightailed it to the toilet, hoping she'd figure his breathlessness for excitement.

"If it's a boy, can we name him after Dad?" she had asked through what sounded like happy tears.

He loved her. He wanted to give her everything. He told himself he'd never deny her deepest longings, but to name their child after the man he killed? What sort of cosmic fuckery was this? He could wish for a girl, but the way things were going, he knew better than to bother with wishes. What was done was done. Rory would be a father, and his secret...what about that? The truth would accomplish nothing except to destroy the good in his life.

For Delene, there was no such thing as a "good lie." No number of extenuating circumstances could be the alchemy that would change a lie into something good. She would teasingly ask Rory: *Does this dress make me look fat?* And that was code for: *I want you* and was usually asked when she wore nothing, except maybe a stringy negligee.

Rory's answer was an emphatic and fiery, *Absolutely, fat as hell.* Code for, *I want you, too.*

At 5'6" and a hundred thirty pounds, Delene couldn't don a dress that made her look anything but desirable. And they'd crash into one another and fall like bowling pins, kiss hungrily, and do all the rest that made for babies. Between them was truth, yes, and a growing number of lies. Why were they so heavy, the lies?

Several hours into a sleepless night, Rory got out of bed and rifled through the deepest recesses of the crawl space until he found the firebox. The key was secreted on a nail behind a wall stud and could not be seen, only felt, and only if one knew where to reach. Cross-legged in the muted glow of the crawlspace lamps, he opened the firebox that held his childhood (and some adult) drawings, cards and photos, and some unsent letters that could destroy him. Whenever he was confused or heavy with guilt, he'd paw through the nostalgic treasure and jot down his thoughts. A measure of peace would eventually come to him. Writing down his mind, while risky, helped him remember his priorities.

He pulled out a card from his parents. They had sent it after the marathon assault. It wasn't the get-well card, though they had sent one of those, too. This card had arrived weeks later when he was floundering in a state of helplessness, feeling one hundred percent victim and not knowing what his next step should be. He'd been considering a return to Taekwondo, and the card was his answer. The card was unremarkable, your basic sunset over the ocean, a few seagulls. His mom had scribbled *One fight at a time...* at the bottom. The phrase was a play on: How do you eat an elephant? One bite at a time. His mom had said it when young, impatient Rory lamented that he'd never get his black belt. "Yes, you will," she told him, "*One fight at a time.*" It became her refrain to all of life's challenges. Unscientific, but such things required a degree of faith.

Rory's firebox did its usual magic when he came across a Telluric coaster, a gift given to new employees. Life was like beer brewing, he thought as he fidgeted with the coaster. You put in the right amount of hops and spices. You heated. You stirred. You mashed and drained. You clarified. And yet, even if you did everything right, infections somehow got into the process. Did a brewmaster go around shouting to the world an infection had got into his brewing process? No. The brewmaster quietly took care of the infection and kept on brewing.

Rory was no quitter. He was a blackbelt, a marathoner. He would deal with this...*infection* and push through it—wait, what had he just thought?—that his unborn child was an infection? He took the horrible thought back and begged God or whatever forces held the strings on his life. He begged that nothing bad would happen to his unborn child because of his terrible deeds and ungrateful thoughts. A comforting image came to him. Delene had taken him to see his first Broadway musical: *Les Misérables*. In the character of Jean Valjean, Rory found an example to follow. To protect his adopted child, Valjean, an escaped convict, had crafted an entirely new (and false) identity for himself. Rory couldn't help but see a parallel to his own, unborn child. And had he not tried to prevent this exact scenario? He prayed God would help him keep his secret and give them a healthy child, whatever the sex. He wrote his thoughts into a prayer that the child would be all Delene, better than Rory. He put his secrets and wishes into the firebox and locked them up.

Benji sprinted the birth canal, almost beating the doctor on call. Other than a broken collarbone, which wasn't so rare, he was born healthy and had a robust cry. Rory cried too, at the magnificence of his wife, her strength, and her capacity for breathless profanity. Who knew agony was such a creative, prolific muse? What love he felt for that slick, wrinkly, little life and for the woman who thrust it from her with a triumphant roar.

Delene took his hand and gave him an exhausted smile.

He planted a kiss on her sweaty head. "You're the bravest, most beautiful creature in the world. And that guy, he's runner-up," Rory beamed.

There were many things Rory could say that were utterly true, like that. They were the two most gorgeous creatures he'd ever laid eyes on.

Arthur sent a stuffed goldfish as a baby gift. Delene thought it was adorable, thoughtful, and outside of Arthur's usual style. Rory said nothing, but he "accidentally" spilled coffee on it then threw it in the trash.

"I could've washed it, you know," Delene scolded, but Rory had already poured bleach into the trash bag, ruining it.

"Why would you pour bleach in the trash?"

"Because...I didn't need it anymore."

Even though the logic made no sense, Delene let it drop. It was just a stuffed goldfish, after all. They had "bigger fish to fry," she'd said. Life with a new baby was myopic and draining. Arthur and Rory had "agreed" Rory would consult for Telluric until his teaching contract was up. In May, school ended. In June, Rory started back at Telluric full-time. In August, Delene had the baby. One, two, three. Bam. Life became beautiful and gritty and exhausting, especially because Rory held himself to his promise to be the perfect partner to Delene, which meant he had to be the perfect partner, perfect father, perfect worker.

Though Rory had run a marathon and passed his blackbelt tests, fatherhood proved to be the most challenging endeavor of his life.

Chapter 20

BY THE TIME BENJI turned three, Rory and Delene were on a first-name basis with the intake nurses in the emergency room, Telluric had climbed out of the financial pit, and Rory's demons took a back seat to the real and pressing demands of family life.

Rory's unique and delicious recipes kept customers coming back to Telluric, and his conservative business philosophy resolved the unsustainable practices Arthur had created in the immediate aftermath of Dubrow's passing. By expanding distribution into local grocery and convenience stores and gas stations, Arthur had put Telluric into the hands of more and more customers—got their name out to the masses, but it came at a high cost. Even Rootsville's Asphalt Jungle served Telluric's flagship beer at beach concession stands. Telluric had become synonymous with Rootsville. It fell to Rory to figure out how to make Arthur's grand scheme profitable.

Nights, Benji didn't much care for sleeping. A solid day-sleeper, he was also on a mission to maim or kill himself and underscored for Rory how dangerous the most innocuous things could be. Who would've thought dryer sheets could be so tasty? And the magnet fidget sculpture Rory displayed on his desk—a couple of medium-sized chromium steel balls and one hundred sixty itty bitty balls the size of peas and just as desirable to a toddler. The ingestion of foreign objects, multiple ear infections, and a coffee table head injury were some of the memorable moments in Benji's first three years.

In that arduous, confusing, and sleep-deprived time, the pull of alcohol on Rory was strong. When Benji woke in the middle of the night, Rory would rock his son and throw down a couple 9% IPA's, enough to knock most anyone out. After getting his little guy to sleep again, Rory would stare into the amber fluid and wish he could go to Telluric and dive into the huge steel drum the fresh brew was stored in, dive in and drink himself into oblivion. But no. He had people counting on him. Benji. Delene. Neither could ever know the storm inside his heart or the lies that held their precious family together like a fragile web, catching more and more debris in it every day. If Delene noticed Rory's increased thirst for beer or the reemergence of his belly, she made no comment other than to offer to push the stroller so they could take a jog together. Of course, he'd turn her down. Delene's ever-energetic can-do attitude, once a source of admiration, now made him roll his eyes. Nobody had a right to be that bouncy.

"Spar at Moon's—we could get a sitter?" she'd ask.

"Maybe."

But he knew they wouldn't. She knew it, too. She'd take a run while Benji napped which ticked Rory off for two reasons. One, that Delene possessed the energy to run (how?). And two, because she waited to do it until Benji was asleep. Like she didn't trust Rory to watch him or didn't want to ask. On her return, she invariably asked, did *he* want to take a run, too?

Might as well ask, did he want an anal probe?

Even her offers of *want-to-run?* had morphed into *you're-a-fat-ass* in Rory's mind. He wasn't anywhere near his old weight, but without a change, he was headed there. Arthur had food served in every Telluric staff meeting, always in arm's reach for Rory. Cookies. Donuts from Thigh High. Pizza. Brisket or buffalo chicken sliders. Overloaded fries.

"You have to get creative, Slim. And we both know you do your cleverest work on a full stomach."

Rory shoveled in whatever delicacies were put before him. It was as if Rory were turning into Dubrow, little by little. He wondered if he'd eventually, through some karmic justice, suffer Dubrow's fate, too.

Arthur surprised him one morning by standing in the doorway and knocking, as opposed to waltzing into his office and throwing himself into one of the accent chairs like he owned them.

"Come in," Rory ventured, sizing Arthur up and feeling unease as he noted Arthur's red-rimmed eyes and even redder nose. Arthur did something he never did: he closed the office door. He sniffled and dropped into his usual chair, looked as defeated and forlorn as Rory had ever seen. Had one of his parents died? Did he even have parents? Rory always assumed Arthur spontaneously generated, like a billion-year-old bacteria that crawled out of the swamp, barbaric yet fully formed, heartless but driven and hungry.

"I don't usually do this..." Arthur began. "I..." His face crumbled at whatever word his tongue couldn't produce. For a few seconds Arthur was wracked with silent sobbing.

Rory had a strange brew of conflicting feelings sloshing around in his heart. Pity. Revulsion. Angst. Curiosity. He pushed back from his chair and braced himself for whatever tragic news Arthur was about to deliver.

Arthur wiped a sleeve across his nose and took a deep, steadying breath.

"It's okay. Take your time," Rory said.

"Right," Arthur sniffed. "It's Hans, he...he needs an operation. It's an emergency."

Hans? Arthur hadn't mentioned the man in months, years even. Rory figured the relationship was a friends-with-benefits thing or maybe a figment of Arthur's imagination.

"I'm so sorry," Rory began, "I didn't know you were still together. He didn't come to the wedding."

"Why would he?" Arthur gave a sideways look. "He was hit by a car this morning. His hip's fractured, and they think he might be bleeding internally, but they won't know till they open him up." Arthur stared out the window at Lake Erie but didn't seem to see it.

Rory released the breath he'd been holding.

"Take the day. Go be with him."

"I need money."

"What for?"

"Hans might *die*."

Rory handed Arthur a tissue, though the sleeve had already done the work. What sort of hospital was this? The tears were real, but the story was fishy.

Arthur blew his nose. "I need money."

"What? Why?"

"Seven thousand dollars for the surgery."

Rory blinked. The doctor gave a price up-front for surgery?

Arthur continued, "I need it right now or...or I go to Delene with your Senna." He looked up, teary-eyed.

"That doesn't make any sense."

Arthur blew his nose, glanced out the window, then, some sharp thought made him wince and pushed him standing. He balled the tissue in his fist and looked at Rory with glacial resolve. "Cash, or I talk. I love Hans."

Love?

Over the three years since Rory was forced to return to Telluric, Arthur's insults had succumbed to the laws of economics. Too many and each was worth less. Rory found himself not even hearing Arthur's voice when the content didn't include work words. A sieve in his consciousness filtered out all but the necessary vocabulary. The intersection was still a nerve-wracking experience, but Rory learned to cope by allowing himself a coffee mug of whatever beer was presently their highest alcohol content product. The consolation prize of a beer made him almost wish for intersection assholery. Almost. It was amazing what a person could accept as normal. Occasionally—Rory had no idea what prompted it—Arthur would remind Rory of exactly what the stakes were if he didn't do this or that. Until today, *this or that* had been for Rory to create new recipes or find a solution to a drainage issue or for Rory to use his charm to convince a supplier to give Telluric preference. Why should Rory be surprised if Arthur kept turning the screws? Arthur was Arthur, after all. This intense love for Hans came out of left field. Maybe Arthur was making it up and needed the money for something else.

It was as if he read Rory's mind.

"How old's Benji now—three? Imagine if he found out what his daddy did...and Delene. She'd go off the rails. Shit man, what if you lost Benji or Delene. Is $7000 so much to ask when you have the perfect little family? Hans is all I have."

All he had...

In the end, Rory took a cash advance on his personal credit card. How he'd cross that bridge with Delene, he'd figure out later.

"We're a great team, aren't we?" Arthur sniffed and slam-patted Rory's back.

That night at dinner, Benji puked his spinach quiche back onto his plate as a protest. The little guy wanted the peaches and cream oatmeal and was doing a Gandhi fast until he got it. Rory wanted to throw down the entire cheesecake variety pie that was sitting unopened in the fridge. Delene was on the phone with the principal about something or other. The screeches and pukes of Benji were probably not helping her concentration, as evidenced by her dash to the bathroom and the slam of the door.

Must be nice to shut out reality, darling.

Thirty minutes later, she joined them for "dinner." For Delene, dinner was a sandwich because she didn't like Rory's quiche, either. She slipped Benji little pieces of shaved turkey while amassing her sandwich supplies. Delene had the annoying habit of leaving the refrigerator door ajar, always. Rory got up and closed it. She needed mayonnaise, opened it, and left it ajar again. Rory sighed loudly, and she either didn't hear or ignored his agitation. The cool air emanating from the fridge was money down the drain. Was his wife that unaware of waste? By the time Delene finished making herself (and not Rory) a sandwich, Rory had eaten half the cheesecake and was downing his second chocolate stout, a Christmas recipe he brought home to do pairings with various foods. Tonight, he was pairing the stout with his anxiety about how in the hell he was going to hide a $7000 cash advance from Delene, who was blithely letting money flow out the refrigerator. Benji finger-painted his masterpiece in the viscous green-yellow slops on his tray.

Rory's phone buzzed with a text.

Hans is fine. Surgery was a success.

Delene read it and arched an eyebrow. "What's that about?"

Rory put a huge bite of cheesecake into his mouth so he could have a chewing moment to craft an answer. First, he waved it away, like, no big deal. "Arthur's partner got hit by a car this morning, but he's okay."

Delene put her fork down. "His partner?"

"Hans."

Delene's face scrunched in confusion. Her shoulders hitched. She slammed her palms on the table and threw back her head. Laughter erupted in bursts and was as annoying as machine gun fire.

"What?" Rory's throat was tight with the effort of keeping an even tone. Being laughed at did something to him. It felt like being stung by bees, on the inside.

"Hans...(laugh laugh laugh)...his (laugh laugh)...partner (laugh laugh laugh laugh)."

"What?" Rory glared.

In the time it took Delene to get control of herself, Rory's blood pressure went up perceivably. His ears burned. He was about to yell things at his wife, things he'd regret, but not until much, much later. Instead, he gritted his teeth and put his hands beneath the table and balled them into fists.

Delene wiped tears from her eyes. "Hans is his *dog*."

Rory almost threw up his beer. A dog. He paid for a dog to have surgery.

She finally quieted. "But how strange, Arthur sharing that with you, like you're buddies. You didn't even know Hans was a dog, and he's keeping you in the loop about his surgery?"

Rory did more procrastinatory chewing, as much to steady himself as to formulate an answer. Hans? A dog? But yes, Arthur had brought an enormous dog to Dubrow's funeral. Before answering, Rory gulped half the stout.

"I meant partner as in *dog*. I knew Hans was a dog."

Delene arched an eyebrow.

"I did. I do. And we've worked together now for three years. The guy doesn't have anybody, except Hans. Who else would he tell?"

Delene's phone buzzed and lit up with a text from Arthur. She glanced at it. "Me, I guess." She winked.

Rory wanted to throw her phone across the room. He rolled his eyes instead.

Earlier in the day an idea had come to him: how he'd pay for Hans' surgery and keep it secret from Delene. It was a hidable thing, a painful, sort of altruistic thing like he did in the past. Rory would donate plasma until he made the $7000. One plasma company had a promotional special: $1000 for first-time donors. Unlike The Red Cross, they allowed plasma donations more than once a month, every week, in fact. If he donated once a week, he'd pay the credit card off in two years. The time could be "lost," as far as Delene was concerned, in late hours spent working at the brewery.

Anyway, Delene didn't deserve to know about the seven thousand dollars. She'd laughed at him.

Chapter 21

The harder Rory worked, the more Arthur pushed. Or maybe it was the plasma loss sapping his energy. Rory felt like a character in one of Delene's "church" books, *Animal Farm*. Rory read it at her request so they could "share thoughts on politics." To push back against the intellectual ennui that accompanied parenthood, she was intentional about having deep, edgy conversations to "keep things exciting." A sweaty romp in bed would've been Rory's way of keeping things exciting—that's what he told himself, though it had been an awful long time since he felt up to sweaty anything. Still, the books she suggested were interesting, if provocative. The horse in Orwell's *Animal Farm*, Boxer, was worked to death and sold for glue. Rory felt every bit Boxer as he woke earlier, worked longer, and never once refused Arthur's demands. On top of his responsibilities at Telluric and his clandestine plasma donations, Rory had a personal goal to never deny a request of Delene's for help with Benji, or anything, really. Like most goals or resolutions, it sounded great when it was conceived. He stayed awake half the night if his honey-do list required it. Fixing the leak under the sink, changing the water filter, unclogging the sink drain. She had no idea he was working, not napping in his man cave. Or that he'd sneaked out to donate plasma. Oh, and there was Benji, sick with a fever and crying at two in the morning. "Would you get him, darling? ...read him a story and rock him to sleep? I have a parent conference in the morning."

Rory never let on when exhaustion burned behind his eyes and weariness (or beer) garbled his mind. He took another drink, gobbled a couple crullers, plied himself with caffeine shots till he finished his work, and then drank himself to sleep. If he felt any bitterness toward Delene, he tucked it away, into the farthest corners of his mind and let it rot there. Never, under any circumstances, did he admit to feeling small or tired or limited. He loved Benji more than he'd imagined possible, but in the wee morning hours when his cries plied Rory from a drunken slumber, the love was somewhat eclipsed by irritation.

Benji couldn't help it he was needy, but Delene could.

Delene's intimate book club had begun to work Rory's patience. Her attempts at conversation felt desperate, like a forced reach for Rory, who had no time for cerebral extravagances and was growing bitter that she even suggested he read a book. Books? Who had time for books?

Carl knocked on Rory's open office door. It had been months since Rory had any meaningful conversation with any of Telluric's staff, including Carl. Rory would grab his coffee or beer or whatever supplies he needed and swiftly close any conversations before they took a turn into the personal.

"Do you have a minute?" Carl asked.

"Just barely." Rory made no eye contact and continued typing.

Carl closed the door behind him and took a seat in one of the accent chairs across from the desk, ignoring Rory's cue for brevity. "How's life?"

"Fine." No eye contact.

"Fine?"

"Fine."

"I'm worried about you, right? You haven't been yourself lately."

"*Myself* is busy." Still no eye contact. "What's up?"

Carl snorted. "Exactly. What's up, Rory? You won't even have a decent conversation with me. Or with anyone."

"Exhibit A." Rory snarled and spread his hands out before his computer screen. "And B." He gestured to the picture of Benji.

"Yeah, yeah. You're busy. We all are. But you don't talk to anyone anymore. I don't know when the last time was you stayed after and had a beer with the rest of us, or even ate lunch in the kitchen." He cleared his throat. "And the numbers, they're turned around. They've been coming in that way for a while now, and everyone's assumed you're distracted or something." He took a deep breath, and Rory glanced up. "A server told me you're drinking on the job, said she sees you filling your coffee mug from the tap when you think you're alone in the brewpub."

"Servers are spying on me?"

"Rory, listen to yourself. You were caught, and you're not even sorry. What sort of example are you setting for other employees?"

"Fire me then. Oh, I forgot, you can't fire me. Because you're not my boss." Rory feigned immersion in his computer screen. He knew it was rude, and his heart ached for his friend, but only a little. Mostly his heart wanted to stop beating. How had Rory become that scumbag Delene had described years ago when they sparred? No, he was worse because he kept his dirty secret from his wife. Rory had asked Delene while they sparred: Should the cheating husband shoot himself? Or drink himself to death? The latter was the correct answer, apparently. It was easier and less messy for everyone.

Carl was still blathering on when Rory re-engaged in the conversation.

"...I knew you'd be mad," Carl said, "But I came anyway because you're a friend. Friends don't stand by and watch each other self-destruct. Nobody loves beer more than me, right? But you can't let your responsibilities slide like this."

"Let them slide? Carl, I let *nothing* slide. I'm trying to be a loving husband, the perfect father. I've got my wife's company strapped to my back, and it feels a little like the rock of Sisyphus, so if I take a drink or two, give me a break."

"You ever think about talking to someone...like a therapist? Or a priest?"

"That's it. Get out."

"Why'd you come back to Telluric? You had a good job at the high school. You said you were happy there."

What could Rory say? That Arthur had Rory by the throat? His lies were turning into switchbacks, bending in half and making it so nothing he did made sense—not to him and not to a watching world. Rory tried deflecting. A sprinkle of truth.

"Delene asked me the same question. The hours were better for our family, and I did like my work with students. But...Telluric, it was her dad's. Nobody else can work with Arthur. Even Delene said so. The place is slowly turning around. I'll get out...eventually."

Despite Rory's turned-around numbers, Telluric had seen profit grow for a straight year. Carl knew it. Everyone knew it. Delene, too, had asked Rory why he worked himself into the ground, had shouted it through tears, actually, when Rory had fallen "asleep" on the couch with Benji and accidentally nudged him off the edge. Benji's scream had rocketed Delene from bed, but Rory was too deeply under for it to permeate into his pickled brain. Delene found Benji crying in a puddle of old beer and Rory snoring loudly on the couch.

Her first question was: why are you drinking yourself into oblivion?

Unanswerable.

The second was: why are you working yourself to death?

Also unanswerable. But Rory made a valiant effort, spun an internal landscape of *best lies are mostly true* about the pressures of providing for his family, of the desire to keep her father's legacy as glorious as it was when he lived, of not wanting to let her down. But he *was* letting her down. Gone were the deep, edgy conversations over books, the walks, the playful grab of her ponytail and passionate kiss on her surprised mouth. They'd not been intimate for months. At three years old, Benji slept through the night, so they had opportunities. Rory wasn't sure: Was it because of his sullenness? His burgeoning weight? Or because most nights he flopped into bed drunk as a skunk? And just as stinking.

It bothered him that Carl, too, could see him floundering. That meant Rory would have to redouble his efforts at being the perfect everything to everyone. And the idea of *redoubling* made Rory want to jump up from his desk, race to the brewpub, and pour himself a coffee stout. Toss it back with a couple of French crullers.

Instead, he opened his drawer, pulled out Bruce Lee III's fish food, and sprinkled a few granules into the tank. He addressed Carl but kept his attention on Bruce's elegant swiveling movements and deep-purple fins. He decided to use the same excuse with Carl that he'd used on Delene the night before: that he drank because of the pressure. It seemed to work here, too. He could see Carl soften.

"Look, Carl, I appreciate you coming. I admit, I've let myself go. You know, the beer does go down easy. We make it so."

"That it does, my friend, that it does."

"This is a wake-up call. No more drinking until five o'clock (*a lie*), I promise." With that, Rory snapped the canister lid closed, pushed back from his desk, and rose.

Carl didn't move.

Rory looked at the door, willing Carl to get up and go through it.

"Rory."

"Hmmm...?"

"Do you ever wonder about Dubrow?"

Rory's attention snapped entirely to Carl. "What do you mean?"

"What he would think of all this? Of Arthur? Of you and Delene? I think he'd want you to put your family first. He did love Telluric, yes, but he had the time to put into it because his wife was dead. *Dead,* Rory. And out of the blue he was dead, too. Life's too short to waste on dead men's legacies, even if that man would've been your father-in-law."

"Noted, Carl." Rory didn't even try to keep the contempt out of his voice. He was done with this conversation.

Carl left. Finally.

Rory had barely focused on the numbers on his monitor when his phone buzzed. A text from Delene.

What's this about plasma?

What do you mean?

Benji tore it up. I didn't mean to open it. You're donating plasma???

He set the phone down and stared out the window at the lake. Seagulls screamed as they hobbled in the sand or bobbed in the choppy waters. He put his phone in airplane mode, strode to the brewpub, and filled his mug with coffee stout without bothering to check who saw him do it. Thus anesthetized, he set his mind on work, pulling the numbers and data sets into reverent focus.

When Arthur called a spontaneous all-staff meeting promising "a big announcement," Rory wanted to pull out his hair. It was as if Arthur had a peephole into Rory's mind and could tell exactly what would most annoy him. Today Rory wanted to be left alone. So...all-staff meeting. Of course.

The upshot was that the sous chef served a sampling of appetizers, some from the menu and some that were being tested: bacon jalapeno bites, sliders, brisket nachos, and soft pretzels. Everyone was encouraged to grab an alcoholic beverage and take a seat in the brewpub's private party room. Arthur stopped Rory in his tracks and asked him to stand beside him.

"I have something *special* for you," he said.

Rory figured Arthur was going to test him to see if he could guess a flavor. The last time Arthur said those words, Rory had won a thousand dollars. And Dubrow had been alive.

The color was lighter than most IPAs. Was Arthur handing Rory a lager? He knew Rory hated lagers. Rory sniffed the beer. It didn't smell right. Arthur sent a dagger look at Rory that said he'd better keep his mouth shut. Then the enormous grin grew right back. The staff dug into the savory appetizers, but not Rory. Had Arthur called everyone here on the pretense of some grand announcement, when, in fact, he intended to expose Rory? Arthur was known for day drinking. *Rules for thee and not for me.* Surely he wouldn't come down on Rory, but what was this announcement, so big and yet Rory didn't know what it was?

Carl looked sheepish as he nursed a water, a bad omen.

After quieting everyone, Arthur stood on a chair. "I want to make a toast." He raised his glass. "To Rory, our *beloved* chemist and grand recipe designer who works tirelessly to bring the best brews humankind has ever tasted. Benjamin Franklin said he believed in God because God made beer... I believe in Rory Harper because he makes the *best* beer."

Where was this effusive praise coming from?

Arthur continued, "May he live long and prosper and take Telluric to the next level of productivity and efficiency. Raise a glass with me to celebrate Rory...and Telluric's incredible first-quarter sales growth... Music, Dennis."

And AC/DC's "Back in Black" pulsed from the speakers.

Over the din, Arthur shouted, "We're making money hand over fist, thanks to your hard work, and thanks to Rory Harper. Rory, come up here beside me."

Rory reluctantly obliged.

"Bring your beer."

Rory hesitated. It smelled wrong.

"Well, go on," Arthur said.

As Rory stood on a chair next to Arthur, out of the corner of his eye he saw Carl walk out.

"A toast to Rory, to us, and to Benjamin Dubrow, may he *rest in peace.*" It wasn't Rory's imagination Arthur stressed the words. Arthur held his stein to Rory's and clinked the glasses hard enough to slop some beer out.

Rory took a gulp.

And almost vomited.

It was beer, yes, beer and—unmistakably—urine. Arthur had served him a stein of piss.

Under his breath he said, "Drink it, or I go to the cops, Slim. Your little stunt with Carl, that'll be the last time you blab your mouth about being overworked. I've publicly worshiped your fat, hairy ass. Now get out there and deserve it."

All he had was in Arthur's grip: Delene, his young son, the glowing faces before him, the respect and admiration of his colleagues shining like a mirage. The life he knew could be gone in an instant if Arthur wished it so. Benji would be fatherless. Delene would be married to a convict, divorced from a convict. Telluric would be under Arthur's control and once again, bankrupt.

Rory hesitated with the stein.

"Do. it," Arthur growled.

Rory glared icily and knocked the stein back. He swallowed the puke that pushed at this throat, stepped falteringly down, and joined the staff in celebrating the company's good fortune. First though, he poured himself another beer, a good one to wash away the shame. Arthur grabbed his arm and pulled Rory's ear toward his despicable mouth.

"Your wife is trying to reach you. Says she texted and called. Sounds like someone's in the dog house."

He checked his phone. Still in airplane mode.

Chapter 22

For the "celebration," Rory chugged several—he couldn't remember how many exactly—beers and drove home without turning airplane mode off. Face to face was better, more honest. Delene was all about honesty.

That thought made him laugh sourly.

She had Benji on a hip and was on her phone when Rory crossed the threshold. He caught the tail end of her conversation. "...right. He's here. Thanks, Arthur."

"Sorry." Rory folded himself into the couch and pulled off his shoes. He leaned back and closed his eyes, let the spin of the room take him for a ride.

Delene sat beside him. He felt the cushions bow, and Benji's little fingers tickled his arm. "Dada..."

Rory cracked open his eyes. "Hey, buddy." He reached for his son, and Delene reluctantly handed him over.

"You ignored me all day."

"I'm sorry. I accidentally hit airplane mode on my phone. I got so busy I didn't even wonder why I wasn't getting any calls or texts."

"And the plasma? What's that about?"

"I donate plasma. No big deal."

"I agree, no big deal, but you might've told me." She shook her head. "You seem so distant these days, Ror. Is something going on?"

"I'm spent, is all...the brewery." That was all he needed to say because Delene knew what it was like, what it had been like for her father. He loved that about her, that she respected an arm's length between them sometimes. Since truth was so important to her, Delene didn't push to know his mind at every turn. Rather, she waited for him to come around when he was ready. Except, the plasma thing threw her.

She grabbed his hands–clutched and dug in–and looked him squarely in the eyes. "If things are so busy at the brewery, why are you taking time out to donate plasma? And not telling me?"

"I...don't...know." He stared right back. Even pickled, he knew a lot rode on how he answered her question.

"You don't *know*?" Her voice was more panicked than he'd ever heard. "Rory, that doesn't make any sense. That's like me saying I don't know why I wash my hands, or I don't know why I eat or why I sleep. We do things for a reason. You do know why. You don't want to tell me."

"You're right. I hid the plasma from you." How sincere his words came out was everything in this moment, so he dug deep. "I feel like I need to do good things sometimes. Selfless things. And I don't want anybody to know." Those were true words. He *did* have to do good deeds. Just, she didn't need to know why. Not now, not today.

She visibly relaxed. "Some people are paid for their plasma, you know."

"Really?"

"Of course, the man who donated a kidney would donate his plasma. I should've known you're so modest, you wouldn't want me to know. Why am I even surprised?" She kissed him on the cheek.

It burned.

Later that evening, Carl called. He had gone to Arthur, he said, but not to tattle. To ask him to consider giving Rory some vacation time or to divvy out some of his responsibilities. Carl told Arthur Rory was on the road to burnout, that Rory's family needed him. Arthur balked, and Carl had blurted that Arthur couldn't possibly understand the pressures of fatherhood because all he ever had to take care of was a dog.

"For some reason mentioning his stupid dog put him over the edge."

"How'd you know he had a dog?" Rory asked.

"Everyone knows about Hans. He's all he ever talks about."

Rory was glad Carl couldn't see him through the phone.

"I said nothing about the day drinking," Carl continued. "I was sure I'd be fired then and there, but Arthole told me to get out, and that was that. When he started toasting you, I figured something bad was coming. I left. Not my finest moment. Sorry, friend."

Carl missed the toast.

"Well...I guess your meeting with Arthur had a positive effect after all," Rory slurred.

"It did?"

"He toasted me and announced Telluric's record profits. Who would've thought?" Even hammered, Rory could still feel the way his throat wanted to close at the thought of Arthur's piss beer. No way could he tell Carl the truth. "Maybe Arthur gave some thought to what you said, once he calmed down. Or he got the good news about the profits and forgot about it. Either way, thanks, Carl. I luff you, man."

"You're ripped, aren't you?"

Carl could always tell when people were ripped. Took one to know one.

"I'm celebrating."

There was a long pause. "Celebrate easy, okay?"

After they'd hung up, Rory wondered exactly how much alcohol it would take for a person to drink himself to death. His research told him that for a "normal, healthy man," five drinks in a two-hour period could raise the blood alcohol level to mortal toxicity. Rory was neither normal, nor healthy. That night, he doubled the recipe to ten drinks in a two-hour period, which was exactly one bottle of Skrewball Peanut Butter Whiskey.

The result was nothing more than the terrible headache he owned this morning.

So much for research.

Here he was, back at the Telluric traffic light again. Rory's head pounded in time with the turn signal. How many times had he sat in his car, waiting to turn left at the intersection of Telluric Lake Brew Works Drive and Lakeside Boulevard? How many times did he slam on the brakes to avoid colliding with Arthur? While hangovers had become par for his morning commute, Arthur's piss-beer and the fight with Delene had driven him to consume new, outrageous quantities of spirits last night, and the resulting headache was a mouth full of teeth gnawing away at his brain. Lava sloshed in his belly. He could hardly think and spaced out through several iterations of the intersection light.

No one was behind him, so no one beeped.

When he came to himself, he noticed the Trans Am across the intersection, waiting to make the right turn. How long had Arthur been there watching for Rory to attempt the turn into Telluric so he could cut him off? Like always. This had happened too many times to count. Rory inching through the intersection pumping his brakes, aware he was a spectacle, trying to close his ears to the angry motorists and their beeps, jeers, and middle fingers. Rory had lost the New York in him. Or more precisely, he'd let Arthur take it.

He was so defeated, he'd tried to drink himself to death last night.

What if he'd been successful? Arthur would be pulling into Telluric right now, no drama. He'd hear of Rory's death and smirk and strut and tell everyone Rory was a weakling who couldn't hang in a real man's world. Imagining his own death superimposed over what he recalled from Dubrow's, Rory saw a lifetime of exertion, suppression, joy, sorrow, and regret parboiled into one meaningless word. *Tragic*. The idea of his colleagues talking about him post-mortem, decreeing him as gutless or soft or a pussy, or using that word, *tragic*, it cut through his paralysis. Rory would not be tragic. Not any longer.

There was more
than one way
for a man
to destroy
himself.

Rory gunned the gas.

Arthur, as expected, moved his car into Rory's path, playing chicken like every other day. Except it wasn't every other day. Arthur smiled wickedly, head out the window like he owned the road–

–right up to the moment when his mouth dropped open in a fearful and shocked "O," and Rory had the pleasure of feeling his own body thrown forward (an object in motion stays in motion), the burning rip of the seatbelt (unless acted upon by another force). He heard the high-pitched crunch of metal, and an explosive cloud of airbag smacked him in the face. A glorious sting and a little cloud of powder.

Arthur would get the message. After all these years of harassing Rory at the traffic light, Arthur would eat his "little" joke, and it would taste like the thorny stems of a dozen roses. In that moment Rory forgot Delene and Benji and everything except his hate for Arthur. Arthur would learn, a man driven to the end of himself was a monster of a man.

Chapter 23

Firemen pulled Arthur from the wreck. As they shoved Rory away from the stretcher, Rory heard one of them call for "tranexamic acid to keep his internal bleeding at bay." Oops. Who knew a low-speed crash could do so much damage? But really, how bad could it be?

And...darn, no tête-à-tête with Arthur. Oh, he wanted a look, wanted to see the whites of Arthur's eyes, the recognition. Rory had set the glare in his own eyes to: *Yes, I did that. That just happened.* He willed Arthur to look his way but was unsuccessful at getting the attention of his nemesis. No matter what Arthur said about the accident, even if he accused Rory of intentionally hitting him, he couldn't prove it. It was his word against Rory's. Arthur was at fault because he went on his own red light. Rory (wink, wink) didn't see him. There were witnesses. The cop was taking their statements. The fact that Rory hadn't hesitated at the light only served to make him look that much more innocent.

The police officer who responded to the accident scene took Rory's statement.

"Poor Arthur," said Rory-the-actor, said Rory high-on-adrenaline, "The sun was in my eyes, and the light turned green. By the time I saw the car, it was too late. We work together. Do you think he'll be alright?"

The officer glanced at the wreck, emotionless. Trained, probably, to keep his thoughts under wraps. "He's in good hands," was all the cop said.

Other than some tenderness where the seatbelt pinned him, Rory was unscathed. He refused medical care, telling the paramedics that Arthur would want him to "hold down the fort." *Haha*. The truth was Arthur would want the fort to fall squarely on Rory's head.

But not today, Arthole, not today.

Telluric's staff was in a grieving buzz, and everyone wanted to hear the details of the accident. Realizing Arthur's absence made him the de facto person-in-charge, Rory called an all-staff meeting, affixed a sorrowful expression, and solemnly addressed the assembly of servers, cooks, and lab techs.

"You've all heard...my car struck Arthur's as he was turning into the parking lot. The sun was in my eyes, and apparently, Arthur wasn't paying attention and went on the red light. I didn't even have time to hit the brakes. I T-boned him." Rory let the lovely fact sink in. He absently settled his hand on the chair, the very one Arthur had him stand on yesterday for the piss beer toast. "It's hard to stand here before you—alone—when I think about how yesterday we stood here together, Arthur and me, toasting our success. Life sometimes is a bitter brew to swallow, I know, but Arthur's getting the best care. The police told me he'll be taken to Mercy Hospital. If he were standing here instead of me..." Rory choked. Arthur almost *was* standing there instead of Rory. He would've been had Rory been capable of drinking himself to oblivion. "If Arthur were here, he'd tell you not to feel sorry for him, to work hard. I'll give an update when I hear something."

Hopefully that came off as: *Poor, poor Arthur. No one, not even him, deserves a morning like that. And after the great day he'd had yesterday (pissing in my beer). Unfair.*

Rory hoped Carl couldn't see through his charade. Last night's lie helped today's lie. Finally, karma was working with him and not against.

The hospital called to ask about Arthur's family. Who should they contact about his status?

Rory hesitated. "His parents?"

"Mr. Clifton's parents are deceased and he has no siblings. Does he have an emergency contact on file with you?"

Just Hans. "No," Rory said.

"Oh," spoken at a lower octave. "Okay, thanks."

"Wait," Rory said. "I'm his colleague. He can call me if he needs anything."

"He has no one? No girlfriend?"

"Nope." It gave Rory great satisfaction to tell that to this stranger. Could she tell?

"Really? Okay then, thank—"

"My wife has known him longer than anyone. Go ahead and ask him."

"I can't."

"Why not?"

Silence, then, "I'm sorry to say Mr. Clifton isn't capable of communication."

"What does that mean?"

"I can't say any more than that."

"When will he be...communicating?"

"I don't know, sir."

Rory peppered her with questions. She was tight-lipped about Arthur's condition, but revealed that any medical decisions would be made by the doctor in charge and would be in Arthur's best interests.

"Is it that serious?" Rory asked. "What happened?"

"I can't share Mr. Clifton's medical information. I can only tell you he's not able to communicate and I don't have an estimate as to when he will."

"A coma, then?"

A long pause, heavy with *yes.* "I can neither confirm nor deny that."

Rory released the breath he didn't know he'd been holding. "Arthur, in a coma?"

"I'm sorry, I can't say anything more."

"He's got the tube thing down his throat, right?"

The nurse ended the call by assuring Rory Arthur was in capable hands, and everything was being done that could be. For some reason, that didn't comfort Rory. A war went on inside him. He hadn't meant to seriously harm Arthur, only to scare the shit out of him. But oh, how tidy his life would be if Arthur slipped out of existence? Would his death weigh on Rory's conscience at all?

He'd been going about this all wrong. He'd been trying to keep Arthur at bay, paying whatever price he exacted. Rory's hopes and dreams were hijacked and held for ransom. He'd been paying. And paying. And paying until there was nothing left. But the real solution was to take the extortioner out of the picture. Why had this not occurred to him before?

Because you're not a murderer, Rory.

For sure, Arthur would go to the cops about Dubrow, once he woke up. Or to Delene. Either one meant the end of Rory's life as he knew it. But maybe Arthur would never wake up. Or maybe Rory could make sure he didn't.

Forever ago, Rory told Carl and Silas he wanted to get Arthur in a rear naked choke hold and recite the poem "Invictus." Rory loved the Rocky Balboa spirit of the poem, the go-ahead, make-my-day steel balls of "Invictus."

Out of the night that covers me
black as the pit from pole to pole
I thank whatever gods may be
for my unconquerable soul.

"Invictus" wasn't only Rory's favorite poem. It had been the beloved inspiration of two men—one good and one evil. The good: Nelson Mandela. The anti-apartheid activist often quoted phrases from "Invictus," to himself over the twenty-seven years he spent in prison. He became South Africa's first Black president.

In the fell clutch of circumstance
I have not winced nor cried aloud.
Under the bludgeons of chance
My head is bloody, but unbowed.

Rory often felt as if his head was bloodied. By Arthur. By fatherhood. By Delene and responsibility in general. By his lies. There. He said it. Rory wanted to be "unbowed," so he chanted the poem to himself.

How appropriate it was to learn that another man also claimed "Invictus" as his favorite poem of all time: Timothy McVeigh, who exploded the Alfred P. Murrah Federal Building and with it 169 souls; 19 were children. McVeigh, too, drew inspiration from the poem's go-ahead-make-my-day spirit.

Beyond this place of wrath and tears
Looms but the horror of the shade.
And yet the menace of the years
Finds, and shall find, me unafraid.

McVeigh was a bad, bad man, the kind who thought nothing of killing when it suited him. Even so, the cadence and power of the poem coursed through Rory like a high-voltage current. He wanted to feast upon the traits of William Ernest Henley, the author who conceived such bold thoughts. As if he could ingest the spirit that penned them. Was Rory Mandela or McVeigh?

It matters not how straight the gate
How charged with punishments the scroll.
I am the master of my fate.
I am the captain of my soul.

What would it look like–Rory being the master of his fate? At this moment it looked like Rory choking Arthur while he was still unconscious and vulnerable in the ICU. A choke hold compressed both the carotid arteries and the jugular veins and could cause unconsciousness in seconds. It cut off oxygen without compressing the airway, so it would look like a stroke.

Who would miss Arthur?

Hans, the big oaf.

"I'd take him in," Rory mused to himself. "I'm no McVeigh."

"Who'd you take in?" It was Carl, in Rory's office doorway. Exactly the person Rory did not want to see.

Rory shook the stars from his head. "Oh, I was daydreaming."

"About Arthur? You going to nurse him back to health?"

Rory shuddered, but the shudder was real, when he imagined following through on the blood choke with Arthur. "I can't believe how fast it happened. One minute the sun's in my eyes, the next I'm crashing into Arthur."

"There's a poetic justice to that," Carl said. "I hate to say it, but it's true."

You have no idea.

"You shouldn't say that," Rory rebuked his friend, and the deceit churned in his gut. "He's in a coma. It might be pretty bad."

Telling Delene about Arthur's accident was easier than Rory expected. Since it was a phone call, he had only to guard his voice and not his face. Also, he made it sound like a little fender bender. She was relieved Rory hadn't been hurt. Ever pragmatic, her focus quickly shifted.

"His dog. Someone will need to take care of Hans in case he doesn't make it home tonight."

"I'm sure he has neighbors." Rory said through gritted teeth.

"No one who likes him."

"That should tell you something."

"Rory."

"Fine, we can keep him."

"Just till Arthur's better."

Or forever.

Delene continued, "I'll be home late, so can you pick up Benji from daycare?"

"Why?"

"I'm going to visit and let him know we're taking care of Hans."

"I don't think that's a good idea," Rory said, "Besides, only family's allowed in ICU."

"ICU?!"

"He's in a coma." Rory tried to sound casual, but not heartless. He was sure he failed.

"What!? I thought you said he'd be alright."

"He will be, eventually."

"Oh Rory, a coma! I should go to the hospital. People in comas hear everything. And I want to put some flowers by his bed with a card and a note. When he wakes up, I don't want him to worry about Hans. You know how much he loves that dog."

Rory knew.

Delene went to the hospital every day for two weeks. One of the nurses was a beer-lover, and when she found out Delene owned Telluric and Arthur was a brewmaster, she allowed the rules to be bent.

"Someone should be there when he wakes," Delene told Rory, "You know he has no family."

"None who'll claim him. Why should it be you?"

"Rory. You know how much he meant to Dad. What if..." She didn't finish.

Rory knew the words hanging in the air were *What if he dies?* What if Rory accidentally killed him?

There would be a poetic justice to that. He had rebuked Carl for saying that, but it was true. Rory didn't supply an answer to the *What if he dies?* question. The years of traffic chicken, the many times he had almost run into Arthur at the intersection, those he'd kept to himself. Even when—over the course of dating Delene when Rory didn't work at Telluric—Delene would share her frustrations about Arthur, even when Rory was tempted to paint the full picture of Arthur for her, he always held back, and now he knew why.

Nobody, not even Delene, would expect Rory had purposefully rammed Arthur's Trans Am.

But when Arthur woke, what would he say? He couldn't prove Rory crashed into him on purpose, but he could spill the beans about the Senna. And—Rory wished he'd considered the possibility before ramming Arthur's Trans Am—he probably would.

That evening, the ventilator was going to be taken out, and Delene wanted both of them to be there. Arthur had been weaned off the coma medications, and his lungs were working on their own. Rory tried to use Benji as an excuse. A hospital was no place for a toddler. Delene solved that by arranging for a babysitter. Rory felt like his life was a train, and he could see ahead the track was torn to shreds, and it was on a bridge, and the remaining ride was short, but he'd see it through. What choice did he have? There was a chance Arthur wouldn't tell Delene about the Senna. If he had amnesia, for example, and didn't remember how he ended up in the hospital, things would go on as they had before. Trauma—especially head trauma—could render a person witless. Rory prayed for severe brain damage, or that Arthur would remain incapacitated. Rory had not followed through on the choke hold, of course he hadn't.

Seeing Arthur with a tube down his throat, having air pushed into his lungs, his mouth propped open by the one-inch tube, the delicate blue veins in his temple pulsing, it almost could've been another person. They were going to pull the ventilator out, and the process was so excruciating it usually woke patients who'd been recently weaned off the coma meds. The nurse said it was likely, but not certain, Arthur would be jolted back to consciousness with a raging sore throat.

That was why they were there, to witness his resurrection and soothe him.

A grim, thick-armed orderly ushered them out of Arthur's room. From the other side of the curtain came a groan and a wet sucking sound. The trashcan was visible, and into it went the ventilator tubing and a large disposable cloth, slopped with pink and rust-colored fluids.

"You can come in now," a nurse said.

A tear tracked down Arthur's cheek. His eyes were closed, but his mouth remained open like it didn't realize the tube was gone.

Delene wiped away the tear with the edge of his blanket. "Look, he's crying." She questioned the nurse, "Even when he's not conscious. Or...is he...conscious?"

"He may be. Hearing is the last to go when a person is under. It's also the first to return. Talk to him as you would if he were awake."

Delene mouthed to Rory, "Told you so."

Rory didn't want to leave, especially now, but Delene asked him to grab her something from the cafeteria. She'd been so concerned about taking care of Benji and arranging the babysitter, she forgot to eat.

The cafeteria had crappy pizza but a decent-looking taco bar. Rory hastily made a salad for Delene and got himself enchiladas, refried beans, and a plate of warm, salty nacho cheese with jalapenos. Arthur was still unconscious or asleep or whatever—thank God—when Rory returned with the trays, and a dinner had been accidentally delivered for Arthur. Covered plates, skim milk, ice cream—chocolate. It was more trouble to take it back. The hospitality worker said they could have it.

Delene barely ate her salad.

"Not good?" Rory asked.

"I can't eat. I feel so bad."

Rory ate his dinner and Arthur's too. With his tongue, he mopped the cheese sauce that got away in his initial passes with a spoon. He had the plate to his face when her glare caught his attention. Like it was a crime to clean his plate.

"What?" he asked.

"Don't *you* feel bad?" She flung her salad into the trash. "He's here because of you. I know it was an accident...but still. How horrible."

Rory reached for the ice cream.

She glared.

He challenged her silently, opened it, took an extravagant, mouth-filling spoonful. Once it was down, he mumbled around the ice cream, "I eat when I'm sad."

"Not buying it," she said. "You're acting strange."

"I'm not acting like you, Delene, that's all. I'm acting like me, and *me* knows the sun was in my eyes. Arthur ran the light. Feeling bad doesn't change what happened."

"I'm sorry, I'm taking it out on you." Her eyes filled, and emotion squeezed her throat. She looked at Arthur, at Rory, out the hospital window at the broccoli-like tree tops in the distance.

"What?" Rory asked.

She whispered, "It could've been you, on life support."

She said no more, didn't need to. Rory should've known that was why she took great pains with Arthur, why she couldn't eat here, at his bedside. Her black-and-white moral code was rocked. She was surprised and sickened by her own relief—that it happened to Arthur and not to Rory.

"It's hard to see him banged up like this." She patted Arthur's hair. "Arthur, wake up."

Or don't.

After a while of cooing and petting Arthur's greasy hair, Delene dropped back into her chair and said, "I want to be here for Arthur the way he was for me at Dad's funeral. And after."

"After? What do you mean?" The arthole brought his stupid dog to Dubrow's graveside, that's what Rory remembered. A dog who cost Rory gallons of plasma.

Delene rubbed her eyes. "I guess I never told you. After Dad died, I received all these anonymous gifts and cards."

"Really?"

"Like tickets to the art museum, and cards about Dad, long after he died when everyone else seemed to have forgotten him. Arthur made sure I knew Dad wasn't forgotten. He never signed his name, of course, but I knew it had to be him. He can be—" she lowered her voice, "—an ass, but beneath the monster act he's got a big heart."

"Arthur? ...a big heart?" Rory stared at Arthur, the outline of his body barely visible beneath the white hospital blanket. Arthur's chest rose and fell, rose and fell. His even breathing was the only sound in the room. Some patients stopped breathing and died when the tube was removed, but no such luck with Arthur. Rory clenched his fists, fists that wanted to strangle that vulnerable neck, to choke the life out of him while he slept. Arthur got the credit for Rory's kindnesses?

"Rory, what's wrong?"

"Nothing. Why?"

"You're crying."

Chapter 24

Arthur didn't wake that evening or the next, but it would happen any day now, said the doctors, and when he woke, Delene would get a call from the hospital. She was ready to bolt at a moment's notice. Every notification buzz of Delene's phone torqued Rory's nerves. Indecision locked him up. One, he could vomit the truth on Delene before she could hear it from Arthur. Or two, he could get on the freeway and drive nonstop forever, maybe drive his car over a cliff like Thelma and Louise. Or three, he could stay silent as he had these several years and hope he wasn't discovered. He saw hawks circling in the sky and wished he were a hawk and not himself. Even the dead squirrels on the roadside—he wished he were them, too. Anything but himself.

Rory cut his drinking in half so he could think more clearly—half so he could think at all. Cold turkey would render him insensate. Each morning he went for a painfully slow jog and banged around in the kitchen of his own head. What would Arthur say when he woke? Rory hoped for the longshot—that it would be unintelligible garble. There was a chance Arthur was brain-damaged, but Rory couldn't count on it. Arthur could have forgotten what had happened. Trauma amnesia was a common thing, but he'd learn soon enough Rory had crashed into his beloved Trans Am, and would he believe it was an accident? Wouldn't it be wonderful if Arthur woke with a five-year-old's mind? If he was sent from the hospital to a rehab home, never to work at Telluric again? Could Rory go back to the life he had before—the one where he kept a secret safe in the darkest corners of his heart? It was the best way, the easiest way.

Certainly, it was better than going to Delene with: *Delene, I killed your dad, but it was an accident...Arthur's been holding it over my head all this time...I wanted to tell you. Every day I thought of telling you, but I knew you'd leave me, and I love you—you understand, right?*

He remembered their sparring conversation and how Delene thought a confession wasn't worth its weight in breath. At this late stage and with her thinking Arthur was her anonymous angel...

Hell no.

On the window ledge, a box of Thigh High Donuts was open slightly, and Rory could see they were half powdered, half sour cream, both Moon's favorites. A dozen. Or, a dozen minus the three that had been eaten. On his way to work that morning, Rory had made the snap decision to take a detour to Moon's. Life couldn't just erupt all over him. He had to take some sort of action, have a strategy. Where else could he go for advice on how to dispatch his enemy, but to Moon?

Rory greeted Moon with as much enthusiasm as he could muster, which was almost none.

"You look like you need a donut," Moon motioned to the box, and Rory took a sour cream.

Moon could tell Rory wasn't right in the head, but even Moon couldn't read minds. The master had a donut in one hand and a dust cloth in the other. Half the shop window was free of little handprints.

"I thought maybe you hired someone," Rory gestured to the half-cleaned window.

Moon shook his head and finished chewing. "Simple work is good for the soul."

Rory should ask Moon if he had other, simple work around. A hundred years of simple work ought to do it. Instead, he brought up the subject of the rear naked choke hold. He hoped he didn't launch into it too soon, so as to be awkward. Had Moon ever needed to use it on someone?

"I used it once. Things went bad, very bad." Moon's eyes were pinched with regret. He looked sadly at the half donut, watched mesmerized as powdered sugar dust dropped lazily onto the floor through the shaft of sunlight.

"When?"

Moon shook his head. "You ask a hard thing."

The polite thing to do would be to back down, but Rory was curious. He grabbed a damp cloth and took it to the other side of the window. "I'm sorry, I didn't mean to be rude. I want a distraction. I feel like I can't...*manage* everything."

Moon chuckled sadly, "When you're starting out as a family, it's a hard, hard time, like breaking boards for your belt tests. You have to expend so much effort, and there's a ton of pain. You know how we fast for belt tests? You do your challenges on an empty stomach because that makes them even harder. Fathering is like a belt test that goes on and on. But someday you'll wake up and realize you earned the Dad Belt, which is a higher level than black."

“What if I let Delene down?”

“Bah. You shorten your life with your what-ifs. My people say, ‘Love forgets faults.’ If you’re not free to make mistakes, it’s not love. Love forgives. If there’s no forgiveness, there’s no love. That simple.”

“Is it now?”

Moon swiped his cloth over the remaining handprints. “Yes. That simple.”

Rory sighed. “So...the choke hold?”

“Why you want to know?”

“So I can kill someone?”

Moon arched an eyebrow, but he thought Rory joked.

Rory spread his hands out. “Defense.”

Moon had Rory stand, and he demonstrated the choke hold. Even in the two seconds (Moon counted out loud) that Moon squeezed off his airway, Rory's adrenaline spiked. Fear shattered his nerves.

"Thanks...I think," he eked out.

Moon sat on the windowsill. “I used the choke on my big brother. We were sparring. He always beat me, and he was an infuriating winner. I was sick of getting beat, and I’d learned about this ‘unbeatable’ move, the blood choke. No one was watching, and I tried it on him. I felt him struggle, but thought he was pretending. With his back to me, I couldn’t see his face and didn’t know he was suffocating. His brain went too long without oxygen, and he was never the same, never fought again. He couldn’t think right. He died years later in a car accident that was his fault.” Overcome, Moon tossed the rest of his donut back in the box.

Rory blinked away the emotion Moon’s story evoked. His phone buzzed with Delene’s ringtone, “Lost in Space.”

“Hello?”

"He's awake." Her breathlessness said she was on the go, probably running through the halls of Chapman Elementary School.

Rory's tongue became a stone, his throat choked by dread. He could feel Moon's eyes on him as he dropped into a seat to digest the words he knew would come, but irrationally hoped never would. Somewhere in the back of his mind, Rory held onto the hope Arthur wouldn't wake, ever. If there was any justice in the world, Delene would be crying and telling Rory Arthur was dead.

"Rory?" Delene piped, "You there? Arthur's awake. I was starting to think he wouldn't, but the nurse just called—can you believe it?"

"Is he talking?"

"What? I don't know. I'll find out when I get there. I took the rest of the day off, so meet me when you can, okay?"

Rory was working up an appropriately happy response when she made her customary kiss sound and hung up.

"Your friend wake up?" Moon asked.

Rory had to smooth out his expression so Moon wouldn't see how disappointed he was. After all, it was Rory who put Arthur in a coma. If anyone should be happy to see a recovery, it should be Rory.

With a nod, Rory pulled himself standing, tried to smile, but he felt it was a grimace.

Moon stood and continued spraying and wiping the window. "Your 'friend' reminds me of Leslie, how she kicked you. Just because a person is broken doesn't mean they have the right to break others. When he recovers, you should fire him, too." Moon saw everything. He met Arthur exactly once, at the wedding, and Rory had never confessed his troubles with Arthur to Moon. In the dojang, Arthur was an invisible presence, the imagined recipient of the blunt force of Rory's fist or foot, but never, ever had he mentioned the name Arthur.

"He...makes things difficult for me," Rory admitted.

Moon licked the powdered sugar off his fingers. "He's jealous, so he steals your joy."

"I'm sorry about your brother," Rory said.

"Me too. No matter how sorry I am, I can't bring him back."

Dubrow.

"Hey. Cheer up." Moon patted Rory's shoulder. "What? You don't like donuts anymore? You barely ate a bite."

Rory shook his head.

"Hmph. I don't believe that. Donuts didn't stop being sweet. They didn't change. You did."

Moon had no idea. No idea how much.

Chapter 25

ON THE WALK THROUGH the parking lot and the labyrinthine halls to Arthur's room in Mercy Hospital Rory's legs were lead. Arthur was with Delene, and he might be talking. God, please no. Let his tongue be tied a little longer, so Rory could tell Delene first. But who was he kidding? He'd had these weeks while Arthur slept, plenty of time to confess his crimes. Even if Arthur ratted on him, Rory could deny it. He'd respond that Arthur's nonsense must be a result of his head injury. People coming out of comas were delirious, weren't they? Rory had done an internet search and had been relieved to read that awakening coma patients were often "agitated and confused." He'd use that if he needed to.

The nurse's station buzzed with activity. A tech pushing a cart exited while another entered Arthur's room. Rory hesitated, but a nurse excitedly waved him in with a cheery greeting. Arthur's awakening was a little like Christmas fucking morning. Delene occupied the chair facing the door. The outline of Arthur's body and one arm was all Rory could see. The curtain obscured his face. Rory hesitated in the doorway. Delene hadn't seen him; her attention was on Arthur. She leaned in. Her brow furrowed. The mood in Arthur's room was not Christmas.

Arthur's hand didn't move, not even an inch.

The machine beeped, but Rory couldn't hear whether Arthur spoke. A nurse stepped between them, so even Arthur's hand was hidden. She appeared to check something under the blanket. Maybe his catheter.

Rory remembered when Delene had brought flowers to him in the hospital. Rory "wet the bed," Nurse Ratched had said, and still, Delene crossed the threshold and entered the hospital room and Rory's life.

Just then Delene found Rory in the doorway. Her eyes, shiny with tears, met his.

What could he do but take a step toward his wife and his enemy? One step, another, another. He continued to meet her eyes, did not ask what was wrong, for he knew many things were wrong, and his habit of giving nothing away was hard to break. As he rounded the curtain, he could see Arthur, propped up by the bed and several pillows. Small tubes still ornamented his nose and were lost in his gown. A clear and stony visage regarded Rory. Hatred seethed behind Arthur's narrowing eyes.

Fuck.

Brain damage was not going to fly. A nurse had combed Arthur's hair, and he'd had a shave. Rory hoped Delene or Arthur would say something first, but the seconds stretched into an awkwardness that stretched thinner and thinner and impossibly thinner like an unbreaking string of glue.

"Arthur, thank God you're awake. How do you feel?" The words were forced and terribly performed.

Arthur arched his brow, pursed his lips.

Delene abruptly stood and leaned over Arthur's bed. Rory hoped he was getting a kiss for a greeting, but she got in his face and whispered hoarsely, so the nurses wouldn't hear, "He says you rammed him with your car, that you intended to crash into him...Rory!? You didn't do that, did you?" She and Arthur stared him down. Her words were fishhooks meant to catch him giving away his secrets. After a few seconds, she tried again. "Rory...?"

Why wasn't Arthur saying anything? The fact that she was so angry about the car crash meant Arthur hadn't spilled about Dubrow. Yet. Even just woke from a coma, Arthur had the cunning and malevolence to hold the cards of Rory's life and wave them around.

"You tell her that?" Rory didn't even bother looking Arthur's way.

"You tried to kill me." Arthur's voice was cracked but robust; he'd make a full recovery.

Infuriating.

"Oh, don't be so melodramatic, Arthole," Rory growled. "You play chicken with me every chance you get, almost slamming into my car every time I pull into Telluric. It only makes sense, one day you'd get hit. Everybody knows you've run the light trying to annoy me. This time...I didn't see you. The sun was in my eyes."

Arthur chewed on that for a moment, his just-woke brain calculating the chances of Rory being believed. He opened and closed his mouth several times before speaking, "It's not the first time he tried to kill me, Delene."

Rory's heart stopped. Here it was.

"Delene," Rory controlled his tone. "Please come with me into the hall."

She hesitated, waited for Arthur to say more.

"Don't go," Arthur said. "He's going to lie to you. He's been doing nothing but lying to you. I can prove he tried to poison me, and he killed your–"

Rory lurched over the bed, found his hands cinched around Arthur's neck of their own accord. He had to choke Arthur before anything more could come out. Initially, that was his thought: silence the man. But a surprising delight flickered inside Rory at Arthur's eyes blowing up like white bubbles and his tongue protruding from his mouth. The other sounds—the screaming and *nurse...nurse...someone help.* And the order to *get back, get away...get security*—were muted. Arthur's delicious *-eck -eck* and his pathetic attempts to make Rory release his airway were Rory's whole world. The coma made it so his arms were like bird wings or a child's swatting. Delene also tugged at Rory's arm, but it did no good. She and the nurse tried to tear him away, and still more nurses and several orderlies came. Rory kept them at bay, intent on silencing the *-eck -eck.*

Stronger arms than his eventually overpowered Rory. Somebody swept his legs and dropped him. First his cheek hit the plastic side rail then the linoleum. All sounds gave way to the flash of pain in his head. Sneakered feet ran around and a knee dug deeply into his back, pinning him. He could see only floor, and his neck was turned away, but he heard Delene sobbing and Arthur hacking. He was immobilized by who knew how many would-be heroes until hospital security cuffed him and yanked him upright. He wanted to see Delene's face, to know if there would be any love there, any mercy or understanding.

She shook her head, folded her face in shock and...disgust? ...And horror? Yes, she looked at Rory the way one looks at a monster.

From his bed, Arthur gasped and vomited. Rory failed to finish the job. He was ushered to the end of the hall and questioned. His lack of answers got him aggressively wedged into the back of a police cruiser. "Till you decide to cooperate," said the officer.

About thirty minutes later, the back door opened, and Delene slipped in beside him. Her eyes were red and haunted like Rory had never seen before and held no trace of affection.

He began, "I didn't mean to–"

Without warning, she came at him with her fists. Cuffed, he couldn't deflect her fury, not that he would. Everything she dealt he deserved, and much more. The cop's back was to the cruiser. Right outside he stood, hands on hips. When Delene stopped screaming curses and took a breath, the cop's humming of Metallica filtered through the crack in the window.

"You–" Slap. "killed–" Slap. "my–" Slap. "dad." Slap. Slap. Slap. She drummed against his chest until, out of energy, she slumped against him and sobbed. "And to think, I loved you."

Loved.

There it was. What he hoped would never happen, what he knew would happen if the truth came out. Delene's hate tore him open. His nerves became high voltage wires and still the current rushed too strong and too fast. Where was the air? An invisible python squeezed his neck, his ribs, the soft tissues of his guts. Tighter and tighter he felt the constriction of her loss until the crushing emptiness forced a groan from him. A ringing in his ears became the scream of buckling and mangled steel—but no, it was a memory: Arthur crushed in his Trans Am. Just a memory, but how big and sharp were the teeth of Rory's memories.

The back of the police cruiser was real, the sting where his wife's hands and fists made contact. Delene's hateful glare sent a hot and coppery flow of blood over his mouth where he clamped his tongue between his teeth. Here in the back of a cruiser was his crash.

Chapter 26

Hans. Big, stupid Hans, the one thing Arthur loved. Hans would make a surprise entry into Arthur's home impossible. Rory had to have the element of surprise. The pound of ground chuck would see to that. He worked the Midazolam into it, squeezing the bag of meat like a stress ball as he surveyed the home and property.

Could he go through with this? Hans' sharp teeth could make Rory look like the meat he was holding. The steel dog leash, the hammer, and the handful of tent spikes stashed in his trunk were insurance, but the idea of using them gave his belly the squirms.

Hans. The $7000 priceless dog, agile as ever after a successful surgery.

As for Arthur, he had himself quite the castle. Floor-to-ceiling windows provided the A-frame log cabin with expansive views of Myrtle Lake. An enormous telescopic camera was the centerpiece in the largest window, and beside it sat Hans with his big nose pushed up against the glass. He had no idea he was about to have a very bad day. One thing was gloriously missing: a ring camera. No ring camera meant no one would see what Rory was about to do.

The sun sank below the tree line.

As he knew they would, Hans' yelps brought Arthur hobbling to the window. Arthur pressed his broken body against the second-floor window, wearing nothing but loose boxers with football helmets on them. His hair stuck up in crown-like spikes. Arthur banged on the glass and called for Hans, who lay out of Arthur's line of sight at Rory's feet, the tainted beef still in the folds of his maw. Darkness, the enormous rhododendron, and Rory's camouflage garb obscured him completely.

Arthur's body language showed he was both annoyed with Hans for not obeying when called and also concerned something had happened to his beloved. He smacked the window and marched out of Rory's line of vision, coming out to search, no doubt. That was the plan. *Thanks for playing along, Arthur.*

Rory crouched beside the unmoving Hans, waiting until Arthur drew close.

Arthur called out, "Hans!?...Hans!? You son of a bitch. Where've you gotten to?"

In contrast to how robust Arthur came off in the hospital room in Delene's presence, the accident and coma had done him a good turn, wore the guy out, what, with all the energy he needed to expend in the service of ruining Rory's life and taking every ounce of happiness he had.

Rory silently approached from behind and put Arthur in the rear naked choke hold. Ahh, the choke hold. It was so unbelievably easy. No words, not even a grunt. The hold instantly stole the breath. The silence of it was elegant. Arthur would be unconscious in a few seconds.

Rear naked choke hold. Thanks, Moon.

Rory let Arthur fall to the packed ground, slashed with roots. He'd feel that when he woke. While Arthur was zapped by the hold, Rory shoved Midazolam tablets into his mouth and washed them down with water from Arthur's own hose because he forgot to bring water. By the time Rory dragged Hans and Arthur into the house, he'd worked up a sweat. The steps were the worst. For Hans, Rory carried him honeymoon style, but Arthur was too heavy and had to be lugged, step by step with rests for breath and an extra long rest on the landing. It was a miracle Arthur didn't come back to himself with the jostling and with Rory dropping him—oops—several times. There would be bruising. Rory dropped Arthur just inside the doorway and decided to take a beer break, but first he used the industrial zip ties on Arthur's wrists, noting the seepage of blood when he yanked with all his might.

Arthur's fridge, as expected, was full of good beer. Rory helped himself to an IPA and reclined in what had to be Arthur's favorite chair, a plush leather throne facing a huge television. On an adjacent wall, Rory was surprised to see a canvas picture of Arthur and Delene posing in front of Telluric. It was an older picture, looked to be around the time of Dubrow's death. Delene's hair was whipped by wind, and her smile was glorious. Even Arthur looked like he belonged on a movie poster, his white button-down open at the neck, the sun glinting off his necklace. They stood back-to-back, arms crossed, the traditional business partner pose. Must've been a shot for a joke or something because back in those days Delene wasn't involved in Telluric. Delene had never mentioned it and didn't have the picture. Not that it mattered anymore, anyway.

Nothing did.

A spirometer and various medicines cluttered the end table, as well as the TV remote and a plate of smokies sliced into dime-sized medallions. From the enormous television screen, a muted cartoon threw various shafts of light around the room like a disco ball. Rory didn't recognize the show, but TV wasn't his thing. Never had been.

Mirrors were the decor of choice, in all shapes and sizes and colors. Clear pendant lights hung from braided cables, and the natural hardwood floor had plush rugs in complementing colors. The furniture was upholstered in a bold, modern style. *Civilized rustic,* Rory thought. Except Arthur wasn't civilized.

A puddle of urine pooled at Hans' rear end, took a course along the knotty wood floor, and soaked into the nearest rug. Arthur was on the floor beside his beast, his head turned so the first thing he'd see upon waking would be Hans. They were nose-to-nose with only inches between them. No way was Arthur getting out of the industrial cable ties without wire clippers. Rory left his enemy's feet unfettered, imagining he'd get a chance to trip him and cause spontaneous damage. Because Arthur was face-down, Rory could see the abrasions on the backs of Arthur's calves where he had dragged him along the concrete walkway. No small feat, Rory had clasped his hands around Arthur's chest, a mercy because the alternative would have been to grasp his feet and let his skull drag along the cement, let it shave a bald and bloody spot on his already-balding head. All that stood between Rory and happily-ever-after was this despicable man, who'd caused him so much grief, who loved no one except this beast. And only the beast loved him.

Rory grabbed another beer and loafed around the rest of the house waiting for Arthur to wake. The bedroom wall was papered with photos of women sunbathing beside Myrtle Lake, obviously taken with the camera in his front window. How had Rory believed Arthur was gay? That Hans was a man and not a dog? Clearly, he didn't pay close enough attention. He'd been mired in his guilt, self-absorbed, even as he tried to work his penance. He had known Arthur liked women, but he thought of Arthur as a give-me-one-of-everything conquistador. As in, who cared which flavor it was, as long as he got the ice cream? And by his own words, he had a partner: Hans. Arthur had said *partner*, or had Rory inferred it?

On the refrigerator hung an ancient, curling, and cracked photo. A family of three, parents and a tow-headed son. It seemed impossible Arthur had parents, that he'd ever been little and vulnerable. And yet, seeing him face down in nothing but boxers, he was pathetic; he'd lost the blocky aspect of his physique in the short hospital stay. Comas did that.

Rory pounded the beer.

And another.

By the time Arthur's eyes fluttered open, a line of soldiers eight strong were on the floor.

Arthur's eyes unstuck with difficulty. He moaned. As Hans came into his view, Arthur gasped. His body jerked and flailed as he became aware of his bound state.

"Hans, oh, Hans! What...? Oh my boy!"

"I have a boy, too. Thanks to you I can't visit him."

At the sound of Rory's voice, Arthur flipped over. "You! What've you done to Hans?"

Rory smiled with what he hoped was malevolence. His head felt fuzzy, and his belly had that delicious distended quality accompanying the ingestion of lots of beer. He willed his mind to sobriety. Then hiccupped. And quashed a giggle.

Arthur strained at the cable ties and kicked his feet, sweeping the beer cans and making a parlous stand. He rounded his dog, bent over, searching for signs of life. He dropped to his knees, put his cheek to Hans' nose, and rested his head on the dog's ribcage.

"He's alive," Arthur said.

"Of course he's alive. What do you think I am, a monster? I couldn't break in with the brute barking his head off, could I? How you feeling, Art? You're looking weak."

"Untie me, you bastard." Arthur ran toward the kitchen, presumably thinking it held something of value that could assist him in escaping.

"Sit down or I'll tie your feet as well."

"Go to Hell." Arthur tried to open a coat closet with his bound hands. Rory let him fumble around in the coats for a second, until it dawned on him Arthur might have a weapon in a pocket. Rory stumbled to his nemesis and flung him to the floor. Sure enough, a hunting jacket held a gun.

"Do you know, I've never fired a gun in my life?" Rory mused. "I could accidentally shoot you with this. You deserve it. Or maybe I'll shoot your dog? You better hope he doesn't wake up at an inconvenient time." Did Rory's face betray his true thoughts? He couldn't possibly hurt an innocent animal, not even a dog who loved Arthur. Hans couldn't help who owned him. What a thrill it was to see fear on Arthur's face. Justice, after all this time.

"Don't hurt my dog. Please."

"How about I show him the mercy you showed me? I have nothing to lose, thanks to you. Delene kicked me out. She fired me, won't answer my calls. I can't even see my son until the lawyers arrange it."

It worked. Arthur paled and took a swallow of fear. "You already put me in the hospital. You got your revenge. Don't hurt Hans. He won't hurt you if I'm here. I'll make sure he doesn't."

"Sure you will."

"I promise."

"Why should you get to have your boy when I don't have mine? All I wanted was for you to leave me alone, but no. You couldn't let me have a single moment of happiness. Why should you have happiness? I'll make it painless for him." Rory aimed the gun, nuzzled Hans' nose with the barrel. His original intention originally had been to tie Hans outside with the tent peg and chain, but he changed his mind last minute. Game day decision: extra sedative. And as it turned out, a way to inflict pain on Arthur.

"Nooooo!" Arthur rushed like a linebacker into Rory's chest. Rory, even buzzed, swiveled away, and the freight of Arthur crashed into the television, cracking the screen. A jagged bloody line coursed down his face, pooled in one eye and kept on going.

"I didn't kill Dubrow, but I'm going to kill you," Rory said.

Arthur slumped onto the TV table and tried to clear his eye. "Don't hurt Hans. He didn't do anything."

"Neither did I!" Rory hadn't meant to lose it so soon. "But you treated me like shit from day one. Why!?"

Arthur's answer was an empty glare.

"Fine. The dog dies." Rory wedged the gun in Hans' jaws. Did it have a safety? He didn't know a thing about guns.

"Because you're...fat?" The question on the end—was it to ask if the answer was acceptable? Or had Arthur made fun of Rory simply because he was fat?

"That's not the reason," Rory said. "It can't be."

"Once I got started..." Arthur held his hands out and shrugged. "You're easy to mess with, you big p—" Arthur cut himself short.

Rory's ears were aflame with rage. He could feel his blood pressure pounding, rising. Even now, Arthur didn't back down. Even when Rory held all the cards, he still felt like he was losing. Could he harm Hans if it meant causing Arthur pain? Back and forth from man to beast, or, *from beast to beast*. Only one of them was innocent. He'd never harm the dog, but he enjoyed allowing Arthur to believe he would. Crouching beside Hans, Rory looked him over as if trying to decide where to strike.

"Please, no," Arthur put his tied hands out, pleading for Hans.

"Because I'm fat? Didn't your mom teach you beauty's on the inside."

"Only ugly moms say that."

Rory threw his empty beer can at Arthur's head. "How'd you know—about the Senna?"

Arthur rubbed the spot of impact with the part of his arm that could reach. "When I got a little bit sick..." He wiped away the beer splashed on his face. "...and Dubrow got a lot dead, I knew you'd done something to the beer."

"Then you know I didn't mean to kill him."

Arthur made a mock ignorant face. "Do I? Cops'll say you poisoned him because you planned to marry his daughter and take his fortune."

"I didn't even know Delene then."

"Do you need to know a piece like that, in order to want a bite?"

Rory launched himself off the recliner and tripped on his own feet. He righted himself and kicked Arthur in the face. "Don't disrespect my wife." Another hiccup popped out of his mouth.

Arthur looked confused. "I meant it as a compliment."

Rory shook his head. The idiot probably did. Just then, a powerful urge hit Rory. He put up the *one moment* index finger and staggered to the bathroom where the too-many-beers came back up. He could hear Arthur working the doorknob.

From the toilet bowl, Rory choked out a threat to kill Hans if Arthur wasn't there when he got out. When he returned, Arthur was there, beside Hans, petting his belly.

"Crackers are in the pantry," Arthur said.

Rory eyed him. It was too late to play nice.

With a long sigh, Arthur began, "I was not happy when Dubrow hired you. It felt...insulting. We were doing fine without you."

"At any time, you could've stopped being an asshole," Rory said.

"You tried to poison me. Who does that?"

"Just a little. I didn't want to kill you."

"Do you know how Dubrow got the Senna? I gave it to him, but I didn't know."

"But you *suspected.*"

Arthur shrugged.

All the answer Rory needed. Arthur suspected something was up but didn't know until later when he got sick. He didn't know what he was giving to Dubrow, but he didn't think it was pure beer. And then he held onto the secret until Rory married Delene.

Arthur continued, "I took one of the steins Dubrow drank from and prepared a couple of microscope slides out of the residue. A friend of mine works in a forensics lab. He analyzed it for me as a favor. Senna. Causes the shits. Would've made my night a living hell if I'd taken more than a couple of sips, but somehow it interacted with whatever meds Dubrow was on or just that his old body couldn't handle it, and poof—you killed him. I didn't know it at first, but later I did. Please, Hans is innocent. Don't take it out on him like you did to Dubrow."

"Shut up."

"Maybe you didn't mean to kill him—"

"Maybe!?"

"–but it's my word against yours. I can make it go easier for you, Rory. I won't tell anyone you were even here, and you'll have a sympathetic witness at your trial. You got me. You got me, good. There. Happy? Don't hurt Hans."

Rory? That was the first time Arthur had ever called him by his given name. He glanced at Hans. The dog would be fine when the anesthetic wore off. Unless Rory made his move right now, struck while the two of them were incapacitated—that was his plan. If he didn't strike now, Arthur would live his happily-ever-after while Rory rotted in a jail cell.

Arthur won. Or Arthur died. It was that simple.

Rory needed another beer. Liquid courage, that's what Carl called it. On second thought, Rory chugged two. He pulled the buck knife from his back pocket, opened it, and asked, "What do you call a man with no arms and no legs hanging on a wall?"

Chapter 27

Rory sat on a bench outside Chapman Elementary School and watched a woolly bear undulate its way across the sidewalk. The end-of-day release bell blared, and seconds later the doors burst open, accompanied by joyful squeals and chatter.

"Better get a move on," he said to the black and rust colored caterpillar. "Or you'll be squished."

Kids skipped and ran about, zigging and ducking in spontaneous games of tag. A train of cars idled in the drive, and an even longer snake of buses waited. Rory's wife led her troupe to bus #33. As the littles boarded, she high-fived them. One flung himself at her, surprising her with a hug. She responded by patting his head and ushering him unto a bus.

Benji waited on the stairs, hands cupping his chin in that bored, comfortable way of children. He flung his backpack to the side and followed something on the ground with his finger. Probably another woolly bear or an ant. Benji had a soft spot for every living thing, even stinging bugs. Rory remembered how Benji had cried when Rory killed a bee that had gotten into the house. After that, Rory had been more careful to kill pests when his son wasn't around. How many ants had he scooped up and placed outside to the applause of little Benji?

Should Rory call out to him? Shout his name?

A pack of children ran in Rory's direction. The woolly bear was almost across the sidewalk, had inches to go when the children dashed past, and a sneaker pressed a portion of it into the cement. The rest of it writhed and curled into a little ball. Rory sighed and picked it up, placed it in the grass beneath his bench.

Delene approached Benji and stood over him as he crawled after whatever had caught his fancy. Her shadow caused him to raise his eyes. She took his hand and they walked together back inside the school. Benji, in kindergarten already. Where had the time gone?

About fifteen minutes later, after the cars and busses had departed, mother and son emerged together and walked to her black sedan with the license plate TCHEVRY1 (the car changed, but not the plate). Rory watched them pull away, knowing they'd go to the home on Montclaire Drive, the one he once shared with them.

An unmarked police car pulled up next to his bench. So Delene *had* seen him sitting there. O'Deens joined Rory. He didn't offer his hand or make small talk. In silence, the two men sat for several minutes.

"You shouldn't be here," O'Deens said, "You're violating the restraining order."

"Can't see my own kid. Yeah, I'm violating it."

"Look, that's a tough one, I hear you. Your wife's seeing nothing but black, but you did kill her father."

Rory arched an eyebrow.

"I know, I know, it was an accident. Everybody knows that, but that doesn't bring the guy back to life. Make it easy on your wife and cooperate."

"I have one request."

"Not that you're in a position to bargain, but I'm listening."

“Benji. I want to see him before the trial. Not like this. I want to talk to him.”

O’Deens shook his head. “Not even my department. I can’t promise you that.”

Rory stared into space.

O’Deens leaned forward. “Why didn’t you come forward when I was at the brewery? It was an accident. There was no intent to harm Dubrow. That’s what your Affidavit says, anyway.”

Rory snorted.

"Harper, help me out here. There's only one thing I like more than donuts. You know what it is? Understanding. I like to understand why people do the stu— the things they do. Especially when it comes to breaking the law. Give me a little something, off the record."

"You guys never mean it when you say that."

"You're thinking of TV. Half the shit cops know we can't use in court because of this or that law or technicality. It's infuriating, frankly. And besides, your testimony is already admitted as evidence."

Rory sighed. “I intended harm, just not to Dubrow. I told myself I held my tongue because I wasn’t sure I was responsible—why go waving my arms around? But the truth was, I didn’t come forward because I didn’t want Arthur to know I’d failed. I thought I’d try again. And do better.”

“You intended to poison Arthur Clifton again?”

“I don’t know. I wanted to keep the option open. To make him suffer.”

“And now?”

“He’s suffering, but not enough.”

“He’s refusing to testify against you for the hospital assault. The DA wants to drop it, to focus on Dubrow. What do you think of that?”

“Hmph. Arthur grows a heart. Could be the title of a book.”

O'Deens scoffed. "Speaking of organs...didn't you donate a kidney? Your wife mentioned it in our little Q and A."

"And bone marrow. And double-red blood donations as often as they allowed. I tried to pay on my own terms with good deeds and acts of kindness. Now I'll pay what's actually due. Of course I'll cooperate. But I want to see my son. Please, if you can."

"I'll try to make it happen. I can't promise it will, but you have my word I'll give it my best shot."

Son-in-law Confesses to "Involvement" in Beer Giant's Death Seven Years Ago

ROOTSVILLE, Oh. (AP)—A 31-year-old man was arrested in connection with the death of his father-in-law, Benjamin Dubrow, founder and CEO of Telluric Lake Brew Works. River County Sheriff's deputies took Harper's voluntary statement on Friday, at which time he confessed he "may have been responsible" for his father-in-law's death seven years ago. The death certificate lists the cause as natural (cardiac event); however, in light of Harper's confession and additional witness testimony obtained by sheriff's deputies, an investigation was opened by the state attorney general. Harper allegedly tampered with what he mistakenly believed was his co-worker Arthur Clifton's beverage because "he [Clifton] was difficult to work with." Harper claimed the tainted drink was a prank. Clifton told deputies he believed Harper held a "grudge" against him. Harper, who was released on bond, has waived a jury trial. County Prosecutor Jorell Lanonica described Harper's arrest as "better late than never justice and closure for the Dubrow family." Harper's wife claims she had no knowledge of her husband's involvement and was not well-acquainted with him at the time of her father's death. The couple has a five-year-old son.

Chapter 29

"Why do you have to go?" Benji wept freely but silently. Rory had been granted an hour of in-home visitation accompanied by sheriff's deputies. He was restricted to the living room. One hour to say goodbye and to say everything else. O'Deens had come through.

Rory used his thumb to wipe each cheek and held his son's head in his hands, blinked away his own tears before they could fall. "I don't want to go away, but I have to. Remember what I told you before? I did something bad, and bad behavior has to be punished. You know that's true, right? Bad behavior has to be punished so we learn a lesson."

He waited for his son's almost imperceptible nod before going on. "Like when Mom and I send you to your room. You don't want to go, but you have to. And it's the right thing to do...after you've done the wrong thing."

"Your room's right there." Benji flung his hand toward the bedroom Rory hadn't slept in since his confrontation with Delene in the back of the police cruiser. "Me and Mom could make sure you didn't come out till the time was up," he begged.

This was because Rory had explained he had to go away to a place where someone would make sure he didn't come out before his time, as Benji sometimes did. Rory had used the parallel to when Benji sneaked out of his room, having decided he'd spent enough time learning his lesson, how Rory corralled him back until the entire time was served. For adults, this was a place where other adults would keep him in his room until the time was up. What could Rory say that hadn't been said? He hugged his son, focused on the way his little body folded in his arms, the baby shampoo scent of his hair, the way his tiny hands gathered at the back of Rory's neck and tried to dig in.

"Did you and Mom talk about this?" Rory asked. He wasn't sure what Benji was told. The boy never knew his grandfather.

Benji nodded. "Mom said you wanted to hurt someone, but you accidentally made them die."

Rory let out a breath he didn't realize he'd been holding. "That's...about...right. Did she tell you *who* it was?"

"Grandpa." Eyes, big as oceans.

"Yes."

"But he was old, wasn't he?"

"Oh son, don't say that to your mom, okay?"

"But it was an accident, and he was old already! I don't want you to go." Benji eyed the deputies and especially the silver cuffs held by one of them.

"I need you to understand. When adults misbehave and are sent to...that place we talked about (he could not say prison, did not want that word on his son's tongue), we stay there longer. It will feel like a very long time to you. Don't ever think I've forgotten you—" Here, Rory broke down, choked on the idea of how many nights Benji would go to sleep without a hug from his father. He didn't want to scare Benji, but he had to impress upon the boy that his love was bigger than his absence.

In the end, the deputy pried Benji from Rory. The last image was Benji, screaming and thrashing in the deputy's bear hug.

Every moment of every day since coming clean with the truth, Rory longed to hear from Delene. Anything. Even the *go to hell* that had kept him from telling her the truth in the first place. Even that would be welcome. Oh, to hear her voice. But after the confrontation in the back of the police cruiser, she didn't come to the hearing, didn't answer his calls, and changed her phone number. All communication had to go through the attorneys. He didn't blame her. She told him exactly how she felt that day when they had sparred. Rory knew what he was getting with Delene. It was Rory who pretended to be what he wasn't.

Because Rory pled guilty, there was no trial and his sentencing was expedited.

Over his reading glasses, the judge gave Rory the stare down and asked if he had any final remarks.

Rory took a deep breath. "Your Honor, I was reckless. I hurt someone. At first, she was just someone. Only later, she became someone I loved. I thought I could be 'good' enough to make up for what I'd done—what I wasn't even sure I had done—to Benjamin Dubrow. I hoped it was coincidence. And I wished like hell I could make up for it. I thought, if I had enough time, I could."

The judge did not look impressed. "Watch your language, Mr. Harper. Is that your way of apologizing for your actions? I didn't hear the word 'sorry,' and I have an ear attuned to that word."

"Your Honor, I am sorry."

"For what? Accidentally killing Benjamin Dubrow?"

"Yes."

"How about for attempting to poison your co-worker, Arthur Clifton? Are you sorry for that?"

Rory pressed his lips together.

"You intended harm toward Mr. Clifton. Your actions caused the death of an innocent man, and knowing that, you sentenced yourself to *your idea* of community service. In your own words, you thought you could 'make up' for your actions. You show some degree of remorse, I'll give you that, Mr. Harper, but you have a problem. You're not the authorities or the judge or the jury. You don't get to make this up as you go along." The judge cleared his throat.

Rory refused to look over at his parents. Instead, he locked his eyes on the overhead lights. He concentrated on staying upright on his feet, not buckling. That his punishment was deserved didn't make it any easier.

"For the crime of involuntary manslaughter, I sentence you to..."

That another person besides Rory should decide his punishment...that was the way justice worked. Criminals didn't decide their own sentences. Vigilantes didn't receive medals, not in the real world. How had Rory thought he was above the law? His knees buckled as the judge spoke Rory's future reality into existence.

"...two years."

Benji would be seven years old by the time Rory was released from prison. Everything else fell away: the feeling in his arms and legs, the breath in his throat, the floor beneath him, fluorescent lights above, the faces, the wood panel walls, even the judge. All Rory could see was two years' worth of days without his son or his wife. He did not have them in his life before he committed his crime. He did not have them now, but oh—having had them and to lose them.

He didn't know what to expect from a prison cell, but the filth was more than he imagined. An emotionless guard led him along a badly lit corridor and up an airless stairwell. Old, rotting chunks of food studded every stairstep, gathered in corners, and drew flies to overflowing dustbins. Grime coated the walls, and the ceiling had a chaotic pattern of water spots and black mold. Rory had no idea the slam of a cell door could be so devastating. He stood, transfixed before the stained mattress. His favorite poem made a surprise showing in his consciousness.

It matters not how straight the gate
How charged with punishments the scroll.

The once-white prison walls were stained a sick shade of yellow, from cups of coffee hurled in rage and thousands upon thousands of cigarettes. Smoking had been banned for years, but no one *ever* cleaned the cement block walls, and they held onto the cloying, rancid memory of years-old smoke. His cell had one window, but it was caked in filth to the extent the pane looked like ash-colored parchment paper. The first night Rory got zero sleep. Men shouted to one another, cell to cell in the pitch blackness, the spare, smooth surfaces not absorbing any of it and, in fact, tuning it to deafening levels and giving the chorus the quality of lunatics squawking and screaming. If every night was to be like this, Rory would join them in their deranged cackling soon enough.

My head is bloody but unbowed.

Was it? Bloody, yes. Cut off from all he loved and aware his punishment had begun, Rory could finally get perspective on his choices. In the dark, shrieking nights, the loss overwhelmed him, but each new day dawned, the sun clawing its way through the dirty window reminded Rory there still *was* a bright sun out there. He couldn't see it until yard time, but it was there.

Unbowed, yes.

Benji was beyond those cement block walls too, and Rory ached for his son. In prison, most inmates practiced self-protective amnesia. The heart had to forget the love beyond the walls, that any sweet innocence could exist. O'Deens had gotten him a last visit with Benji as promised, but Rory could not allow himself to remember the hurt and confusion in Benji's eyes.

And Delene. Those first weeks incarcerated, Rory couldn't open up the idea of her either, would not allow himself to picture her heart-shaped face or her tiny hands or the way her neck looked when she slept. He banished what was impossible for him to have.

Before rising from the sweat-smelly mattress each morning, he recited the poem "Invictus." He looked toward the ceiling and asked how–*how* was he to keep going? And the poem answered:

I am the master of my fate.

I am the captain of my soul.

Which was not a call to self-annihilation, but to overcome. A blackbelt knew how to choke an opponent, to take on a wide, strong stance against whatever threatened him. Strangely, it was "Invictus" coupled with images of Moon and the practice of Taekwondo that strengthened Rory. Running the prison's yard perimeter helped, too. Rory trained himself to concentrate on the present moment. The hum of the heater vents, the shadows made by the bars. The gentle touch of wind on his face, the sun. Even the flies. He'd never noticed before the striking iridescence of fly eyes, the green, more exotic than grass or trees or ocean water. He could stare at fly eyes for hours. He'd almost come to love them for the beautiful diversion they were, the way men on the outside thought of women as beautiful diversions. If a fly landed on Rory's arm, he allowed it to scuttle wherever it wanted to go. Something alive had touched him, and the company was welcome.

It didn't take long for his Taekwondo skills to be of use. Prison was a microcosm of the dinner table. Each one took turns stabbing, carving, and devouring. No one got a pass. When your number was called, you were served. How you tasted was up to you: tough and chewy and worthy to be spat out and never eaten again. Or soft. Juicy. Tender. The sort of meat that draws predators.

And the predators scouted for your weak spot. That's why it didn't happen right away. First, they studied you. Rory came into prison overweight, but the 2,500-calorie-per-day prison diet was already thinning him. Though he tried not to scarf down his meals, anyone could see food, even the vile prison grub, was dearly held as one of Rory's few pleasures. On holidays, inmates were given desserts. The Thanksgiving tray had a slice of water-added turkey product, canned corn, mashed potatoes, and stuffing. Dessert was a slice of carrot cake the size of a deck of cards.

Had they tried to take anything but the cake, Rory would have let them.

In the old days when he was a free man, Rory would've thrown that cake down without an ounce of gratitude. One bite. How things changed.

I thank whatever gods may be...

He intended to immerse himself in the eating of cake, to sit with it like art and allow it in slowly, majestically, as cake deserved. Rory would make that itty-bitty bite of cake last until they rang the bell for dismissal.

A fellow inmate had other plans.

From behind, a beefy, tattooed, hairy arm came across Rory's plate and swiped the cake.

Initially shocked, Rory sat and stared, disbelieving.

From the table next to his, a bald, towering man spit cake while guffawing. Rory's metal chair legs shrieked as he stood. The cafeteria silenced as Rory beelined for the thief. Same feeling as when he crashed into Arthur's Trans Am, as when he choked him. Yes, this is happening.

I am the master. I am the captain.

Rory had his ass handed to him by the bounceresque prisoner, but not before he got in a good punch and a roundhouse kick that broke the guy's cheekbone. Contrary to what Rory expected, the cake-stealer, Cube, respected Rory's maniacal counterattack and the force a foot could apply. Cube rubbed his jaw and chuckled. Rory, it appeared, was tough meat, not worth anyone else's time. To earn that privileged status, he spent three days in cell confinement. Cube did, too.

Rory was still sad about the cake, though. It was a long time until the Christmas meal. Cube was known as a person who could get things, and a week after the cake fight, Cube slipped Rory a chocolate bar and a joint as a sign of goodwill.

"Share," Cube directed. He meant the marijuana.

Rory did. Prisoners had a code, and Rory was a quick study. After that, Cube never spoke to him again. When their paths crossed, Cube gave Rory an almost imperceptible nod. That was what it looked like to be in Cube's good graces. Being allowed to exist unmolested was the kindest, most royal treatment a prisoner could hope for. Others were not so lucky.

Chapter 30

TIME IN PRISON WASN'T like regular time. It was time till. Time till breakfast. Time till lunch. Time till yard. Time. till. release. Or for some: time till death. Once engaged in even moderate enjoyment like walking the track in the yard, time did a curious thing. It snapped, broke from its cables or girders or whatever held it moving at a steady pace and—poof—activity over. Surely it was over before the time had elapsed in the normal fashion? Even the injustice of time had to be accepted in prison. The lack of privacy. Lack of silence. Of touch. Just when he thought he'd gotten used to one depravity, another loss stepped up to take its place. Given enough time, a person could get used to the absence of just about anything.

In the rest of the world, paper letters were all but dead. In prison, the slower pace and the excitement of receiving something tangible meant snail mail was a favorite. Paper letters could be read and re-read without having to go to the computer lab. Sometimes, they had a fragrance of home. Perfume. Or a grease stain. The waxy smell of crayons or the bite of markers. When Rory heard the whoops and hollers of inmates getting this or that from their wives or families, he coached himself not to look expectantly for packages in his cell. Managing expectations was what Rory Harper was about.

Sometimes, upon coming back to his cell, he was greeted with a pleasant surprise. His parents, bless them, sent him books *to pass the time*. And once a week, they communicated with Rory through the prison email system. He didn't want to seem ungrateful for whatever they were willing to give, but how he wished they'd send something paper, something he could put in his desk drawer or beneath his pillow. Maybe even on his wall. He wanted to be able to touch something that had come from outside the prison, to smell it.

It was through email he heard Benji got a puppy. His parents attached a photo of Benji hugging the Rottweiler mix, a rescue from the local shelter. Hopefully, the puppy would be enough love for his son over the next—oh, what was Rory saying? A puppy would make up for an MIA father? His parents didn't say it, but the dog was obviously Delene's substitute for Rory. Still, anything that gave Benji joy was a good thing. And Delene? Her spirits? Herds of rescued puppies couldn't fix that. Rory had written and asked his parents to snap a picture of her, but they wrote back she had refused, and they thought it disrespectful to take one without her consent. She'd never agree to a picture, not for Rory.

Since his arrival two months ago, he'd had emails from only two other people besides his parents: Silas, the intern from Telluric, and Rory's attorney. The attorney's was a summary of the court sentencing, a breakdown of his billable hours and a receipt showing his account had been paid-in-full, a gift from his parents. Silas' unexpected but pleasant news was he had finished college and was accepted into medical school. He'd apparently changed his major because Rory thought he remembered Silas was going to school to be an engineer. Whatever his major was, it had nothing to do with beer. That, Rory remembered. The tone of Silas' email suggested there had been other communications. He referred to past letters, but there were no other letters Rory knew of. Perhaps the prison email system wasn't so great. Why should it be? This wasn't the Taj Mahal. Apparently, it was Silas who had transferred money into Rory's prison account, not his parents, as he had thought. How generous, especially for a college student. He asked Rory to visit him when he was released. *Ithaca has a great microbrewery,* Silas wrote. *Imperial stouts to die for and whiskey to resurrect any ghost.*

Silas' lighthearted emails were exactly what Rory needed. Silas wanted to share the ups and downs of college life, and Rory enjoyed writing to Silas some of his stories, even the one about Delene and the elevator; now that all was out in the open, why not share it? He told Silas Arthur hadn't blended Mr. F as they thought, but it was a video of another goldfish. Silas wrote back that it *was still a dick move.* Rory returned with: *Not a dick move. An Arthole move. Takes one to know one, I guess. :)*

How Rory wished he could email with Carl. But where to start? More than anybody else, Rory had lied to Carl about Dubrow, about Arthur, about everything. No doubt Carl wondered who he'd been "friends" with all those years. More than once, Rory started letters to Carl—and Moon—who, he figured, had the same thoughts: How could we be so wrong about Rory Harper? But as Rory put words on paper, they didn't feel like enough. Everybody bandied about that phrase, *words don't do the feelings justice*, but in this case, it was true. There were not adequate words to breach the chasm created by Rory's actions and lies. The combustion of every relationship made it impossible for Rory to reach through the emotional smoke and try for restoration.

When he got out, he'd contact Carl and Moon in person. Yes, he would.

Rory used some of the money from Silas for extra pairs of underwear and socks and for markers, crayons, pens, and paper. And stamps. Benji would have a stack of love from his father, proof he was not forgotten.

Rory asked his parents to send him a book on how to draw, a beginner's guide meant for kids, and before long, Rory was creating animals and landscapes, cartoon renditions of Benji's new puppy and father-son portraits. In two months, Rory ran through a package of markers and a book of stamps and found he had a talent for drawing; it comforted him. He could forget his heavy feelings in the creation of the whimsical. He held out hope he'd receive something from Benji eventually.

One day, he was rewarded with an over-stuffed manila envelope on his desk.

He handled the package as if it were a Faberge egg, brought it to eye level with reverence and care. "Stadium mustard," Rory breathed. In prison, Rory found himself comparing everything to food, especially food he didn't get. The ceilings were the color of pizza cheese; the water stains were where the mozzarella mottled with broiling. His bedsheets were pistachio ice cream. The blanket was not a reddish-brown but German chocolate cake. It was one of his many mind games that kept him from depression or despair.

This stadium mustard envelope was from a person, not a book company. It gave when he gently squeezed. Full of papers. The address was written in Delene's handwriting with black marker. He kissed the address. The tang of marker, the idea of her writing his name gave him goosebumps. And what could be inside? Pictures from Benji? Divorce papers? It wasn't one letter. The envelope was stuffed. *Stuffed.* Rory held it to his heart. Wanting but not wanting to open it. Like Christmas, once it was open, the mystery was gone. And Rory wanted to imagine, to daydream Delene had found it in her heart to forgive him. He could only have that illusion if he kept the envelope sealed. Anything was possible, so long as Rory didn't look.

But wait—what if it was his letters to Benji, returned?

This first tangible, spousal communication was sacred. For two hours, Rory left the envelope unopened. Finally, he could bear it no longer. As much as he dreaded what might be a *go-to-hell* from Delene, he had to face reality. His hands shook as he carefully peeled apart the glued tab. He closed his eyes and dumped the contents onto his desk.

His little Benji had made him cards and pictures, a ton.

Delene. Thank you.

My first communication from Delene. That thought set him to panicked rifling through the stack. And then he let out the breath he didn't know he'd been holding. No divorce documents. Thank God, none of those. Some folded, lined pages were tucked between Benji's drawings and a letter from Silas addressed to Rory's old home—an old one, dated before they started emailing each other. Also included was a letter from Carl, and a blank, bulging envelope. Rory's blood pounded. A letter? From Delene? Or maybe inside were the dreaded divorce papers.

He unfolded it.

No.

It was his own handwriting. He'd forgotten. She must have gone through his possessions with extraordinary thoroughness because these letters-to-self were buried in a huge metal cabinet with bills, insurance policies, appliance instructions, beer notes, cards, and recipes. They were in a locked firebox inside the locked cabinet. The keys to the firebox had long ago been lost, so it had remained a sort of time capsule. To get to these, Delene must've called a locksmith or used a sledgehammer. His guess was the latter.

He'd always admired her determination.

Rory knew the letters could get him in a heap of trouble if Delene ever found them. Why had he kept them? They *were* incriminating. But a part of him wanted to keep evidence of his journey, to remember what he was like when he was bad so he'd never, ever be that person again. Each letter was a snapshot of Rory's mind. And when you forgot history, you were destined to repeat it. Even your very own.

With great apprehension, he'd kept the letters. Locked securely, he'd thought. And then he had bigger fish to fry. Keeping his secrets took more work than he had imagined, and the letters were forgotten.

His hands trembled as he read.

Chapter 31

Delene! OMG we just had coffee. I made you laugh. You want to jog with me. WTF?! I'm sorry. There's no way. No way I can do that. I have to figure a way out of it, but I don't want to. I don't. How did Dubrow make such a beautiful creature? I'm going to keep you at arm's length, Delene Dubrow, and I'm going to continue to do my small kindnesses in the shadows. This will fizzle. I've never been good with the ladies.

He sucked in a big breath. How different things were when he wrote that note to himself. What did Delene think when she read that? Did she hate him even more? The picture he'd kept on his refrigerator was the next thing he pulled from the manilla envelope. There she was, jumping out of an airplane in her Winnie the Pooh suit, all joy. If he could step into a time machine and go back to the day she came with lasagna and wine...what? Would he have thanked her and closed the door? Not let her in?

He set down the envelope and took Carl's letter. It looked like he'd hand-delivered it, maybe to Delene, because it had only Rory's first name on the front.

Rory, Sorry it's taken me a while to write. I started a bunch of letters. Mostly with what-the-fuck, man? And I couldn't think of much else to say. Every day I look in the mirror and I think what a dumbass I am, right? How could I be so stupid? I was your best friend, and I had no idea. But lately I'm thinking, you didn't think you had a choice, and I get that. I reviewed some of our conversations in light of what's come out, and I see you wanted to protect your family. I mean, you married her? After what you did?! WTF man? (There it is again.) Word is, you guys aren't on good terms. Don't worry, she'll come around. Anybody who knows you knows you'd never kill a guy on purpose. I admit, I wonder what you're going to be like on the other side of jail. Can we grab a beer? Or six? Haha. I want to hear the deets. I'm guessing them martial arts are coming in handy in the showers. Don't drop the soap, if you get me. Anyway, the money's for stamps if you want to write me back. Arthole's sort of a changed man. Or maybe it's just you're not here. He seems kind of sad, to be honest. – Carl

Rory smiled, and, feeling rejuvenated, dug back into the manilla envelope that represented his thoughts. That's what the letters were to him: photographs, stills of his mind at any given time. That was why he couldn't destroy them. He feared if he did, he'd forget what was true and what he needed others to believe was true.

To the thugs who assaulted me, You think you got away with something? My family and friends, they're frustrated you haven't been caught, that "justice" wasn't served, but I deserve what you did to me at the marathon and so much more. You're tools in the hand of karma, and while I'm not going to thank you for kicking my ass, I wish you all the best.

You think you had free will in our little confrontation, but nothing could be further from the truth. You are tools, tools, to a man.

I wanted to do something nice for somebody, and you stopped me. That's the extent of the wrong you did. My body's healing. Time is magical. I've already forgotten your fugly faces. Maybe we'll meet again sometime and you can try to finish the job. I'll give you more of a fight, I promise. Our scrap on the sidewalk reminded me why I wanted a blackbelt. Going back for it, now, thanks to you bitches.—R

Oh, the bravado when young Rory was writing to people who would never read his words. Next, he pulled out an envelope, torn in half and scrawled on the fragment in furious black marker was a stick figure stabbing another, taller stick figure. Rory titled his art: Arthur gets what's coming to him. It smelled mildly of beer. And another gem written on a fancy napkin:

My love, Delene - I should leave you, should run out that hotel door and never return. It would be the loving thing to do for my new bride.

On a piece of spiral notebook paper:

Delene, I can't sleep. I've become an actor and convinced myself I can have this dream-come-true life, but my guilt won't let me rest, much less dream. I tell myself all that matters is your happiness. And how is that accomplished? Lies. But they're loving lies! Your joy is my life's goal. I intended to be kind to you anonymously, to never see you and still atone for what I did to your father. You don't know what I did. Hell, I don't know what I did.

Fate put us together. I tried to <u>*not*</u> *love you, remember? But your kindness, the way you raised the bones of my miserable life and clothed it with passion and energy, I would do anything, anything to not have done what I did. Even if it meant never having met you, Delene. I'd give it up. But I couldn't undo what was done. I could only go on, trying to right my terrible wrong with acts of good. I wonder: can I be an actor as long as it takes? To the end? When I think of coming clean, I know it would mean losing you. You've told me as much. Remember when we sparred—you told me then. How close I was to telling you that day. If only I had...*

It's our honeymoon, and my heart is broken. I thought I'd feel better when you were my wife, but I feel worse. Confessing would relieve this burden from me, but it will land on you, a beautiful angel who believes I'm a good man. And I will try to be. In every way possible, I will try to make up for what I've done, to love you perfectly.

I can't go back in time. Wishing and regretting—they do neither of us any good. I've got to get busy if I'm going to be the best thing that's ever happened to you. For starters, only I can know that I am the WORST thing that's ever happened to you. The prison of my mind is no place for a beauty like you. I must keep you safe from it.

The next letter had a note on the envelope. Rory remembered writing it one night when he was particularly loaded. His handwriting was miserable. *File with last will and testament.* He'd sealed it, but Delene had torn it open.

Dear Benji, If you're reading this, I'm dead. I love you more than you'll ever know. My hope is when you are older, you'll read this and—even if you don't understand, you'll see things how I saw them, in the distorted way I saw them.

It started when I didn't stand up for myself.

This guy at work, his name doesn't matter, he was sort of an asshole (excuse my French, but you're old enough now). His mission was to ruin my life, at least, that's what it felt like at the time. I was young and dumb (not that I'm old now, but I've aged a lot in the past few years) and all I could see was how mean he was to me and I didn't deserve it because I'd never done a thing to him. People are like that sometimes, people mostly broken. But I couldn't see this guy as anything but dirt. I decided to get revenge on him, anonymously, but with the possibility he'd know it was me. I devised what I thought was the perfect plan: I found a substance that caused diarrhea and put it in his beer. That was it. He'd drink the beer, spend the night on the toilet, and I'd be the winner.

As you know, it didn't work out that way.

I committed the worst act a human being can by causing your grandfather's death. The fact that I didn't intend to doesn't matter. Not a day goes by I don't wish I'd acted differently. I used to wonder about people who did terrible things, how they could live with themselves. Then, one day, I knew. What a dark day. I had no one to blame but me. I'd gladly take a thousand gut punches, be bullied, be his victim again and again in perpetuity if I could go back in time and not be the guilty one.

A man who lives with this level of regret has only two choices: to kill himself or not. If he will continue to draw breath, he'll have to find a way to exist inside his dirty, despicable soul. Maybe clean it up, if he can. I tried to make up for the wrong I did, but on my own terms.

Your mother took me to see my first musical. Les Misérables. I was introduced to a fictional character named Jean Valjean. He stole a loaf of bread to feed his family, went to prison, and was released many years later. No one would give him a job. He found himself in charge of an orphan girl, needing to provide for her. The only way he could exist and take care of the girl was by taking on a new identity, throwing off his past in one grand lie, and forging ahead, giving his life as a ransom for his foster daughter.

I have managed to live, telling myself I am Jean Valjean, but in the nights when I can't sleep, I know I'm not. I could have told your mother the truth before she married me, but I adored her and wanted so badly to be her husband. Selfishness kept me from telling the truth, not love. Love would have been willing to lose her. Jean Valjean would have lost her.

Valjean lied to protect his daughter because he had no alternative. Although in time my lie became like his, especially when you were born, I knew that by not telling your mother what I'd done I had missed an opportunity to love. I squirmed in the shadow of my lie, in the fear I'd be found out, that you and your mother would be hurt because of my lie. The longer I went without confessing, the more it felt selfish to do so.

I have to say this plainly: I am responsible for your grandfather's death. That is a hard truth, but the sooner you accept it, the better. That is the legacy I leave you, Benji, I am sorry.

The man I tried to hurt, I wasn't trying to kill him. I wanted revenge. I tell you this so you know. Face your enemies head on in one act of bravery or face the dirt a thousand times as a coward. If you're reading this, I was never brave enough to come forward. Most days, I felt the damage I'd cause with my confession was simply too great. Even as I write this, I am ashamed. A good man faces the catastrophes he is responsible for creating. As to what sort of man I am, you can decide. What sort of man you become is also your decision. Be like your mother, Benji. Have no regrets.

I only wish I could have lived better for your sake. Love, Dad

Rory gulped. The next letter also Rory's handwriting on lined paper, but it had been balled up and re-smoothed. He hadn't done that, so it had to be Delene. There were water spots all over it.

Dubrow, Does it matter I didn't mean to kill you? You're dead after all, and the fact that it was an accident doesn't change things. If I could go back in time and not put the Senna in Arthole's beer, I would. Best case scenario is I'd have stood up to him, not taken his bullshit. Worst case: I'd let him shit on me. I thought I could get revenge and only Arthur would know. I mean, he'd guess it was me, but he couldn't prove it. That was the beauty—it could be denied. How could I foresee the Senna getting into the wrong glass? But that's me, Nearsighted Nelly is what my dad called me. Play with fire, and you will be scorched, he'd say. Had I been man enough to punch Arthur in his stupid head, you'd be alive. I'd be fired. Oh, how I wish for the day when that was my biggest dread.

Even if I was more of a coward and let Arthole be Arthole, you'd be alive. But no, I'm exactly the man to cause your death. Now I find myself in a relationship with your daughter, trying to make up for what can never be made up for. She's a nice person, didn't deserve to lose you, btw.

I'm no murderer. But, here I am. If I could trade places with you, I would. But would I? The closest I can get to dead is to turn myself in. So why haven't I? Because I can do Delene no good rotting away in jail. I can never make up for what I've taken from her, but I will live trying. The most peace I ever feel is when I'm doing something for your beautiful daughter. Do I lie to her? Yes, but even parents lie. What is Santa if not a loving and wonderful lie that gives joy? What is the tooth fairy? The Easter bunny? What is

The letter stopped mid-sentence. Rory guessed he had passed out while writing. That would explain it. He couldn't imagine a sober him writing any of that.

A plain envelope addressed to Rory's home had been delivered by post, and judging by the postage date, had been written months ago. It was still sealed. Aha...evidence Delene didn't indiscriminately open his mail.

Rory, I can't take it anymore. I don't know why I didn't tell you this sooner, but partially it's because my classes are so fucking hard, and if you're going to do something to me, I wanted to be accepted into medical school first. (Yes, I changed my major!) It's important I finish college before I go to jail, I don't know why. But I finally earned my degree, which is why I'm writing again. Until I was finished, I refused to look at anything related to your trial. I had to get into medical school, even if I never get to go. I had to. I hope you understand. You're probably wondering what the heck I'm talking about.

I originally wanted to come see you in person and tell you. But I don't want to see your face. I mean, I don't want to see your reaction.

The day of the tasting, I switched the beers. I found a capsule on the bar. I tasted it. I know Senna because my dad hated fiber, and he used Senna all the time. My dad ordered Senna tea and drank it daily. I tried it once, giving myself what I'd seen him take...and I paid the price, if you know what I mean. I knew if I gave Dubrow a little Senna, he'd be making out with his toilet. And I was supposed to meet with him the next day to "discuss" me mixing up the ale recipe. Can I tell you how much I did not want to have that meeting? All that work, my whole summer, and he was possibly going to give me a bad reference over one mistake? You know what a hardass he was.

My Telluric internship was just a shit job. To sit there and take crap from Dubrow and get a poor review could be avoided if he was too sick to come in the next day. I'm sorry. I took some of the beers I knew you meant for Arthur and gave them to Dubrow. I figured you had lots of time to get revenge on Arthole. I had one night I needed to control.

> *Do you remember how you used to tease me about not drinking beer? I've swung to the other extreme. Some time in jail where there's no beer would probably be good for me. I looked it up. A misdemeanor doesn't stop me from practicing medicine, and did you know? I changed my degree because of what happened to Dubrow? At first, I thought I wanted to research drug interactions, but the more I was around patients, I feel a call to general practice. If the fates allow. I am ready to serve as a doctor or to serve time. I wanted to finish school first—before I told you. I hope you understand. I'd like to visit after...*

Rory could read no more. Silas, too, spiked Dubrow's beer with Senna. Silas *and* Arthur. No wonder the man died. Rory saw stars and his vision dimmed. A biting, sparkly feeling spread through his legs and arms, and he knew he'd better lay down before he fell. How many times had he stared at the mozzarella cheese ceiling and asked how it was possible, what happened to Dubrow? How many nights spent trying to learn the lesson his mistake had taught him? And to learn Silas deserved to be here, too. But no, Silas didn't hatch the plan. Silas made a snap decision, a bad one. And who knew what the threshold was for Dubrow to die? Maybe the Senna Rory gave would've been enough to kill him? Either way, what good would it do for Silas to be implicated in Dubrow's death?

What was missing was a letter from Delene telling him she missed him, that she was thinking of forgiving him. Rory spread out the pictures from Benji and the letters from Carl and Silas. On second thought, he shoved Silas' letter into the envelope with his own private thoughts.

Rory still had friends. When he served out his time, he had something, *someones,* to look forward to. And he had Benji. His son hadn't forgotten him, didn't hate him yet, and Rory would make it his life's mission to deserve Benji's love. Honestly. Not as he'd done with Delene. This package sent by Delene had made him rich. She could've withheld it, but she didn't. That was something. Maybe he and Delene could—someday—be friends again. For the first time in years, Rory felt strangely light. As if he'd been carrying those letters around in his chest, each one made not of paper, but of lead. Everything was out now, out in the open. Those letters were Rory's soul turned inside out.

Chapter 32

One year later.

Rory adjusted the foil blanket to be snug around his shoulders and torso. His marathon medal bounced softly against the tissue-thin material. The sizzly rustle harmonized with his triumphant stride. His second marathon, complete. No one would call him greased lightning, but that was partially a result of less-than-ideal training during his sixteen-month prison sentence, out early because of good behavior. The marathon was three days post-release, so he could not train for distance. He coped by slowing his pace. It worked.

It was irrational, he knew, but during the race he had searched for Delene and Benji. The work of running distracted him from the disappointment of not seeing them.

A sign had caught his eye. *May the course be with you.* He stopped. The runner behind had plowed into him and cursed. Rory mumbled an apology and veered toward the sign, hoping, hoping.

It wasn't them. Of course it wasn't. They wouldn't even know he was at the marathon. On he had run. And on. And on. It was more of a shuffle, but each step brought him closer to the finish line. One step, another, another. Eventually, he reached it. Not so different from prison.

Irrationally, Rory had even hoped Delene would bring Benji to meet him when he was released from prison. Like on television where loved ones were parked on the curb, and they ran toward each other and hugged and kissed and cried happy tears.

The reality was his parents met him in a gloomy waiting room, painted grey with grey-flecked floor tiles. They sat on old but sturdy chairs, the kind with rows of buttons holding the leather upholstery together. Rory tried not to show his disappointment that Benji, especially, wasn't there. Benji and his mom were on vacation at the beach, planned by Delene months ago. Ever the optimist, Rory's mom said the week would give him time to get settled. "It was a blessing in disguise," she had said. Moms always said things like that, but Rory wondered if the vacation was purposely timed so Benji couldn't possibly be there. What mother wanted her son to see Daddy walk out the prison gates?

Even more disappointing was Benji couldn't be here, at the marathon, to see Rory cross the finish line. He'd signed up for the race so he'd have an *appointment* of sorts, something he *had* to attend once he got out. Something challenging. As if walking out of prison with his ass intact wasn't accomplishment enough.

The prison yard hadn't been big enough for a decent long run, nor was there enough yard time. Even so, Rory's feet had sanded the prison yard grass, creating a packed earth "track" around the fence perimeter. The actual running track was simply too small and congested with walkers. Rory guessed (because GPS watches were not allowed) the yard perimeter was about a half mile long. For the entire two hours of yard time, Rory ran.

The marathon was a breeze, really—the running part, anyway.

Post-race, Rory continued to search the crowds and runners, hoping Delene would surprise him, that the vacation was a ruse.

A Trans Am parked along a side street caught his eye. Black, like Arthur's. Until that moment Rory hadn't thought about Arthur's car.

Had he fixed it? Could it be fixed? Or had he bought a new car? Rory's mind went to the intersection at Telluric. He could picture exactly how he felt in the moments before he stomped on the pedal, finally taking his revenge openly. That act brought everything else out into the open, too, and all Rory feared had come to pass.

And he survived.

The Trans Am had tinted windows. Try as he might, he couldn't see inside.

Clusters of silver-mantled runners chatted merrily as they made their way to their cars. Ahead and walking his way, was a rough-looking posse with tattooed faces, dressed in black. As they neared, they shot him challenging stares. The proximity of a hard-eyed group of youth in an unpredictable section of the city *and* after a marathon—separately those things wouldn't bother him, but churned together they made his mouth twitch reflexively with the memory of thorns.

I am the master of my fate.

Rory straightened and flashed them a genuine smile.

Some shook their heads, like *this be a strange man...*

It was the prison time. People who'd done time knew their brothers. Prison stuck to a man's aura, maybe forever. They could see it on Rory; he was sure.

The very spot where he'd been abducted was a few blocks south of where he was now. The marathon was the same one he'd come to watch Delene run those many years ago, the race that had whet his appetite for running, and the assault that had led him back to his love of Taekwondo. But it started with Arthur. With his stupid provocations...

No. That wasn't true.

It had started with Rory, not being strong enough to stand up to Arthur's stupid provocations, which was a different thing entirely.

Rory's decision to take anonymous revenge on Arthur rather than have it out, man to man, was where it started. He'd admitted it in his letter to Benji, and now finally, he admitted it to himself.

Would he do it again—knowing what he knew now?

In a New York minute.

Well, yes and no.

He'd fight. Against Arthur. For Delene. He'd give Benji a worthy legacy.

But so much good had come from Rory's bad decision. The worst thing Rory ever did was the best thing to happen to him. Arthur was the catalyst but not the cause. It was not Arthur's or Silas' fault Dubrow was dead. Not their fault Rory went to prison. Now that it was over and his time served, the actual prison wasn't as bad as the prison of his lies. Who would have thought?

God. Probably, God knew.

That evening as Rory was elbows-deep in his aquarium, there was a knock at his door. He'd been smoothing the gravel and adjusting the rock formations and live plants when he heard the sound—one he hadn't heard in over a year—such a normal sound. One taken for granted. A knock at a door. His very own door. He could open and close it at will, in his home he could remain in or leave, at will. Crossing a threshold would never feel blithe again.

The knock. Who could it be?

For a moment he was paralyzed. He put his hand on the edge of the aquarium and gripped it with white knuckles. The tank's filter hummed along, and his new fish were acclimating in their plastic bags. A handful of iridescent tetras flitted in one bag, and a cory catfish in another, as well as two angelfish. The muted light and the gurgle of water had instantly turned his apartment into a home.

The knock. Had Delene returned from the beach early, before their scheduled visit? Rory hadn't seen Benji since before his incarceration. The thought sent bolts of angst through his body. How different little Benji would look. The last communication from Delene had been an envelope of Benji's drawings, ones he'd done using the same how-to-draw book Rory owned. He was able to send Benji the book as a Christmas gift, along with two other art books. Rory had written Delene many letters, and she answered none.

His hand trembled as he turned the doorknob.

He felt the blood drain from his face, his arms, and legs as his disappointed heart stole it for a moment. He could feel his face fall at the sight in his doorway.

Arthur.

Arthur's reaction was to hold up his hands as in, *don't shoot.*

Rory held the door, didn't swing it open and didn't slam it closed. Prison had taught him many lessons.

"I came to talk," Arthur said.

So many images flashed through Rory's mind at those four words. Senna, Dubrow, Mr. F. the taste of piss, the feel of Delene's hair, a seatbelt cutting into him, digging into his belly, a cold shower in the fermenter, beers with Carl and Silas. (Silas, argh...) All of it.

Rory opened the door, stepped back to allow Arthur into his apartment. It wasn't so different from the unfurnished studio he'd had when he started at Telluric. Rory had a camp chair and an overturned milk crate he used as an ottoman. He offered Arthur the camp chair and pulled the milk crate beneath himself as he sat.

A thick, dusty silence waxed between the men. Arthur surveyed Rory's place. Empty walls. No television. A stack of books in the corner, those too precious to give away to his fellow inmates. *Watership Down, Lords of Discipline, The Four Agreements.* A handful of others. Thin blades of sunlight warmed the room. Rory watched dust particles flutter.

"The brewery's doing well," Arthur began. It wasn't his usual bragging, more of a grateful declaration, spoken with the flavor of praise to a higher power, an *amen* or a *hallelujah.*

"I'm glad to hear that." And he was. Delene and Benji stood to gain from its success.

"You see the family yet?" Arthur asked.

"Saturday."

"Oh...Where you working?"

"Amazon. Carl knew a guy. I start Monday."

"Sales?"

"I'm a picker. It's mindless." An eighteen-month time gap didn't look great on a resume.

"Right," Arthur said. "Maybe you could get back into the business. You were the best, you know."

"What do you want, Arthur?"

Arthur cracked his knuckles. He'd never done that before. He looked around the apartment and settled on the aquarium as if it would inspire him. "I don't get something," he said. "You never told Delene about the money for Hans, did you? I waited for her to fire me, and she never did, never even mentioned it. I expected to get my ass handed to me. I thought maybe she was waiting for me to recover from the accident, but she kept on, nice as pie, business as usual. She asked me if I could do a little work from home while I convalesced because things were falling apart in her life, and she didn't have the bandwidth to deal with Telluric. I thought she'd fire me once she had her head on straight, you know, after the trial. I updated my resume just in case—oh, and I put the seven thousand dollars in a 529 for Benji. Actually, I put in ten thousand total, for your pain and suffering. By the time he goes to college, it'll pay for a class or two. But money's money. And it's yours." Arthur nodded at the modest apartment. "Had I known, I'd have given it to you."

Rory waved off the charity. "I'll be okay." And it was true. Rory had plans next week to meet Carl for lunch, not for beer, as the terms of his parole forbade alcohol, and that was fine by him. Next up: Moon. Of his friends, Moon was the only one who hadn't written. Rory knew Moon's Martial Arts had hemorrhaged students in the aftermath of his arrest, and although it would be easier to never see the man again, Rory was no longer in the habit of doing the easy thing. He had an apology to make, and he would make it.

"Why didn't you talk—about the money for Hans?"

"Maybe for the same reason you didn't press charges for what happened at the hospital." Rory shook his head. "Someone has to stop the madness, am I right? Someone has to let himself be wronged. Dubrow had said something like that on my very first day at Telluric, something about vengeance being weak. I didn't understand what he meant, back then."

"About that, I have a confession," Arthur began, eyes downcast.

Rory waited impatiently while Arthur struggled for words.

"I...was...jealous. Of you. There. I said it." Arthur pursed his lips, as if to make sure no more confession came flying out.

Rory shook his head. "I don't get it. Why?"

"Nope. Not going there, Slim. We're not going to have a heart to heart. I don't do that mushy stuff." Arthur stood and put out his hand to shake.

Rory didn't want a heart to heart. Arthur's half-assed idea of an apology would have to do. It wasn't like they'd ever not be enemies. This was a stalemate. A ceasefire. He still hated the man.

But he willed himself to stand and grip Arthur's paw, and it didn't kill him to do it. No, on the contrary, Rory felt more alive and stronger than ever.

Saturday came, and with it the jitters. The agreement was for Rory to pick up Benji, and they'd spend the afternoon together. Rory wasn't sure what they should do. He'd let Benji decide, but in case the little guy was tongue-tied or shy (as Rory had been at that age), Rory had some ideas: the art museum, the zoo, go-carts, and of course, Thigh High donuts. *Donuts to thigh for.* From now on, Rory would live a life that deserved Benji's love. Delene's too.

Seeing his old home, what was his and what he'd lost, brought the eighteen months down onto his head like so many pianos. The porch light was no longer crooked (he'd been unable to straighten it, no matter how he tried). The laurel shrubs beneath the windows were symmetrically pruned; the flowering dogwood was a fluffy white against the red brick. The grass—his grass—was lush and green and weed-free, and the sidewalk was edged. Had Delene acquired a green thumb?

When the stranger opened the front door, ruffled Benji's hair, and sent him toward Rory's car with a wave, Rory understood. The man's tie was loosed; his button down was open at the collar but still tucked into his slacks. He offered a wave to Rory. Confidence and good nature radiated from the man, even at a distance. Rory swallowed and raised a hand to wave. It felt like the blood in his arm had turned to lead, but he did it. He waved back.

She'd told him. Delene had told Rory not to lie to her. Some things could be put back together, but not all things.

Benji rocketed from the doorway, all unhindered joy and genuine delight. "Daddy!"

Rory bounded from the car and scooped up his son, spun him around, and didn't even bother about the tears he felt tracking down his face. He wanted to hug his son forever, to hug him for eighteen months to make up for his absence. As Rory turned toward the house, he thought he saw the upstairs curtain fall back into place.

Delene. Watching.

In case she still watched through a slit, he waved to her as well. Everything would fall back into the place it rightfully belonged. He'd be strong. Do hard things. Be honest. Pursue what he wanted. He hugged Benji and gazed at the window. Up to that point his life had been out of order, but it was never too late to put things right. Never. With time and truth and as many good deeds as it took, Rory was sure he could be a good father to Benji and the sort of man Delene could love again, even as friends. He simply would not give up until he won her over.

Epilogue

TEN YEARS LATER.

Delene sneezed and wiped her sleeve across her face. The crawl space beneath her home had become engorged in the fifteen years since she and Rory had purchased the home as newlyweds. Fifteen years' worth of dust and spiders and those little cloth-eating silverfish had kept her from ever probing the farthest corners of the crawlspace where her dad's effects had been deposited.

The house had sold.

Downsizing was long overdue, as she was single and likely to remain so.

Old and never-to-be-used Christmas decorations, pickleball, cornhole, and several sets of luggage had to be cleared so she could sort through the boxes of who-knew-what. She should've gone through the crawl space when she put the house up for sale, but it was a heart-heavy project. It was easier to paint the front stair rail, power wash the vinyl siding, or weed the driveway.

But here she was on hands and knees, crawling around the crawl space, not wanting to throw away Dad's awards, Dad's phone, Dad's favorite tie. The sniffles were not from the dust. Delene missed him. He'd be over the moon to know Telluric flourished once again. With the help of a new CEO, Arthur kept the company profitable with the existing recipes. People loved constancy.

Hop Rikki had a cartoon image of Rory on the can, and the oldest Telluric staff still considered him a legend. He hadn't meant to kill Benjamin Dubrow, they said (behind her back, but she knew), and those who worked with Arthur could understand why someone would want to poison *him*. According to Arthur, he was referred to as *Arthole* so often he believed his tombstone would be engraved with that name.

Rory was gone from Telluric, but his legacy wasn't.

And Rory was ever in her consciousness because, when she looked at Benji it was like looking at Rory, like he was cloned. And like his father, Benji practiced Taekwondo and ran cross country in high school, eschewing any other sports Delene suggested.

She pulled out a Rubbermaid tub of mementos and shook her head at a picture of her dad and a younger, fatter Rory. It was a newspaper article about the rollout of the Hop Rikki flavor, Rory's recipe. She gazed at the old photo and tried to remember the last time Rory had sent her one of his I-still-love-you cards. Her birthday, months ago. That had been the last time.

Was he seeing someone? She didn't know. She didn't care.

Not having to squash Rory Harper's hopes on a weekly basis had come as a relief. He picked up Benji on time for his visitation weekends; he had stopped coming to the door and waited in his car, in the driveway; he dropped Benji back home on time. Rory's texts were polite but all business. No, *How are you?* No emojis. Not anymore.

Delene had brushed off his advances for years, and he finally got the picture. Her eyes glazed again, and she dashed at them. The man had loved her, that much was obvious. But love was not enough. He'd killed her father and lied about it. Someone who lied would always lie.

After Rory, Delene found it difficult to trust anyone. Her therapist bill was as constant as the electric bill. Her singleness, too. Men had come and gone. She was tired of the dating scene. Selling the house was her way of accepting the cards life had dealt.

She pulled out a manilla envelope with a hand-printed label in Dad's handwriting: MEDICAL and was about to toss the contents when a letter caught her eye. His insurance company wrote asking for the contact information of his new prescription supplier. He'd stopped filling his prescriptions, and the company wanted the name of whoever was filling them now. The letter stated they'd tried to contact him by phone and this was their last attempt at connection.

She read on.

...claims unsubmitted. Benefits will not be paid on claims submitted more than a year after the date of service. Our records show no claims for service or pharmacy...patients are responsible for keeping appointments and following through on preventative care.

A twisting sensation began in her belly. What did this mean? Her dad's phone and charger were in the container. She fished it out and plugged it into the extension cord that powered lights for the crawlspace. Would it work after these many years? Would it show his call history? While she waited for it to charge, she went through his paperwork more thoroughly. Several letters were from his family practitioner warning he was *...overdue for your yearly screening.* His cardiologist sent a letter with his bill for several missed appointments. A folded paper looked as if it had been pocketed and read and been carried around a while. Phrases from the text were highlighted. *...doctors may bypass informed consent...altered mental capacity affects a patient's rights...refuse care...know it will be* *painful...side effects...quality of life vs. quantity of life.* And a picture of Mom.

Mom. How Dad must have missed her.

Enough to want to join her?

A bizarre and horrifying connection formed in Delene's mind. Her father was on a cocktail of medications: Acetazolamide, Amiloride, and Bumetanide—no, he *should have been* on a cocktail of medications. According to these letters and against his physician's advice, he'd stopped taking them.

Why?

She re-read the folded article that had Mom's picture tucked inside. *Quality of life vs. quantity of life.*

The medications for his edema and heart issues were what interacted with the Senna extract and killed him. Except, here, according to this, her dad had stopped refilling those medications long before Rory started working at Telluric. Her dad didn't want to end his life, but he wasn't down for prolonging it, either. He wanted to be with Mom. *Oh my God, Dad...*

Her phone buzzed. Rory.

Would you mind if we switch the drop off time?

I'm thinking 8 Sunday?

Want to take B to the game.

She considered the box of profoundly terrible revelation in her crawl space, there all along. Her fingers hovered over the keys to text back. It felt like she was on a precipice and could either fly like a sparrow or jump to her death, and she didn't know which would happen until she took that step off...

She typed: *I found something. Need to talk.*

Her fingers trembled on the send button. A split second, now or never, and she knew if she didn't open the can of worms, it would never, ever be opened. It was too dirty, too slimy, too much to contemplate. She hit backspace to clear the field, typed a different message, smashed send, hit it too hard.

Sure thing, Ror.

She wrenched Dad's phone from the outlet, grabbed the whole lot of effects (didn't even look through the rest) and put the Rubbermaid tub in her trunk. She took it to the city dump because she didn't trust herself not to pull it from her garbage before pick-up day.

On her way home from the dump, she stopped at Mike's Bar and Grill and ordered a Hop Rikki. Then another. A third, and the numbness turned up the edges of her mouth, almost into a smile. Through the amber liquid, she gazed at the people eating, drinking, laughing.

All this time...Rory...

She smothered the thought before it took. Dad was buried in the cemetery, and his medical history was buried at the dump where it belonged. It would disintegrate and become as if it never existed. And with time and distraction and as many beers as it took, what she'd just learned would be buried in her heart as well, would eventually cease to exist. That's how it worked for Rory, hadn't it? He had lied to himself and to her until he didn't know up from down. Would it be a kindness to tell Rory the truth—that his guilt, his self-inflicted pennance, kidney donation, even his prison sentence, was for nothing? Was it kind to withhold his absolution when she had it in her power to give? Giving one meant giving the other, and giving *both* felt monstrous. It was said that the truth will set you free. Delene could see how that would apply to Rory. He would know he was not guilty of murder, even accidentally. But also, the truth could destroy him. Delene herself had been down that road. She ordered yet another drink and wondered what Rory would do if he were in her shoes.

The answer came to her instantly. Forcefully. Blessedly. The answer brought tears to her eyes.

She knocked back her beer. "Cheers."

Cheers, friends! If you enjoyed my beer-drinker thinker, *Spiked*, and are down for darker, twistier journeys with explosive endings, check out ***Bookworm*** or ***Switchback***.

Before you go...

Thanks for reading *Spiked*! It would mean the world to me if you'd leave a review on Amazon and/or Goodreads. Stay in touch at klgriffiths.com where I share my thoughts on everything deep, dark, and droll.

Many thanks to my critique group, the Reds (Laura Kenelly, Mary Turzillo, Rebecca Moon Ruark, Cyndi Hilston, and Jeremy Jusek) whose honest, smart, and critical comments keep me on track, motivated, and encouraged. Neil Sater's thorough critique helped me polish and ground my story in time and space. Bill Wetmore, Dennis Kramer-Wine, and Luke Griffiths graciously answered my beer questions, and third-degree blackbelt Diane DeCaprio was a source of Taekwondo wisdom (and is a great friend!). My brother Kevin Seyer (GOAT principal!) gave me the idea for skydiving as Delene's reading challenge. I also want to mention Nancy, James, and Catie, who believed in my writing from the earliest days. And the same goes for my old buddies from the North Ridgeville Writer's group, especially Scot, Scott (two t's!), Kathleen, Paul, Alexia, Betty, and John.

Gushing thanks to my husband and best friend who champions this writing dream of mine. XOXO, Bob! Love to my children, Katae, Paul, Tory, Luke, and Gabe who make my world a wonderful place. All adoration to my Lord and Savior, Jesus. May this story, even its dark parts, serve a greater good. Jesus said the truth will set you free. Imagine how different Rory's journey would have been, had he told the truth.

www.ingramcontent.com/pod-product-compliance
Lightning Source LLC
Chambersburg PA
CBHW030020260726
48782CB00025B/255

9798988703808